Opening Gates

a novel by

Nancy King

Books by Nancy King

Novels

Changing Spaces
The Stones Speak
Morning Light
A Woman Walking

Nonfiction

Dancing With Wonder: Self-Discovery Through Stories
Playing Their Part: Language and Learning in the Classroom
Storymaking and Drama
Storymaking in Education and Drama, co-written with Alida Gersie
A Movement Approach to Acting
Giving Form to Feeling
Theatre Movement

Opening Gates

a novel by

Nancy King

Plain View Press, LLC

www. plainviewpress.net

1101 W. 34th Street, STE 404   Austin, TX 78705

ISBN: 978-1-63210-015-3
Library of Congress Control Number: 2015945782

Cover photo by Paul Ross, photojournalist
www.GlobalAdventure.us
Background photo by Nancy King
Cover design by Pam Knight

We Find Healing In Existing Reality
Plain View Press is a 36-year-old issue-based literary publishing house. Our books result from artistic collaboration between writers, artists, and editors. Over the years we have become a far-flung community of humane and highly creative activists whose energies bring humanitarian enlightenment and hope to individuals and communities grappling with the major issues of our time—peace, justice, the environment, education and gender.

for Barbara Radov

I'm no longer quite sure what the question is,
but I do know the answer is, "Yes."
—Leonard Bernstein, 1973 Norton Lecture

sometimes the stories take you and fling you against a wall
sometimes you go right through the wall
—Alicia Suskin Ostriker: the volcano sequence
University of Pittsburgh Press, 2005

Prologue

A woman decided that before she died she had to find Truth. So, with the blessings of those around her, she began her journey. She walked for many days, up mountains, down canyons, across rivers, through deserts and forests, asking everyone she met, "Do you know where I can find Truth?" Some said no, others gave directions, but no one really knew for sure. Then, after climbing an unusually steep mountain, she found a cave and carefully entered. There, sitting near a fire, was the ugliest woman she had ever seen. Still, there was something compelling about her, so the woman asked, "Are you Truth?"

Truth nodded. She already knew what the seeker wanted and invited her to sit and eat and rest. For many days and nights Truth shared her wisdom. When the seeker was ready to leave, she asked, "You have given me so much. Is there nothing I can do for you?"

"Yes," said Truth. "When you tell people about your time with me, say that I was the most beautiful woman you ever met."

World Tale

Summer 1956
New York City

1

The director's office in Manhattan was surprisingly small and drab and the air was thick with acrid smoke that burned my throat and made my eyes water. I was barely able to stifle a fit of coughing. The man sitting behind the desk, puffing a fat, smelly cigar, stared at me through hooded eyes. He reminded me of an ancient turtle I'd once encountered on a camping trip. It was hard to imagine that this wrinkled man was in charge of a huge mental hospital.

Don't think about anything except the salary—sixty dollars a week, more than enough to pay tuition and books. Almost twice as much as teaching swimming at a camp.

"Sit down, Miss Weinstein, our business won't take long. I notice that even though you're only 19, you're going into your senior year at college. Very impressive." He began reading from recommendations in my dossier, "Responsible, reliable, resourceful..." then looked up at me and said, "excellent qualities that will be extremely useful when you are working at the hospital. Tell me, what do you expect to do as a recreational therapist?"

I had assumed Mr. Carson would give me a job description, not ask for one. Tentatively, I said the first thing that came to mind. "Take the patients outside and play games with them?" *How difficult could this be?*

"Exactly. However, I should warn you, the job is harder than it sounds. Patients are unpredictable. And, there is a routine to working at the hospital. You come to the entrance. Unlock the main gate. Leave your troubles and problems behind you. Collect your inmates. Take them outside. Play games. Keep track of how many you take out—that's how many you bring back. Don't get personal. Don't get friendly. Don't offer to help. Just keep them moving and busy so they're tired when you return them to the ward. Above all, don't lose anyone! You're responsible for their safety. At the end of the day you lock the gate. You leave the inmates' troubles and problems inside the hospital. You go home and don't give work another thought until you open the gate the next day."

He made it seem like working in some kind of human factory. Where was his concern for these patients as people?

"Concordia Hospital houses six thousand patients and funding only allows us to hire one psychiatrist for every nine hundred patients. But attendants are trained to give excellent care. In fact, we've just begun to use Thorazine with some patients. It's a new drug that calms hysterical inmates and seems to be working quite well."

"Do I have to give patients their medication?"

"Of course not. That's the attendants' job. The new and younger patients receive insulin or electric shock treatments for six weeks. If they respond positively, they're released; if not, they're sent to the general wards for a minimum of three months." He paused. "Any questions?" I couldn't think of any, so he continued. "Your salary will be sixty dollars a week. You begin on May 28th and finish September 14th. Since you've passed the physical, all you have to do is sign the contract. Miss Gibbons will give you the form when you leave. You can sign the loyalty oath in the main office of the administration building in the hospital before you pick up your keys. My secretary is a notary. Any questions?"

"Loyalty oath?" *To work in a hospital? With mentally ill people?*

"It's required for all New York State employees."

"But..."

"Miss Weinstein, if you want to work at the hospital you must sign the oath. I'm surprised you'd even question it. We're lucky to be living in the United States of America, and we need to do everything we can to protect our country from its enemies."

Every moral fiber of my body screamed, "No! I'm not signing." *I have no intention of violently overthrowing the government. Besides, if people wanted to be disloyal, whatever that means, surely they'd sign it with no qualms. What about the land of the free and the home the brave?*

"Well, Miss Weinstein?" He didn't bother to hide his impatience. I needed the job. I wanted the salary. Yet I hesitated. Then, despite knowing I was betraying my principles, I said I'd sign. I left the interview feeling dirty, knowing no amount of water could make me feel clean.

After walking a few blocks, I realized that Mr. Carson had not mentioned an orientation for summer staff. I assumed there would be training before I began working with patients. *How could there not be?*

Even though I was very pleased to have the job, signing a loyalty oath filled me with apprehension. So many people were losing their jobs, even after signing loyalty oaths, just because someone accused them of being Communists—no proof required, no chance to confront their accusers. A classmate even told me to stop being a "Commie sympathizer" after I joked, "Let the Russians come. We'll welcome them with hamburgers, jazz, and dungarees. Who'd want to fight after that?"

My worries about the effects of the political hysteria fomented by Senator McCarthy and the House Un-American Activities Committee interrogations had intensified when my twelfth-grade European history teacher, a man I respected and revered, was accused of being a Communist. He never mentioned politics in class. No one ever offered evidence that he had done or said anything wrong, or that he was even a member of the Communist Party. Yet, he was fired. A few days later he committed suicide. He had signed the loyalty oath. Why hadn't that protected him from capricious charges? For days after I heard about his death I walked around in a stupor, upset that this could happen in a country where you're supposed to be innocent until proven guilty. I kept remembering what he said to me when I came to class one day, visibly frightened by all the political vitriol and witch-hunting. "Rennie, nothing stays terrible forever. People will eventually see that what is happening is wrong." Maybe they will, but they didn't in time to save him.

Although I don't consider myself a political person, I signed a petition at school protesting a new law that required teachers to inform on colleagues if they suspected subversive activity. Later, I learned this was the reason I was not hired as a Resident Assistant in the dorm. The person who told me said, "Rennie, you need to accept authority if you want to be hired." I didn't see how protesting an unjust law had anything to do with being an RA in a freshman dorm.

I never thought the summer of 1956 would see me working in a mental hospital in Queens. It felt as if the world had gone crazy, and here I was, taking a job to work with people who were certifiably crazy. Did that make me crazy for doing it? Everyone else I knew was working in a restaurant or as a camp counselor. *What was I doing?* Maybe it wasn't too late. I had some other skills. I could head a waterfront program, teach dance, take kids out on wilderness trips, even teach puppetry and drama to young campers.

My bad feelings disappeared when I saw Jake drive up on his motor scooter, looking relaxed and confident, just as handsome as when we first met on a ski trip sponsored by American Youth Hostels. I was 16 and Jake was 21. Even after three years, I couldn't help smiling as I remembered how excited I was when he asked me to be his partner in the final event of the trip, an evening ski race that went from one end of the small Vermont town to the other, ending in a long steep icy hill. I was thrilled. Although I'm not the greatest of skiers, his sexy grin overrode my fear of going fast and I zoomed next to him, exhilarated by the crowds cheering us on. We came in second. I got a bracelet. He got a gallon of maple syrup, which we shared with everyone on the bus going home. It was midnight when we arrived in Manhattan and he walked me to the subway, waiting with me until the train came. I was as happy as I'd ever been, and even happier when he called a few days later, asking if I'd go with him to see *The Teahouse of the August Moon*. I loved theatre and immediately said yes. That was how it began—Jake suggesting, me agreeing. I finally had a boyfriend.

While I'm away at college we write to each other two or three times a week, and when I come home for vacation we see each other as much as we can. It's not always easy. He's in law school on a full scholarship so he works hard to maintain good grades. I've seen him flirting with women, even when he's with me, and I'm pretty sure he sees them when I'm not around, but I'm afraid to ask. He likes my enthusiasm and willingness to try things like rock climbing and backpacking in the mountains. I like our shared sense of adventure. Although I was scared when we first started making love, I love Jake and I feel he loves me. When I told him I was worried about getting pregnant, he assured me that if it happened he'd marry me. Although that mostly comforts me, the thought of being a mother is too scary to contemplate.

Stop thinking about the past. What about now? Jake's here. At least for a while.

"Hey Rennie, how'd it go?" asked Jake, grinning with pleasure when he saw me. I felt myself melt. He parked the scooter at the curb and kissed me. "You now a sane and certified recreational therapist?"

"Don't know how sane or certified I am, but I got the job."

"Swell! Now we have two things to celebrate—your job and our third anniversary. Hop on, I made reservations for lunch." His pleasure at my having gotten the job was so contagious I hugged him hard and he responded passionately. Nothing mattered but his smell and the feel of his body enveloping mine.

As I got on the scooter, I still marveled that it held the two of us. It was so small, with little wheels and not a whole lot of power, yet we'd taken lots of trips on it. We had even ridden from New York City up to Maine with all our camping gear and food. Jake was proud of being the owner of the second registered motor scooter in New York City. I was proud of being adventurous enough to ride with him.

I didn't mention having to sign the loyalty oath because I knew what Jake's reaction would be: You want the job, you sign the oath. It's just a stupid reaction to a supposed enemy and won't last long.

He drove us to our favorite restaurant, a tiny hole-in-the-wall with great Greek food. This meal was particularly bittersweet with Jake leaving in less than 24 hours to go wandering around Europe for three months. I didn't like remembering how jealous I felt when he described some of the places he would visit, the hikes he planned to do. "Can I go with you?" I had asked, excited by the idea of traveling with him.

"Are you crazy? Our parents would have a fit! We're not married."

"As if I didn't know," I retorted. There was an uncomfortable silence between us, which I broke by asking him to tell me more about his trip.

After lunch we went to his apartment, the normally neat bedroom a mess. Clothes were strewn all over the bed in piles ready to be packed, a painful reminder of his leaving. There was no way I could ask the one question I wanted answered: "Will you still love me when you come home?" I walked into the bathroom and locked the door, not wanting Jake to see me so close to tears. Washing my face with cold water helped push the tears back to wherever they had come from. I combed my hair, opened the door, and walked into Jake's arms.

We made love for most of the afternoon, snuggling against each other, contentedly tired afterward, his arms cocooning my body. I always missed Jake when we were apart. *Would he miss me while he was in Europe? Would he write? Would he receive my letters? How long would it take for me to get mail from him?* I couldn't make myself stop wishing he had asked me to go with him, even though I knew I had to work during the summer to pay for college.

Reluctantly, after a shower and lingering hugs and kisses, I was about to leave when Jake stopped me. "I have a really big surprise for you." Thrilled that he'd thought to give me a present, I threw my arms around him in such a goofy way he burst out laughing. "You really are crazy." I knew he was teasing so I hugged him again. He laughed and hugged me hard before saying, "Close your eyes and don't open them until I tell you to." He led me down stairs and outside. "Ready for the surprise?" he asked, his voice seductive. I nodded. "Okay, turn around and look." I did. "What do you think?" I looked again. No boxes. No bags. Nothing but his Vespa. "Well?" he asked, his tone less sexy, more impatient.

"All I see is your scooter. What's the surprise?"

"That's it. I thought you'd be excited and pleased."

"Jake, I'm happy to be excited and pleased if you'll tell me what I'm supposed to be excited and pleased about."

"Thanks for taking the fun out of my present."

"What present?"

"My scooter! I'm lending it to you for the summer." He beamed with pride.

"But I've never driven it."

"Rennie, if I didn't think you could drive it, I wouldn't have offered. I can give you a quick lesson, but if you don't want it I'll lend it to Marty. He's been asking to borrow it while I'm gone."

His confidence was reassuring so I said yes, wanting him to be proud of me, but also wanting to keep some connection between us while he was in Europe. I couldn't help wishing he'd given me an engagement ring.

2

The day before I had to start working I was flooded with doubts and worries. Every question provoked more panic: *What if I didn't know enough to do the job? What if a patient attacked me? What if they refused to do what I asked? What if I made a horrible mistake and Mr. Carson fired me? If it's too scary and too difficult and I quit, how will I pay for school?*

When I told people I was going to work in a mental hospital, their response was some version of "Are you crazy?" *Did they know something I didn't know? Was that why I seemed different from people my age? Why so many people told me I was too serious? Why had I let the salary become more important than the job, given my appalling lack of experience working with mentally ill people?* Even though I had taken four psychology classes and too many boring recreation and physical education courses, I knew almost nothing about mental illness or recreational therapy. I tried to comfort myself. Mr. Carson hired me. He must think I know enough to do the job.

I also didn't know how good I'd be at leaving my troubles behind. I tend to mull over stuff, even when I know I should either leave it alone or do something about it. Like going to a college I didn't want to go to, studying subjects that didn't interest me. And just because I didn't think I could get into a liberal arts school, I never applied.

Despite my doubts about myself, when Jake offered to let me use his Vespa while he was in Europe, I knew he expected me to say yes. He often had more confidence in me than I had in myself. I liked the idea of driving the second registered Vespa in New York City, even though it took a while to quell my fears. Driving home the first time, across the striated Queensboro Bridge, I held my breath until I reached the safety of the paved road. There were so few motor scooters on the road that wherever I rode, people stared. I learned to enjoy driving it, except when I had to bundle up in rain gear that never quite kept me dry. Within a few days I taught myself to change a spark plug in less than two minutes, in pouring rain, in traffic. One night on the Queensboro Bridge a kind motorist even stopped his car so his headlights could shine on the scooter and me. Having the Vespa freed me from figuring out bus schedules or asking my parents if I could use their car during the summer while they were in Mexico with my younger sister.

When the dreaded morning arrived—my first day of working at the mental hospital—I couldn't decide what to wear. With half the clothes in my closet strewn across my bed and on the floor, I gave up and walked down to the kitchen in my pajamas. Trying to calm myself I, made my favorite breakfast of scrambled eggs, toasted English muffin with marmalade, a big glass of orange juice, and coffee. I don't particularly like coffee but I had recently learned to drink it and hoped the energy it gave me would counteract my lack of sleep. Unfortunately, the minute I began drinking the juice my stomach tightened, my throat closed, and that was the end of breakfast. I stored the mess in the refrigerator thinking I could heat it up for dinner. Since I didn't know if there was an employees' cafeteria, I took bread out of the freezer to make a sandwich for lunch, but even that was too much. I put the bread back and headed for my bedroom.

First I put on dungarees and a T-shirt, which I usually wear when I play softball, but when I looked in the mirror it felt too casual. I took them off and put on a black skirt and white blouse. Too stark. Time was passing, and the last thing I wanted was to be late, so I settled for a denim skirt and light blue blouse. I had never driven the Vespa dressed up and fervently hoped I wouldn't have to change the spark plug and arrive with grease stains on my clothes.

I didn't know where the right hospital entrance was so I kept driving, following a massive stone wall topped with broken glass, looking for the gate marked EMPLOYEES ONLY. When I found it and turned off the engine, a bored male guard looked up from his newspaper and asked tonelessly, "What do you want?"

I showed him my letter of employment and managed to say, still not comfortable with the title, "I'm a recreational therapist. Where do I park? And could you please tell me where the orientation is?"

His sarcastic laugh unsettled me. "Orientation? You mean where you go to get your keys?" I waited, hoping for more. He shook his head. "You college kids—you got a lot to learn." He opened the enormous iron gate and said, "You can park near building 4 but you have to sign the loyalty oath in the admin building before you register in building 2, the one with the porch." He pointed to an imposing, uninviting, gray stone structure. I had barely driven my scooter through the gate when he slammed it shut. The clanging made me jump, my foot slipped off the clutch, and the engine stalled. The guard laughed. I failed to see what was funny. Construction sounds from a nearby building site added to my anxiety. The high wall that kept patients in, and the public out, felt forbidding. After parking, with no one in sight, I walked through a huge grassy area with a few large trees, under which were concrete benches.

As I headed toward the administration building, my conscience and I battled. According to what I had learned in history class, loyalty oaths were unconstitutional, but what bothered me even more was the assumption that I needed to promise to be loyal to my country when the most "subversive" act I'd ever committed was to sing folk songs, sometimes protest songs, in Washington Square Park in Greenwich Village. I was also a member of the Young Progressives of America, but the meetings I had attended consisted of most everyone but me smoking pot while we talked about the horrors of various blacklists and McCarthyism. Occasionally we made protest signs and joined rallies and marches, a small group among many. I knew I'd sign the oath because I wanted the job, but it didn't do much for my sense of self-respect.

Mr. Carson's regular secretary was out sick. Her bored replacement handed me the form and a pen. Signing the oath took less than five seconds. Without looking at me she took the signed form and put it on his desk, not bothering to say thank you or welcome or hope all goes well. I left feeling depressed and sorry for myself.

After a few wrong turns I managed to find building 2 and walked up the steps to a small porch with more steps leading to the front door. There was no bell so I knocked, increasingly apprehensive about the lack of formal welcome. I was used to working at summer camps where each session began with greeting new and returning staff. My parents, and everyone else I knew, had tried to talk me out of taking this job, but I had waved away their fears and ignored their descriptions of horrible scenarios. Patients were people like anyone else, just needing some help, I told them. Now their voices screamed inside me. *What had I gotten myself into?*

The iron grating on the front door and bars on the ground floor windows did nothing to alleviate my qualms, nor did the heavyset man with piercing eyes who opened the door. Curt and direct, he spat out his words. "You one of the summer therapists?" I nodded. "Go up to room 307. You'll get your keys there." I stood, expecting to hear about an orientation. "What are you waiting for?"

I managed to blurt out, "What do I do after I get the keys?"

He asked for my name and searched through a number of documents on a clipboard. "You're assigned to building 5. After the man upstairs gives you your keys, ask him to show you where to go and to tell you what key opens which door. Your supervisor is Mrs. Langstrom. You'll meet her at four this afternoon in the administration building." With that, he walked away.

I trudged up the flights of stairs looking for room 307. The doors to all the rooms were closed. Were there people inside? I listened intently but heard only a whirring fan behind one door and the sound of typing behind another. I knocked on the door to room 307 and almost fell in when a short, wiry man with a pipe in his mouth abruptly opened it. "You looking for your keys?" I nodded and told him the number of my building.

Although he hadn't invited me in, I followed behind him and then stopped. Shocked. I had never seen so many keys. Big ones, small ones, long ones, squat ones, weirdly shaped ones. Given that I could barely open the door to my house—the lock was old and sometimes the key stuck—how was I going to deal with keys that were five or six inches long? Suddenly sixty dollars a week seemed like no reason to have taken this job.

"You got a chain?" I shook my head, puzzled. *Why would I carry a chain?* He sighed. "Well, I got a couple extra." He went into the back room and returned with a chain of metal links that he draped around my waist. "You need to gain some weight. Scrawny thing like you'll be no match for some of your patients." I tried to stifle my gasp. "Oh well, it's not like you'll be working in building 6. Then you'd really be in trouble."

"What's building 6?" I managed to say, not daring to ask about building 5.

"It's where they keep the violent ones. You need to be real tough to work there." He snipped off a few links of the chain and then, working from a list he held in his hand, put more keys than I'd ever used in my whole life on small link chains that he attached to the big chain, which he then draped around my waist and clasped. I felt my body list to the left, where pounds of keys jangled as he tested to make sure they were on securely. "Okay, that'll do." He showed me which keys opened the big gates, the small doors, and the equipment storage units, but within seconds his words became meaningless. He must have noticed because he told me, sternly, to pay attention. "Walk out the front door, turn left... He kept talking. Too many instructions for me to follow, until he said, "Open the door, walk to the third floor, open the iron grating, and an attendant will tell you which inmates are going with you today." I froze, unable to imagine myself walking into a building full of mentally ill people. Jake's words echoed, "They're crazy people. You must be crazy to want to work there."

"Something wrong?" he asked.

"I thought there'd be an orientation," I managed to admit. "I've never worked in a mental hospital before. I..."

"Guess you thought wrong," he said, amused. He showed me out and shut the door behind me. If I had been thinking clearly I would have knocked, and when he opened the door again said, "Thank you," given him back the keys, and walked out to the world I had come from. Mr. Carson had hired me—I still wasn't sure why—but I was becoming aware that there was much more to this job than I thought possible. I had no idea how to be a recreational therapist, even for three and a half months.

I walked down the stairs, opened the door, and stood on the porch steps, unable to force my feet to move. The construction noise heightened my edginess. How were mentally ill people supposed to relax with constant banging and drilling? My mind told me to go back upstairs and return the keys. My body refused to budge. A middle-aged man wearing rumpled brownish pants and a drab yellow plaid shirt walked slowly up to me. He had no keys. No belt. "Howdy, ma'am, may I help you? You look lost." His high-pitched voice was friendly and welcoming. Before I could answer, he stuck out his hand, "I'm James. Been here a long time. I intend to die here. I don't like all the noise, do you?" I shook my head and briefly held his too-soft hand, trying not to show my shock. *Was he a mentally ill person?* "This is the safest place I ever been. Three meals a day. Movies once a week. It's pretty nice. I empty all the waste paper baskets in this building.

Sometimes I do errands for Mr. Barnwell. He's a nice man." James lowered his voice to a whisper, "But you don't want to get on the bad side of him. No, sir. He's got a temper, a real bad temper. Last week he gave me a magazine. He's a nice man."

"Thank you, I'll remember that," I said, my voice quivering, wondering if the man who had opened the door was Mr. Barnwell.

"Where you going?" he asked.

Before I could answer he leaned toward me and said in a loud whisper, "Don't go near the construction. There's a lot of strange men. Could be dangerous." He looked around then asked, "Where did you say you were going?"

"Building 5," I answered, too scared to wonder if I should be telling him this.

"I got a little time. I'll take you there if you like."

"Thank you." He seemed sort of normal, except for wanting to live and die in a mental hospital, but what was he doing walking around with no attendant in sight?

"You a summer therapist?"

"Yes."

"Want some advice?"

"Sure," I said, aware of the irony of a mental patient giving me what no one in the administration thought I needed to know.

"Just be yourself. People here can see right through you so don't lie. Don't pretend. Don't be mean. And," he added as an afterthought, "don't go near the strange men."

I took a chance. "What if I'm scared?"

"What are you scared of?"

"Well," I lied, "I'm not scared, but..."

"We may be crazy, but we're not stupid," he said indignantly. "I can tell. You are scared. You lied. Why did you lie? I just told you not to lie. Why are you scared? You think we eat people?"

This was not a conversation I ever expected to have, but I was too nervous to make up a story. "I'm sorry I lied, especially after you told me not to, but I'm not used to telling people how I feel." I couldn't stop blabbering. "And now I'm supposed to be a recreational therapist and no one's told me what to do. It's scary."

"I always say, don't confuse new with scary. We're people just like you. Only difference is sometimes we get a little upset and need help. Just be yourself and everything's gonna be okay. And remember, don't be mean." He stopped when we reached a towering black metal gate. "They tell you which key opens this?" I shook my head, not remembering anything the man in room 307 had said. "Lemme see your keys." I pulled them from the left of my waist to the front of my body and held them. "Okay, this key," he said, pointing to one that was at least five inches long, "opens the first gate. Then this key," he said pointing to one that was a little smaller, "opens the front door of building 5." Pointing to a third, bigger key, he said, "I think this key opens the iron grating on the third floor." *How does he know all this?* "If you forget, you can use the buzzer, but attendants don't like when you do it 'cause then they have to get up and answer the door. Remember, don't be mean."

He walked away. No matter how I tried, I couldn't open the door. Desperate, I yelled, "Wait, please."

"What's the matter?" he asked, coming too close. "Are you in trouble? Should I call someone?"

Feeling extremely uncomfortable and impossibly inept, I admitted, "I can't open the gate. Can you help me unlock it?"

He giggled conspiratorially. "Patients aren't supposed to touch keys, but I won't tell if you won't tell." I gave him the small chain holding the key, which was still attached to my chain belt. Much to my relief and chagrin, with a flick of his wrist, the gate swung open. "The trick is not to push too hard."

The trick is not to work here.

I watched him saunter away. It wasn't too late to change my mind. Then I thought about all the *I told you sos* I was bound to hear, took a deep breath, and walked to the front door of building 5. Heavy iron bars protected all the doors and windows. I'd never seen a more depressing place. The key to the front door was only three inches long. I managed to insert it and, with a lot of jiggling, turned the lock. Once inside, I began to sweat. The intrusive smells and sounds in the building were like none I had ever experienced— disagreeable and thick. They seemed to cling to me as I slogged up the metal stairs, terrified of what would happen next.

Judging from the signs on the doors on the second floor, I figured it was a kind of hospital area, so I walked up to the third floor where

I heard people moving around. There was a small landing with a steel gate. While I fiddled with keys I heard raucous laughter and shouts to be quiet. I wanted to run down the stairs but I unlocked the gate; it clanged shut. The next set of doors didn't require a key and I hesitantly opened one of them. As soon as I closed it behind me a tall, skinny woman, her face hideously contorted, made a beeline toward me. Paralyzed, I waited for her to crash into me. Inches from my body, she abruptly turned forty-five degrees and headed toward an inmate with messy hair and clenched fists who was keening, as if someone she loved had died. Just before she reached the keening woman, the skinny woman turned sharply again and rushed toward another woman.

I watched, baffled. A wiry woman in a colorless housedress strode over to where I was standing, glaring at me with angry blue eyes. "What are you doing here?"

I was too frightened to lie. "I don't know."

Her hard, cold laugh was not reassuring. Taking a step back, she snapped, "Well, at least you're honest. That's more than I can say for most of your type."

My type?

A muscular woman in a dowdy blue housedress pushed the first woman away. "Don't scare her, Liz, you can see she's new."

Shaking, Liz gave the woman a dirty look. "Don't push me, Maggie, I don't like to be pushed. I told you before; I don't like to be pushed. Don't push me, Maggie."

Several more women gathered around, staring at me. The first two women seemed about to fight and there was no attendant in sight. "Please," I practically shouted, "Please!"

"Please, what?" sneered Liz.

"I don't know. Just, please," I blathered.

"What's going on?" A large woman in a crisp green uniform, looking very annoyed, marched over and placed herself between the two women and me. "Who are you? What do you want? Why are you causing such a rumpus?"

Her nametag read Mrs. Martelli—no staff designation—but given the way the women deferred to her, and her tone of voice, I guessed she must be the head attendant. I commanded my voice not to tremble but it paid no attention. "I...I'm the recreational therapist for building 5. Until the second week in September."

Her sneer upset me even more.

"Another college kid. Well, you don't seem the type to last more than a day."

"Why is that?" I asked.

"You been here two minutes and already you're causing trouble. Seems you ain't got the sense you were born with." She looked at my nametag. "Miss Weinstein, I expect you to follow the rules, same as everyone else. One more disturbance and I'll have you fired. The last thing I need is another college kid causing problems."

A few of the women standing behind the attendant looked at me sympathetically, shaking their heads in disagreement. They gave me the courage to speak up. "Mrs. Martelli, I've never worked in a mental hospital before, but I'm willing to learn."

"I been here sixteen years, and you want to learn in three minutes what you should do for the next three and a half months?"

Three minutes? Nothing made sense. The person I thought would be my ally was acting as if I were a bug to be squashed. The people I thought I'd be afraid of seemed to be urging me to stick up for myself. I looked at my watch and then at Mrs. Martelli, who was still glaring at me. Desperate, I said, "It's only a few minutes past eleven, I could take some women out and organize a few games before lunch."

"No. There's no time for that, they have to get ready."

"When is lunch?" I asked, taken aback by her hostility.

"Eleven-thirty."

"What time do they finish?"

"Twelve."

"Okay, I'll come back at noon."

"No, come at one."

I decided not to ask why. "Where is the sports equipment kept?"

"Don't you know nothin'?" Her pasty white skin tinged red with rage. She stormed out, leaving a stillness like the eye of a hurricane.

We stood there, the patients and I, in an uncomfortable silence. I was feeling lost, with no idea what to say or do. Maggie came up to me. "Don't mind her, she's just jealous 'cause you get almost the same pay as her. Your title is therapist and she's only an attendant."

"That doesn't seem fair if she's been here sixteen years."

"Sixteen years too long, if you ask me," whispered a lumpy looking woman with a worried expression. "She can be real mean when she wants to. Best to stay out of her way. Even when she seems nice."

I thought about James telling me not to be mean. It suddenly hit me: working here was not going to be anything like playing ball with kids at a summer camp. This was a place where people's wellbeing was at stake. I was angry that no one thought it necessary to give me an orientation—some information about working with patients—and it was scary to think that if I wasn't careful I could cause someone great harm. It was also the first time I realized I couldn't feel two major emotions simultaneously. Anger trumped fear.

3

I forced myself to walk into the ward, which was filled with women of all shapes and sizes, sitting, standing, moving aimlessly. Some were shaking uncontrollably, others mumbled to themselves. Several moved in repetitive patterns. One was talking out loud to no one. A few gathered around, staring at me. I saw Liz watching me, an ironic smile on her face. Desperate to do something, I took a chance and asked her, "Do you know where the balls and sports equipment are kept?"

Before she could respond, a drooling woman began chanting, "Balls, balls, balls." Some of the women joined her. I was afraid Mrs. Martelli would storm out of wherever she was and let me know that not only was I unqualified, I deserved to be fired immediately for continually upsetting the patients.

Putting my finger to my lips, I said, "Sssh," to the crowd around me. Amazingly, the chanting stopped, but having so many eyes on me was disconcerting.

Liz stuck her index finger into my chest so hard I jumped back. "Why are you so scared?"

I was madly trying to think of a response when Mrs. Martelli came back. Ignoring me, she boomed, "Time to get ready for lunch, ladies. Let's all wash our hands and don't forget to use soap." Her voice would have made a six-year-old cringe. Like frightened children, the women lined up at the six bathroom sinks and dutifully washed their hands. If one woman didn't use soap, a chorus of voices chortled, "You didn't use soap. Dirty hands. Dirty face. No soap. No soap."

I noticed there were no doors on the toilets.

"Line up, ladies, two by two," barked Mrs. Martelli. And, two by two, they left the ward. I watched them go, mesmerized. When the last woman disappeared from sight, I let myself out and walked toward the administration office. I had forgotten to ask where the lunchroom was, assuming I could eat there. My list of questions for my supervisor, fueled by fear and indignation, was growing exponentially.

Did the women have any rights? If they didn't obey, what would happen? Would they be moved to the violent ward? Given the tense environment and the women's fear of Mrs. Martelli, how did anyone get well in this place? I hoped the afternoon meeting with Mrs. Langstrom would relieve some of my anxieties and answer some of my questions. Why didn't the summer therapists meet with her before starting work?

I was so lost in thought, I bumped into a tall, lanky guy, almost knocking both of us over. "Whoa! Slow down," he said, amused rather than irate.

"Oh, I'm sorry. I didn't see you."

"Well, you see me now. I'm Bruce. Who are you?"

"Rennie."

"Haven't heard that name before. It's pretty. What are you doing here?"

I had no idea who he was, but he seemed normal and friendly, and he had keys on a metal chain like mine. "I'm a summer therapist. What about you?"

"Me too. Sort of."

"Sort of?"

"Well," he hesitated, "my dad's the chief psychiatrist and he gets me a job here every summer. This year I'm supposed to do recreation but I know nothing about sports and hate everything about them. I've been pushing him to persuade Carson to let me do what I want to do."

"What's that?" I asked. Maybe there was an easier job than recreational therapist—one where I had no contact with patients or attendants.

"Horticulture. I tried to convince the administration to let me start a garden where the inmates could grow vegetables and flowers. Maybe even sell them. So far nothing's changed." He sighed. "Oh well, no matter what happens they can't fire me. Where you heading?"

"The administration office." I told him I'd been assigned to building 5.

"Five." He rolled his eyes. "Martelli. She's the head attendant there, an appalling woman—totally unpredictable. Watch out for her."

"She wasn't exactly friendly."

"Don't worry. Everyone knows she's a witch, but she can be surprisingly nice when you least expect it. Problem is, you never know what will set her off." He sighed and then asked, "What are you doing for lunch?"

"I was told there's a staff cafeteria but I don't know if I'm allowed to eat there."

He laughed. "Believe me, you don't want to. It's amazing the slop they call food. Come to my house, I'll fix us a sandwich." My startled expression made him laugh again. "I live here. Everyone knows me—for good and for bad."

"Will your parents mind?" I doubted that having lunch at his house on my first day was such a good idea.

"My dad's working and my mom's probably drunk, so no, they won't mind."

This sounded like trouble, but it seemed he really wanted me to go with him. "Is it okay? I mean should I sign out or something?"

He rolled his eyes, shaking his head as if I were a creature from another planet. "Listen, let me tell you something for your own good. No one cares what you do here as long as they don't see you doing it. First rule: Don't cause problems—for yourself, the staff, or the inmates. Second rule: Do as little as you have to—work too hard and everyone will hate you because you're showing them up. Third rule: Smile, be pleasant. And, although this isn't a rule, it's good advice: Don't be mean."

Have you been talking to James?

We walked through four iron gates, which he opened and closed with enviable ease. "Do I have keys to open these gates?"

"No, I have to take you back. This is where the resident staff lives. The hospital covers about three hundred acres—bigger than a lot of college campuses. Only good thing about all the gates is if you don't have keys to open them you can't go where you're not supposed to be." This seemed like no comfort since I had trouble opening the gates for which I did have keys. I looked around. The landscaping had changed; houses of varying sizes with gardens replaced the big institutional buildings. *Too bad the patients don't live here.* Bruce's house was a large brick cottage surrounded by freshly mowed grass. Pots of variously colored petunias bloomed on either side of the front steps. The windows were small but unbarred. Although he had more keys on his chain than I did, he had no trouble finding his front door key.

Inside, we walked into a large, well-appointed foyer that smelled as if someone had sprayed a full bottle of room deodorant everywhere. In spite of myself, I gagged.

"My mother thinks if she squirts enough air freshener around the house we won't smell the bottles she empties and then tries to hide." His tone was a mixture of contempt and sarcasm.

I stood in the living room trying to ignore the mess—newspapers and magazines strewn everywhere, pillows on the chairs and sofa in disarray, ashtrays overflowing. I hoped my dismay didn't show. The dining room was worse. Dirty dishes didn't cover stains on the tablecloth, and the remains of food made the idea of eating anything in his house extremely unappetizing. I looked at his ironed white shirt, his pressed khaki pants, and wondered at the discrepancy between how he looked and the way he lived. Bruce seemed oblivious to the mess. In spite of not having eaten since last night's dinner, there was no way I could eat anything made here.

"C'mon into the kitchen. The last time I looked we had some turkey. If not, I can open a can of tuna." He whistled as he walked down the hallway into the kitchen, a bright, surprisingly large room with pots of herbs lining the windowsill. The dirt and chaos made me gasp. I hoped he hadn't heard.

"Sorry about the mess. I guess the cleaning woman didn't come. That's the problem with having inmates for maids; they're not very reliable."

I made a show of looking at my watch. "Mrs. Martelli told me the women would be back after noon. I better go."

He shook his head, took containers out of the refrigerator, then put slices of white bread in the toaster. "They'll wait," he said, taking out a huge jar of mayonnaise.

Even on a day when my stomach isn't queasy I have trouble eating mayonnaise. "Could I have my sandwich without mayonnaise?"

"Turkey's pretty dry. It tastes better with it," he said, slathering mayonnaise on the toasted bread, after which he piled on meat and wilted lettuce. He took out two plates from the cupboard and put a sandwich and potato salad on each. "What do you want to drink? Iced tea, soda, water?"

I never considered myself squeamish, but the glasses he took out of the cupboard looked like they had never been washed. "Uh, nothing, thanks, I'm not thirsty." He shrugged, handed me a plate, poured himself a glass of soda, and gestured for me to follow him. Behind the house was a small fenced-in patio with well-watered grass and lots of pots with brightly colored flowers. I looked around, wishing for a hungry dog to steal my sandwich. "The flowers are pretty," I said just to make conversation.

"I especially like petunias—keep finding new varieties to plant."

"Do you do the gardening?"

"Such as it is. I love arranging flowers and herbs in pots. Besides, if I didn't do it no one would. The place would look pretty bare, even with the grass. Gardening is so relaxing. That's why I wish they'd let me start a garden at the hospital."

"Maybe you should be a horticultural therapist," I joked.

"I wish. I keep asking Jack to put in a greenhouse, but he—"

"Who's Jack?" I asked, feeling as if I should know.

"Jack Carson, the director. What a dismal person he is. He only got appointed because he did a bunch of favors for the Commissioner of Health and Human Services. He knows as much about mental illness as I do about sports. Probably less." Bruce gobbled his sandwich, stuffing down the potato salad as if it were the best food he'd ever eaten. The most I could do was move food around my plate. I was relieved when the phone rang and he went inside to answer it.

While he was gone I barely had time to dump the food on my plate behind an azalea bush and get back to the table to make it look as if I had just finished. I thanked him for lunch and said, "I guess I better be getting back."

He looked at his watch. "You have time. Want to take a walk?"

"I'd rather you show me where the sports equipment is for building 5. I was afraid to ask Mrs. Martelli. She's already upset with me, about what I don't know."

He stared at me. Not like men whose looks mentally undress a woman, but like I was an alien who didn't have a clue as to what constituted normal behavior. "I don't think you understand. This may be a hospital, but the people in charge don't care much about healing. It's a place to keep people safe from hurting themselves or others."

"Then why am I called a therapist?"

"By law inmates have to go outside in the summer and so the hospital needs more people to watch them. The administration gets the extra help by applying for a grant from Health and Welfare, but the grant only pays for therapists. Ergo, you're a recreational therapist rather than an attendant."

"Is there anything you don't know about this place?" I asked.

"Probably not. My advice? Don't make waves. Don't try anything new. Just do the minimum and you'll be fine."

I had no idea what doing the minimum meant, but since he was the chief psychiatrist's son and not at risk of being fired, it didn't seem like useful information. Besides, I wasn't good at doing anything halfway. More than once I've been accused of having only two modes: on and off.

"Would you show me the way to building 5? I'm not sure I can find it from here and I'd really like to know where the equipment is kept."

"Okay," he said tersely, "but I'm telling you, no one wants a goody-goody working here." He led and I followed, watching him easily open and close gates, praying I'd soon learn. When we got to building 5's equipment shed, I eventually found the right key but couldn't open it. "Here, let me do it," he said, using his key with no success. "Either the door's stuck or the lock's been changed. Happens all the time. Guess you'll have to ask Martelli." My face fell. Bruce laughed. "Don't look so scared. She'll help you once she knows you want to take the inmates out. Makes her life easier."

I decided it could be useful to talk with him. He might give me suggestions about dealing with patients or attendants. "Maybe we could meet for lunch tomorrow," I ventured. "I'll bring sandwiches."

"Super. I'll meet you here at 11:30." He smiled. "You like jazz? Louis Armstrong is playing at a club tonight—members only—but I'm a member and can bring a guest. Want to come?"

"I'm tired. Work's been really hard so far and the day is only half over."

"So? His music always makes me feel good. Besides, Satchmo doesn't often play in small venues. Tonight's really special." He sighed. "It would be a shame to waste a ticket, especially such a good one."

I liked Louis Armstrong's music and sort of felt sorry for Bruce. In spite of his know-it-all talk, he seemed lonely. I reluctantly agreed.

Steeling myself for an unpleasant encounter with Mrs. Martelli, I finally opened and locked the gates, all the time planning what to say. Just as I entered the third floor, she saw me and asked pleasantly, "Are you ready for your patients?" I was too taken aback by her changed attitude to ask about the equipment key. All I could do was nod. "Ladies, line up. Miss Weinstein is here to take you out." About twenty women, a variety of ages, sizes, and shapes, lined up two-by-two. "Stay in the inner area and make sure you bring your patients back by 3:30."

I noticed that neither Maggie nor Liz, the only two women whose names I knew, were in the group. I couldn't help asking, "Aren't Maggie and Liz coming?" Mrs. Martelli shook her head and closed the door. Was something wrong? Had I somehow gotten them into trouble? The women were watching me intently, waiting for instructions. None of them seemed in any shape to play ball games even if I could open the equipment door. What was I going to do with them for two hours?

On the stairs, when I checked to see if the group was still plodding behind me, I was surprised to see an attendant, a thin, sallow woman wearing a rumpled green uniform. Where had she come from? What was I supposed to do with her?

I breathed a sigh of relief when I opened the last gate and led the group across the lawn and into the shade of a huge maple tree. Before I could ask the attendant if she had a key to the equipment shed, the women, as if released from years of silence, all began talking at once.

"Miss, where are you taking us?"

"Miss, I don't feel so good."

"Miss, how old are you?"

"Miss, I got to use the toilet."

"Miss, you got a boyfriend?"

"Miss, I got a headache."

"Miss, it's too hot out here."

Their questions and complaints came at me so quickly I felt helpless. I hoped the attendant would rescue me, but she was busy counting, making sure no one wandered off. I was so tense, with no idea about what to do with the patients, who obviously needed more care than I could provide, I decided the best thing for me to do was to quit at the end of the day, regardless of the *I told you so*'s and my embarrassment. The job was just too difficult. Having made the decision, I immediately felt better. Then I looked at the faces of the weary, resigned women, waiting for me to tell them what to do, and my conscience nagged. *What did you expect? You thought working in a mental hospital would be easy?*

The weather was sweltering. It was too hot to play games involving running, even if I had the equipment. "Let's make a circle and sit here in the shade." They followed my instructions so docilely I felt even more uncomfortable. Trying to make some sort of connection, I asked them what they would like to do. No one answered. Perspiration dripped down our faces and bodies.

"Do you like stories?" I asked.

A few of the women sat up, others nodded, several smiled. One woman said, "I love to hear stories."

The attendant frowned. "You're not supposed to be telling stories. You're supposed to be doing recreation. You know, games and stuff."

"I'm happy to play games if you'll open the equipment shed."

"I don't have a key. You're supposed to open it. You're supposed to take out the stuff, and you're supposed to put back whatever you take out."

My temper rose. Too many *supposed to*'s. If a therapist outranked an attendant, I ought to be able to do what I wanted. I ignored her resentful look and began telling a story that I made up as I went along, about a woman lost in a place she'd never been, with no map or directions to guide her, not even sure she knew where she wanted to go. The women had moved closer and I was feeling pretty good about how things were going, even though the attendant was pacing nervously. Then I heard a loud, angry voice. "Why are those women sitting under the tree?"

Mr. Carson was striding toward me, followed by a bunch of men in dark suits. He walked over and squinted at my nametag. "Miss Weinstein, you're supposed to be a recreational therapist. Talking is for psychiatrists. Do what you were hired to do. Get those women playing games. Now!"

The terrified women shrank away from me, heads down, recognizably upset—crying, shaking, muttering, flailing. Flabbergasted and angry, I stood up and said, "The door to the sports equipment is stuck. Besides, it's so hot I thought sitting in the shade and telling stories was a sensible thing to do."

"You're paid to know how to open doors. If you can't, contact security. I want these women moving. Now!" With that he took off, the suits trotting behind him.

The women huddled together, a few of them unable to stop crying, some gibbering, one moving her hands and fingers as if she were playing the piano. It was too early to take them back to the ward and much too hot to run around no matter what Mr. Carson wanted me to do. I looked toward the shady, grassy outer area. "Let's take a walk out there," I said, pointing, "in the shade, under the trees." I knew I was going against Mrs. Martelli's orders, but the outer area was just as protected as the inner area, and a lot more inviting.

The woman on my right gasped. "We can't do that. There's too many of us. You'll get in trouble."

I had no idea what she was talking about, but I wasn't worried. Today was my last day, so if taking the women for a walk would make them feel better, that's what I was going to do. "Let's go." Eventually all the women followed, looking even more panicky than they had when the director scolded me. The attendant grudgingly followed. I told her, tired of worrying about what I was supposed to do, "Don't worry, I'm in charge."

At the gate to the outer area I wrestled with the key until it became obvious I couldn't open the lock. One of the women started to laugh nervously at my ineptness and others joined in. "Okay," I said, embarrassed, "who's willing to help?"

"We're not supposed to touch your keys."

I remembered what James said. "Well, I won't tell if you won't."

The women backed away like sheep being herded by an invisible dog.

"If I can't open the gate, we can't take our walk." I looked at them. They refused to meet my gaze. Shrugging, I said, "Never mind, we'll just walk around the inner area."

"I'll help." A tall woman with a scarred face, who looked to be in her late forties, took the key from me, put it into the lock, and turned it easily. The gate swung open. I stared at her.

"How did you do that?" I asked, amazed.

"If you'd been here as long as I have you'd know too." She walked through the gate and took a deep breath. "It's nice out here. Thank you for taking us, Miss."

"You're welcome, but you can call me Rennie. What's your name?"

"Mary, Miss. We're not allowed to call staff by their first names."

No wonder patients have to spend a minimum of three months here. It takes them that long just to learn the rules. I nodded, managing a weak smile, feeling thoroughly inept.

The outer area was large and the high walls, topped with broken glass, didn't seem obtrusive. Hesitating despite my smiling encouragement, the women, one by one, slowly walked through the gate. Spurred on by Mary's competence, I managed to lock it after them. She gave me an approving grin. The attendant looked like she had swallowed worms.

4

I began to walk. The women timidly fell into line behind me, two by two, like good little schoolchildren. Every time one of them slowed or stopped to look at a wildflower, the attendant herded her back into line with a curt, "No stopping." I was outraged. But if I challenged the attendant, would she take it out on the women?

When I walked toward the attendant she shrank back, frightened. Afraid of me? The women watched. Suddenly the whole business seemed ridiculous. There was nowhere for the women to run, no way to escape. I stopped. "We still have a bit of time. You can walk more or you can sit and rest. I'll stay right here. When it's time to leave I'll raise my arm as the signal to line up so we can go back to the ward." The attendant scowled at me. The women stared. No one moved. "Go! Walk! Go wherever you want. Take some time for yourselves."

Mary came forward. "Miss, we're not allowed to walk by ourselves. That's the rule. We're supposed to stay together." The attendant nodded, relieved.

Shocked, I asked her, "So what's the problem if you walk by yourselves for a few minutes?"

"Miss, we're not allowed," she repeated tonelessly.

"Okay, if that's what you prefer, we'll keep walking, two by two."

"It's not what we prefer, Miss," said Mary. "It's the rule."

"The rule makes no sense. It's a beautiful day."

The women watched, expressionless. I tried again. "Why don't each of you go and look at something and then come back and tell us what you saw?"

No one moved. I could smell their fear.

"Please, Miss, can we start walking again?" asked a short scrawny woman with red hair. "It's so nice to be outside. Thank you for taking us outside. I love being outside. I hope you'll take us outside tomorrow."

I gave up and led them around the perimeter.

When I said, "Time to turn around," I avoided the word "ladies," which sounded so condescending. They seemed to be walking back slower than they had walked out. *What would Mrs. Langstrom say if I was late to the meeting?*

Mrs. Martelli was waiting for me. "It is 3:37. You are seven minutes late!" She glowered at the attendant. The women cringed.

"It's my fault," I said, trying to speak with authority. "It was so lovely walking around that I lost track of the time."

"Walking! You're supposed to be playing games."

"I can't open the door where the equipment is kept. My key doesn't work."

Mrs. Martelli gave me a murderous look. "And you're a college graduate?"

"No, ma'am, I have one more year to go. Besides…" Mrs. Martelli was not interested in what I had to say and left to deal with two patients who were yelling at each other.

I noticed Liz and Maggie looking as if all the air inside of them had been sucked out. I made my way to them, at the same time trying to pay attention to the women who kept thanking me for the walk.

"She wouldn't let us go with you," said Liz.

"She says we're troublemakers," added Maggie.

"She says you won't last two days here," whispered Liz.

"She's wrong, isn't she? You're not gonna quit, are you?" I hated hearing the begging in Maggie's voice. "You won't let her chase you away like she did the other girl, will you?"

I could feel the two women silently beseeching me to stay. We'd barely spoken, and what they'd said hadn't been exactly friendly, and yet I couldn't make myself tell them I decided to leave. Nor could I imagine leaving without telling them.

I took a deep breath, hating myself for not being able to tell them I was quitting. "I'll be here until school starts in September."

"Promise?" asked Liz.

Maggie looked as if she wouldn't believe anything I said. "Yes, I promise."

"You crossing your fingers?" queried Maggie.

I couldn't help laughing. "No," I said, showing her my ten uncrossed fingers. I sensed them watching me as I hurried to where

Mrs. Martelli was beckoning me. She harumphed and stomped her way down the stairs, shaking her head in disapproval as I followed close behind. When she suddenly stopped and turned, I almost fell on her. "Show me your key."

I pulled the chain of keys around my waist, trying to remember which key we had used. To gain time I said, "Why don't we go to where the equipment's stored."

"You don't know which key it is, do you?" she asked, a wicked gleam in her eye.

I gave up. "No," I shrugged. "I don't remember."

She looked at the keys on my ring and, without hesitation, said, "It's this one."

I was amazed. "How can you tell? A lot of them look alike."

"You want to survive in this place, you learn what you need to know, fast."

"How long have you worked here?"

"Too long," she sighed. "But, that's the way it is. No sense crying over spilt milk is what I tell myself. Let's open the door."

No matter how she twisted and jangled her key and mine, she couldn't open the door. I managed to suppress a smile, biting my tongue to avoid saying "I told you so." While watching her struggle, I was impressed by her tenacity. I was also worried. Would she blame me for damaging the lock when I tried to open the door? She muttered something under her breath and then turned to me. "This is a perfect example of what's wrong with this place. Nothing works the way it should and nobody gives a damn. I think the lock's been changed. That's why we can't open it. You'd think someone would have told me, wouldn't you?" I nodded. "You need to go to where you got your keys, give the man this key," she pointed to the key on my chain, "and ask for the right one."

Much to my astonishment, she opened the gates for me. I started to leave, then stopped, turned to her and said, "Thank you for your help," but she had already walked away.

Although I didn't want to be late for the meeting, I couldn't run. The weight of the keys bouncing against my body hurt, so I walked. Pleased that I found the building, I knocked on the front door. No one answered. I walked back full of dread at having to tell Mrs. Martelli I didn't have a new key. Struggling with the key to open the big gate did not improve my mood. I was ready to tell her to take the job and shove it, except that I couldn't rationalize breaking my promise to Liz and Maggie.

Prepared for a tongue lashing at best and being fired at worst, I climbed up the stairs and walked to the ward. Mrs. Martelli was yelling at a woman who'd messed in her pants. "You know you're supposed to use the toilet? Why didn't you?"

The woman was crying, mumbling words that made no sense.

"Speak up! What do you have to say for yourself? You think we like to live in your stink? You know better. Now go clean yourself up." She turned to two women who hadn't scurried away fast enough and bellowed, "Get the bucket and the soap, and don't forget the towels."

The woman hobbled toward the bathroom, her chin on her chest. Two women ran to get supplies. Some of the women dispersed, edging themselves into corners. A few walked to the far end of the day room and stood in small groups looking out the windows.

I was so upset I blurted out, "No one answered the doorbell or my knocking. I couldn't get a new key."

"Well, now you know where to go. Get it tomorrow before you come here." Without waiting for a response, she went into her office.

"I'm leaving," I told no one in particular.

"You saying that to make me jealous?" shrieked an obese woman.

"Shut up, bitch," screamed a sallow-faced woman.

The obese woman acted as if she'd been hit and made a move to retaliate, but the sallow-faced woman had already backed away. I thought I would comfort the obese woman by patting her on the shoulder, but she waddled off, exuding rage, forcing anyone in her way to move aside.

"She doesn't like to be touched," explained Maggie.

"Oh, I'll go tell her I'm sorry," I said, feeling as if I were walking in a minefield.

"Don't worry. She's new, only came a couple of days ago. She'll learn."

Maggie's bitter tone made me uncomfortable. I didn't know what to say to her. I kept thinking: *She's in a mental hospital. She's mentally ill.* "Maybe we could sit for a bit and talk tomorrow."

"It's not allowed," she snapped as she walked away, melting into a group of women staring into space.

More rules. I cursed myself for agreeing to stay. It didn't help that my head was aching and my stomach was making embarrassing noises, reminding me that I hadn't eaten since last night's dinner. *Damn my conscience. Why is this day seven times longer than any other day in my life?*

As I walked toward the door, the obese woman ran up to me and blocked my way. "You're a terrible person," she yelled. None of the patients paid attention to her. "You make me sick." I tried to move past her but she blocked my way, screaming curses and accusations. She was a whole lot bigger and wider than I was and she used her bulk like a defensive football player.

I was resigned to waiting for someone to either take care of her or release me when two women stepped between us. One said in an authoritative, calm voice, "Agnes, go wash your face and hands, it's almost time for dinner."

"They're not dirty," Agnes whined.

"Yes they are. Go wash up. Now!"

I watched in amazement as Agnes shuffled away, crying, "Not dirty. Not dirty. Not dirty. Not dirty."

"Don't mind her. She's just confused. It takes a while before some people settle down and get used to the routine," said the woman. Her hair was neatly curled and her dress, a housedress to be sure, was neatly fitted and bright yellow, not faded like most of the patients' clothing. "I'm Carol," she said, "and this is Barbara."

I nodded. "Thanks for coming to my rescue. I was beginning to worry."

"About what?" asked Barbara. She was tall and emaciated, with piercing black eyes her glasses couldn't conceal. She could have passed for a strict schoolteacher.

I shrugged, trying to seem nonchalant, failing miserably. "She looked like she was going to attack me."

"This is one place where looks are absolutely deceiving."

"But..."

"Look how she behaved when Carol told her to go wash up. Is that a person you need to be afraid of?" Barbara's tone of voice was withering.

Why were Carol and Barbara here? They seemed sane, especially compared to some of the women in the ward. Were they crazy in a way I couldn't see?

As I was leaving, Mrs. Martelli spotted me. "What are you doing here? You're supposed to be at a meeting."

"I was just saying goodbye." *I sound like Agnes.*

"Oh, no, a goody-goody! " She shook her head. "God save us!" Pushing away strands of gray hair that had escaped her bun, she said, "Miss Weinstein, let me give you some much-needed advice. There are rules and then there are rules. You need to learn real quick which ones to follow."

I looked at her blankly.

Then there were screems.

"I'll fix you."

"Bitch."

"Whore."

"Help!" stopped the conversation. Mrs. Martelli hurried away. I slipped out, ran down the stairs, and didn't take a full breath until I was out of the building.

The grounds were deserted. A terrible odor pervaded the inner yard—some kind of food being cooked for dinner. Cabbage, I guessed. There was no way I could even imagine eating anything that smelled that bad. Then again, what choice did the patients have?

5

Despite running to the building, I was late and opened the door to the meeting room with trepidation. A gray-haired woman with tight curls, plaid-rimmed glasses, and a body stuffed like a sausage into her uniform, checked her clipboard and greeted me icily. "You must be Miss Weinstein." I nodded. "The meeting started fifteen minutes ago. I expect you to learn what you've missed on your own time." Four men and three women, none in uniforms, stared at me. I slunk into the closest empty seat while the gray-haired woman, who I assumed was Mrs. Langstrom, spouted rules and more rules. The others were busy writing down what she said. Feeling conspicuous, I looked through my bag and found a pen but no paper. The woman sitting next to me ripped a sheet of paper out of her notebook and handed it to me without looking. When I tried to whisper thanks she turned away. I waited for Mrs. Langstrom to give us suggestions—how to deal with patients, intransigent locks, or difficult attendants—but after spouting a bunch of *shoulds*, *oughts*, *need tos*, and *have-tos*, she closed by saying, "You are summer recreational therapists and you are here to play games with the inmates. Most of you are experienced and know what I'm about to say but, I'll tell you anyway. Take back as many patients as you take out. Make sure you have the proper number of ward attendants with you. Maintain professional distance. Any questions?" I had plenty but was too afraid to ask. No one responded. "Very well, I will see you next Monday."

I tried to walk out without attracting attention, but she stopped me at the door. "Miss Weinstein, I expect you to be punctual from now on." Before I could apologize she strode out of the room. I stood in the empty room, feeling ten years older than I had before starting work. *Where was Bruce? Why hadn't he attended the meeting?* Finally I pulled myself together and left.

Outside, the noise from the construction had stopped but there was a new kind of noise—it sounded like people shouting, but I couldn't see anyone. I walked across the grounds to where I had parked the scooter. It wasn't there. *Someone stole the scooter!* I looked around frantically trying to imagine where it could be. Then I realized the cacophony was coming from an upper level screened-in porch where patients were laughing and yelling at me.

"It's over there."

"No, it's that way."

"Look behind the building."

Apparently it wasn't stolen. That was a relief. Yet it was nowhere in sight. I began to listen to what the patients were yelling. Some of it was nonsense, but a couple of voices kept mentioning bushes. It was like the hiding game we used to play: when you got closer to the hidden person the others shouted, "Hot," and when you moved further away they screamed, "Cold." The patients' voices grew more intense as I moved uncertainly toward a thick clump of rhododendron bushes. When I was about a foot away, I saw a bit of red paint.

More than one person must have put the Vespa into the bushes, because no matter how I tried, I couldn't push or pull it out. *Wonderful! A perfectly miserable end to a perfectly horrible day.* I gave up, walked over to the curb, and sat down, my head in my hands.

"Something wrong?" I looked up and saw a gray-haired, distinguished looking guy wearing a suit and tie, carrying a briefcase.

"Someone, maybe a few someones, decided to hide my scooter. It's behind those bushes, and I can't get it out."

"Where is it?" he asked, looking around.

I shrugged. "Over there." He followed me, studying the situation as if he were a lawyer. Maybe he was a lawyer. Maybe he could sue the bastards—if I ever found out who did it. "I'm sorry," he said, picking up his briefcase, "I can't help you," and walked away. No matter how bad the day had been, it seemed it was about to get a whole lot worse.

I stood looking at the imprisoned Vespa. The silence was eerie. I guessed the patients were eating dinner. *What if the creeps had vandalized it and it no longer worked? What would I tell Jake?*

I heard male laughter and saw hordes of construction workers leaving the worksite. I didn't relish asking them for help but I didn't see any other choice. I walked to the road where three men had stopped while one of them had a smoke. "Hey, what's a nice girl like you doing in a place like this?" one smirked. His bulging muscles were both promising and repugnant.

"Guess I'm doing what you're doing, working," I countered.

"Want a cigarette?" offered another.

"No thanks," I said. "What I need is help."

"What for?" The third guy, tall, covered with construction dirt like the others, looking at me with disconcertingly blue eyes.

I took a deep breath, girding myself for the inevitable jokes. "I drive a Vespa to work. Somebody, or a bunch of somebodies, moved it into the bushes over there."

"What's a Vespa?" asked Bulging Muscles.

"It's a motor scooter, sort of like a small motorcycle. Will you help me?"

"Sure," shrugged Smoker, taking a final puff, throwing his still-burning cigarette to the ground. I couldn't help myself. I stamped it out. He laughed.

Blue Eyes, who kept ogling me, asked, "What's it worth? Us helping you."

"Forget it," I muttered and walked back toward my scooter.

"Hey, Scootergirl," he shouted, "I was only teasing." I didn't stop walking. In fact, I walked faster. He caught up with me, the others following. His tone was friendly. "My name's Mike. What's yours?"

"Rennie," I answered, staring at my imprisoned scooter. The other two joined us. "There it is," I said, pointing. "I think the only way to get it out is to lift it over the bushes."

Bulging Muscles laughed. "Piece of cake. He turned to Mike. "You lift the front end; I'll take the back." Apparently he didn't consider Smoker or me to be of any use. *Well, they tried; I'll give them that.* After a few tries Bulging Muscles shook his head. "Damn, it's heavier than it looks. What do you think, Russ?"

"Maybe Russ and I could lift the front end since it's lighter, and you and Mike could lift the back," I suggested timidly, not wanting to impugn Bulging Muscles' sense of himself.

Mike interjected, "Good idea." He moved to the back. Russ and I positioned ourselves at the front. "Will, you say when."

"One, two, three, lift," yelled Will, aka Bulging Muscles.

It was heavy and awkward, and I didn't like the way Russ smelled of stale cigarettes, but with a lot of grunting and heaving the four of us managed to lift the scooter over the bushes. I released the brake and started to wheel it to the curb. "I'll do that," said Will, a command more than an offer. It was no time for me to object.

"Never saw anything like it before. Will you give us a ride?" asked Mike.

Up till now, the only person I'd let ride on the back was my skinny little sister. These guys weighed a lot more than I did, more than Jake. I wasn't sure the Vespa could hold their weight and mine but I didn't know how to say no. "Okay, but just up this road and back. I need to get home." Russ was the lightest so I thought it best to start with him. "Hop on, Russ, and don't wiggle!"

I started the ignition, he held onto my waist, and we took off. There wasn't enough room for me to make a U-turn comfortably with him on the back so I stopped. "Let me turn the scooter around and then you can get back on." He agreed, got off, I turned it, then he got back on and we drove back to Will and Mike. I was sweating with worry and apprehension.

"That was fun," he said. "How many miles you get to a gallon?"

"About a hundred." The three guys looked impressed.

"Where do you buy one of these?" asked Will.

Hah! Here's my chance. "It belongs to my boyfriend. He lent it to me while he went on vacation."

"How come he didn't take you?" asked Mike.

Good question. "I need to work. Got tuition to pay for."

Why is this day three months long? "Don't know about you, but it's been a long, hard day." I looked at Mike, hoping he would take the hint and leave with the other two. "I need to get home."

Will straddled the Vespa. "It'll only take a few minutes."

"Right," I muttered, and got on the scooter. When we came to the place where I had to turn, I told him, "You need to get off so I can turn. I can't do it with you on it, you're too heavy."

"Sure you can, Scootergirl," he said, making no move to get off when I stopped.

If I were a person who used clichés, I would say this was the straw that broke the camel's back. I yelled, "Get off!"

He laughed.

I turned off the engine and took out the key. "Right! Stay here as long as you like, I'm leaving."

He smirked. "You're bluffing. Besides, you leave this baby here and we'll just put it back in the bushes." I was beyond caring. All I wanted was for the day to be over.

"Have fun," I said, walking away. *Let him do what he wants. Jake has insurance. I'll tell him it was stolen. There are worse things than taking the bus.*

As I walked away, I saw Mike and Russ coming toward me.

"Where's Will?" asked Mike.

"He wouldn't get off so I could turn it around. I'm tired and I'm going home. It's been a horrible day."

"Don't leave. I'll talk to him," Mike said. " He's really a good guy, he just hates being told what to do." I shrugged and started walking toward the entrance. "Hey, Rennie," called Mike, "don't go. He'll get off, he was only teasing. That's how he is." I kept walking. "Wait, he's coming." Mike caught up with me. "Rennie, wait!"

"What?" I could see Will and Russ walking toward me, a big grin on Will's face.

"Go get your scooter and ride it home. It's not a good idea to leave it here overnight," said Will, his voice like a parent talking to a child.

He's right. What if someone really did steal it? "Thanks," I muttered as I walked back. Will still had that stupid grin on his face. I couldn't help myself, "What's so funny?"

"The way you looked when I wouldn't get off your scooter. I like girls with spunk and you got lots. Want to go for a beer with us? Make nice nice?"

I shook my head.

"C'mon, I was only kidding. If you want, you can leave your scooter with us tomorrow. We'll make sure no one touches it."

"Yeah," added Mike, "you don't even have to give us a ride."

"Don't know about that," teased Will.

I looked at the three of them. All in all, they seemed like pretty okay guys. "Sounds good, thanks. See you tomorrow." I started the Vespa with no problem and waved as I zoomed off. I was grateful that I didn't have to change the spark plug on my way home.

When I walked into my house, it was as if I were seeing it for the first time. A quiet, peaceful, place. No unpleasant smells. No nerve-wracking sounds. No commands. No fear that I was breaking a rule. No eyes staring at me. The contrast hit me hard, as did my sense of the responsibility I'd taken on. In a few weeks I'd be twenty, not even old enough to vote, but for the next three and a half months I had the power to hurt or help people two and three times my age.

When I took the job at the hospital my only thought was how much more money I'd make than if I worked at a children's camp. I'd been deaf to the questions and concerns of so many people. Even during the interview I had had no qualms and raised no concerns about the nature of the work beyond the obvious—taking people out to play games, planning recreation for small groups of women. *How could I have been so oblivious?* So stupid? I felt proud of myself when I told people I'd be working as a recreational therapist for the summer. And I'd ignored them when they said, "Are you crazy?" Now I wished I had listened.

I took out the breakfast I hadn't been able to eat and heated it up. The scrambled eggs didn't look very appetizing and I wasn't hungry, but I ate them anyway. I was so full of impressions and thoughts, I wished there were a way to erase or delete emotions and images. I remembered Mr. Carson's directive to leave hospital experiences inside when I locked the gate behind me. I could see the wisdom in this; I just had no idea how to do it. The day's events clung to me like burrs on a wool sock.

As I watched the sunset I was more than sorry I'd agreed to go to the concert with Bruce. Not only did I dislike smoky crowded places with loud noise, I didn't know Bruce, and I was exhausted. I was too full of impressions, as if the women were living in my head.

Vanity kicked in. I managed to pull myself together and changed into my green dress. I even put on the jade earrings I'd found in a secondhand shop and saved for special occasions. When the doorbell rang I opened the door. Stunned, I stared at Bruce. His whole demeanor had changed—seemingly taller, fuller, more sure of himself. He had a big grin on his face. "You look great," he said. Jake seldom paid any attention to how I looked, which I never minded, but being told I looked good on such a bad day lifted my spirits. Maybe the evening wouldn't be so bad.

"You do, too," I said, and he did. His trim charcoal pants and blue-gray shirt were a sharp contrast to the khakis and white shirt he wore at the hospital.

On the way to the club, Bruce told me how much he loved jazz, how he looked forward to hearing the music, how each night was totally different, even if the players were the same. At the entrance, the ticket taker welcomed him by name and asked, "Who's your gorgeous girlfriend?" I blushed. Bruce didn't correct him. We walked up a flight of creaky stairs to a large, crowded, smoke-filled room where a band was warming up. Bruce led me to two seats near the front, marked RESERVED. "They're for us," he said, with undisguised pride. "The musicians consider me a regular."

Bruce braved the crowds around the bar and brought back two cups of ginger ale. He was so keyed up that when the band stopped playing, he jumped up. "Hey, look over there, by the door. Satchmo's coming." Louis Armstrong, elegant in a shiny gray suit, with a huge smile on his face, waved to the crowd with his trumpet as they yelled, "Satchmo! Satchmo!" Bruce cheered and whistled. I looked on in amazement at the change in him. His rapt focus and beaming face radiated ecstasy as Louis Armstrong began to play, moving and shaking in time with the music.

Band members joined in as Satchmo walked to the stage. The music took over and crowded out all thoughts and feelings of my first day of work. I forgot how tired I was, how stressed I felt. I even forgot about the women. Along with everyone else, I clapped and tapped my feet, unable to sit still. When the band closed with a rousing version of "When the Saints Go Marching In" it was impossible to stay seated. Everyone, including me, got up and started dancing to the irresistible beat. Suddenly the music stopped. Shocked, everyone froze. Satchmo grabbed the mike and said, "Folks, this is a wooden floor. If everyone moves to the same beat, I'm told the floor will collapse. You gotta move off the beat."

"Not possible," people shouted, me included.

"Well," he said, grinning, "then clap your hands and shake your booty, but keep your feet still." It wasn't easy.

When the music stopped and it was time to leave, Bruce and some of the musicians exchanged a series of complicated hand gestures that made them all grin. Bruce whistled happily as we waited in line to go down the stairs. Everyone looked joyful and relaxed. No one seemed bothered by how long it took to walk down the steps.

On the way home Bruce said, "It's great to have a friend go with me to concerts. I hope you'll come with me again." He told me about a lot of other musicians he knew and thought I would enjoy. When he pulled up to the curb at my house he got out of the car, opened the car door for me, walked me to the door, and waited until I'd opened it and turned on the lights. He didn't try to kiss me, so I decided it was all right that I hadn't told him about Jake.

I should have been even more exhausted than I'd been before we went to the concert, but the music left me exhilarated in a way I'd never felt before. Even though the day had been grueling, and it was almost midnight, I hardly felt tired any more. With the music still playing in my head, I quickly fell asleep.

6

In the morning I got ready for work humming "When the Saints Go Marching In." I packed a lunch with an extra sandwich for Bruce and drove to the hospital thinking that now I could park the Vespa without having to worry about where it would be at the end of the day. As I wheeled the scooter through a small opening in the fence surrounding the construction site, a red-faced man in a construction hat yelled, "Hey, where do you think you're going with that thing?"

"I'm looking for Mike," I said.

"Mike who?"

I shrugged. "I don't know his last name but he's got two friends, Will and Russ. Don't know their last names either."

"What do you want with them?"

"They said I could park my scooter here and that they'd keep an eye on it." As soon as the words came out of my mouth I realized I'd said the wrong thing.

"They're paid to build, not to babysit scooters. Get it out of here."

So what if I promised Liz and Maggie I'd come back. So what…

I maneuvered the Vespa back into the main yard and looked for a safe place to park. "Park it here." I looked up and saw a male patient out on the screened porch of a nearby building. "I'll watch it for you." He was grinning, shaking his head.

"Thanks," I yelled back, hoping he'd be there when I needed him.

After I managed to open all the gates and doors, albeit with great difficulty, and got the key man to trade my wrong key for the right equipment shed key, I walked into the main room and greeted Mrs. Martelli, practically crowing. "Good morning. Here's your copy of the new key. I thought we should both have working keys for the equipment shed."

I hoped I saw a faint smile of approval before she turned and yelled, "Ladies, line up. Miss Weinstein is here to take you out. Make sure you wash your hands and faces before you go."

I was feeling that things were finally going a little better when a gaunt, grey-faced woman with huge dark eyes and equally huge dark circles under them came up to me. "Miss, will you take me?" she asked. "I promise I won't run away."

Not knowing any better, I shrugged. "Sure, join the line."

Mrs. Martelli strode over to her, glaring. The woman cowered as if she expected to be hit. "And where do you think you're going, Missy? You know you're not allowed outside. You have no business asking someone who doesn't know enough to say no."

Groveling, the woman backed away as Mrs. Martelli strode off. When Mrs. Martelli was out of sight, I went over to her and asked, "Why can't you go outside?" She turned away from me and didn't answer. "Look," I said, "if you want me to take you outside, I need to know what the problem is."

She mumbled, "I'm on suicide watch." I tried to hide my shock. "But if you take me outside I promise I won't run away. I promise I won't hurt myself. It's such a beautiful morning. I just want to listen to the birds."

I didn't know what to do. I understood why she wanted to go out—it was a bright, sunny morning—but what if she did run away or hurt herself? Then what?

"Please, Miss, I promise I'll stay right by your side. I promise I won't hurt myself. Please, Miss. You don't have to ask Mrs. Martelli. If you don't tell her maybe she won't find out." The desperation in the woman's pleading upset me.

"You came back, that's good. And surprising. You going to help Natalie?" It was Liz at my elbow, a challenging look on her face.

"Hello Liz. Are you coming with me this morning?"

"I asked, you going to help Natalie?"

"Where's Maggie?"

"You going to help her?

Shut up! I'm doing the best I can. "Why don't you find Maggie? I'll deal with this." When she didn't move, I said tersely, "If you make a scene I won't be able to help her. What's the point of that?"

Liz stared at me for a long second, nodded, and left.

Mrs. Martelli had told me that a lot of the women didn't want to leave the ward, so as they gathered I whispered to Natalie, "Okay, stand in line. If Mrs. Martelli comes back and questions me I'll do the best I can."

"Oh, thank you, Miss. Thank you. I promise I'll be good." The defeated sag of her body was gone and in its place was a woman with birdlike energy, exuding joy. Liz and Maggie beamed their approval.

No one should have so much power over other another person's happiness.

Trouble came where I least expected it. The attendant scheduled to accompany me spotted Natalie. "You can't come with us and you know it." She yanked her out of the line. I couldn't bear the look of anguish on Natalie's face.

"Just a minute," I said to the attendant. "I'm the therapist and I decide who goes out with me." I had no idea if this was true, but it sounded authoritative. The attendant looked confused. I grabbed Natalie's hand. "Let's go, ladies." I hated that form of address but I didn't know what else to use. Under my breath I murmured, "Don't say anything and don't stare at me, just move with the rest of the women." Her eyes grew even larger. Her fear was palpable. "I'm holding you to your promise. If you try anything, I'll never take you out again. Understand?" She nodded and squeezed between Liz and Maggie, who made room for her.

"It's okay," I told the attendant, "I'll make sure she stays near me. You take the head of the line and I'll take the back." She hesitated. I tried to look like I knew what I was doing and breathed an audible sigh of relief when the women started moving slowly down the stairs. Thankfully, Mrs. Martelli was nowhere in sight.

I felt a surge of triumph as I opened the equipment shed and handed out bats and balls. The women took them with no comment. The whole time Natalie hovered, periodically touching my arm. Every few minutes she'd say, "I'm here, Miss. I haven't run away. I'm not hurting myself." I hated hearing her demean herself.

At the field the women gathered around me, Natalie at my elbow. "How many of you have played softball?" A few raised their hands. I didn't ask how many wanted to play—clearly they didn't care what we did. I managed to organize two teams, but when I suggested they choose positions in the outfield they didn't move. "What's the matter?" I asked.

"Nothing," said one of the women.

Maggie came up to me, Natalie close behind, and said, "You need to tell them what to do." She reacted to my puzzled expression with a mirthless smile. "Miss Weinstein, the only way to survive in this place is to do nothing until you're told what to do. That's the first lesson every person who's forced to come here learns." She added, bitterly, "The sooner the better."

"Even when it comes to playing a game?"

"You're the boss and they know it."

"What about you?"

"What about me?" she mocked.

Before I could decide how to answer, a tall, powerfully built black woman strode up, followed by a breathless attendant. Stepping between us, she spoke with so much authority I wondered who she was. "The women hate games. They hate rules. They just like to be outside."

"How do you know?" I asked, taken aback.

"If you're in this place, you know." Her tone of voice was withering. I felt sorry for anyone who stood in her way.

"Who are you?" I knew she couldn't be a therapist since she was accompanied by an attendant, but she knew exactly what to do, unlike me.

"Shirley. I'm a real good pitcher. I'll get them going." She turned to Liz. "You play first base." Liz nodded and walked out onto the field. Then, one by one, the women went where Shirley told them to play. "Okay, ladies," she said, "let's toss this ball around." She picked up a softball and threw it to Liz, who threw it back with ease. I watched, astonished, as Shirley organized infield and outfield practice. She energized the players by effortlessly hitting the ball to each of them to catch and return, while the batting team waited patiently.

The attendant who had come with Shirley sighed. "That woman is two people living in one skin." Her eyes followed Shirley as she moved around the field. "I promised I'd bring her here when she found out building 5 had a new recreational therapist. She works so hard we try to give her a reward when she finishes her work in the laundry—that is, when she can.

"What do you mean?" I asked, admiring Shirley's graceful athleticism.

"When she's okay, like now, getting some exercise, she's the sweetest, kindest person around, but when she has a spell, watch out! It's like there's a tornado inside her." She moved closer to me and whispered, "We're not supposed to know, but she's in here for life. Killed her husband and baby. Word has it the baby wouldn't stop crying and the husband tried to protect the baby. When the cops came she was standing, cradling the dead baby, crying. Didn't even try to get away. Told the cops to put her where she couldn't ever hurt no one ever again." She looked at Shirley, pitching the ball, easy and slow, encouraging a woman to swing. Giving her suggestions. Shouting with approval when her pitch hit the woman's bat and the ball rolled into the infield while the woman ran to first base.

"Wouldn't think it to look at her, would you?"

"Does she ever have any warning? That she's about to have a spell, or whatever you call it?"

"She gets a terrible headache. Maybe the pain drives her nuts."

"She's such a good athlete."

The attendant shook her head. "Wish there was a way to help her. Seems like she senses when it's gonna happen but the pressure builds up so fast she can't stop it and then she explodes. She's so strong everyone's afraid of her."

"Maybe you should bring her here and let her whack softballs until she uses up her energy. Maybe then she wouldn't have a spell."

The attendant looked at me as if I were a small child making a naïve suggestion. I felt foolish. What did I know about spells?

After almost an hour, when the attendant told Shirley it was time to leave, everyone lost interest in playing. As we gathered up the equipment, Natalie hesitantly touched my arm. She'd been no more than two feet from me the whole time. "I'm here. I haven't hurt myself."

Maggie shook her head. "Jesus, Natalie, you're not a ghost. Yet. We see you."

Natalie gasped and seemed to shrink inside herself.

"It's okay," I told her, wanting to throttle Maggie. I looked at my watch. It was only eleven—we still had fifteen minutes, but I was exhausted. "Let's take a little walk before we go back." From the expressions on their faces I sensed what the women wouldn't say; no one wanted to walk anywhere except back to the ward. I shrugged. I was in a foreign country, and if I wanted to survive I was going to have to learn the customs and language and culture.

The attendant who'd come with us got up from where she'd been sitting and yelled, "Form a line, ladies, two by two!" Natalie, who'd been too close for my comfort the whole time we were out, suddenly grabbed my hand and held it so tightly I winced. When I tried to release it she grasped it even tighter.

I told Natalie she had to let go so I could put the equipment back. Although she reluctantly released her hand she moved even closer, which I didn't think possible. Liz warned me, "You better be prepared. Martelli's gonna be furious. Natalie's on suicide watch, you know."

Natalie started to cry. "I stayed next to you the whole time, Miss Weinstein. Please, tell her I was good."

Liz rolled her eyes and jeered, "Crybaby!"

I threw the last of the balls into the box with so much force it bounced back and I caught it just before it hit Natalie.

"Good catch," jeered Maggie. "You should start a softball team."

I swallowed my anger. "Good idea. Maybe I will."

"We need to go upstairs," said the attendant, scowling at me as she herded the women toward the stairway.

Liz mumbled so low I barely heard her, "We need to go upstairs, '*lay-dees.*'"

Maggie sighed. She and Liz hung back as the others climbed the stairs. "You sorry you stayed?"

"I'm sorry I don't know more than I do."

"Well," mocked Liz, "just remember you can lie as much as you want."

Astonished, I asked, "What's there for me to lie about?"

"Even if Natalie hadn't been practically inside your skin all morning, you could say she ran away, and even if she denied it, no one would believe her. They'd send her to building 6 so fast you'd think she'd never been here."

"You wouldn't tell her that, would you?" pleaded Natalie, paler than ever.

"There seems to be no end of kindness around here," I retorted, after assuring Natalie that I wouldn't tell.

Liz and Maggie ignored my sarcasm.

"You ain't seen nothing yet," said Liz. "Stick around, if you dare." She and Maggie flounced up the stairs, leaving me with a shivering Natalie.

I reluctantly followed them, Natalie hovering next to me, crying. I felt cross and irritated—by her, Liz, Maggie, Mrs. Martelli, by the whole system, but I swallowed my annoyance. "Don't worry, if there's a problem I'll tell Mrs. Martelli how good you were." Even to me, my words sounded ridiculous. Natalie was more than twice my age and she hadn't done anything wrong while she'd been with me, yet she cowered, waiting to be punished for the crime of wanting to be outdoors on a lovely summer morning.

Once again the hospital world turned upside down. Mrs. Martelli was nowhere in sight. The attendant who greeted me asked, as Nathalie slithered away, "Isn't she on suicide watch?"

"Is she?" I responded innocently.

The attendant shrugged, checked her list, and said, "No matter, everyone's here." She walked back into the ward, telling the women, "Time to wash up, ladies." My resentment and frustration threatened to boil over, so I ran down the stairs and out the doors, breathing in air still reeking of boiled cabbage. I found a quiet place under a tree and ate my lunch, which should have reminded me that I'd agreed to meet Bruce at 11:30. Now if I went I'd be more than half an hour late. No sense trying to find him. He had probably given up on me and eaten lunch at his house. I pulled out the extra sandwich and fed what I could to the birds, then threw what was left into a garbage can. I paced around the inner wall feeling sucker-punched by Liz and Maggie, with only myself to blame. The authority I had over the patients made me nervous. Not only did I not know how to how to deal with it, I didn't like it and didn't want it.

Stomping across the lawn, I asked myself why I felt like I had to stick with working at the hospital just because I promised Liz and Maggie. There was the salary, of course, but then I started thinking about Jake and school, and wondered if there was more to my working at the hospital than the pay. While he was in law school in Manhattan, I was going to a teachers' college in the middle of what I called, "cow country," a boring small town, far removed from New York City, where I'd grown up. I hated the school. I hated what I was studying. I hated the town. I had nothing in common with my classmates, yet I hadn't applied anywhere else. Jake was infuriated by my decision and insisted I was just as smart as his sister, who was going to Brooklyn College. He accused me of being afraid to go to a better school. We'd argued about this—too many times. Jake's accusation hurt. Although I pretended not to care, privately I agreed with him. It now occurred to me that maybe it wasn't only the money. Maybe I took the job at the hospital to prove to the world that I could work in a difficult place without giving up. So far, I'd survived, but that wasn't saying much.

Mulling it over, I walked faster, tripped over a fallen branch, and felt too miserable to get up. I rolled over and lay on my back, looking at the sky full of white puffy clouds. The scent from a bank of rose bushes overwhelmed the smell of cabbage. I wished I could have stayed there for the rest of the day. Instead, I got up and walked toward building 5. I knew I should go to a different ward, but which one? What was the point of playing games with patients who didn't care what they did? I had no idea what to do next. It all seemed ludicrous.

7

I peered into the hospital ward. Row upon row of prone, inert, silent bodies covered with white sheets, many with tubes attached to motionless arms. Nothing I could do with anyone there. In the next ward a few women lolled aimlessly while others paced or stared out the window. How was I supposed to play games with people who weren't even aware of one another? At least they were moving. I looked for the head attendant. She was sitting at a desk in a small office with a huge window onto the ward and a smaller window through which I could see the leaves of trees.

"What can I do for you?" she asked. *At least she seems friendly.*

"I'm the recreational therapist for this building, and I've come to work with the women in this ward."

She laughed a deep belly laugh.

What's so funny? I tried to swallow my frustration. "Is there a problem?"

"Oh, Honey," she said, smiling kindly, "these women have been in the hospital for so long there's no way you can do anything with them. They don't even talk to themselves, much less to each other."

I looked at the women and felt a surge of something—pity? Outrage? Shock? I couldn't make myself walk away from them. "If it's all right with you, I'll bring up some big balls. Maybe they would like to play with them."

She shrugged. "If you want, but these women haven't interacted in years and there's no way you can change that."

"Well, I guess it won't hurt to spend a few minutes with them."

"Up to you," she said, shaking her head, sighing.

I went to the equipment shed, still feeling a sense of triumph when I opened the lock, filled a cloth bag with large rubber balls, and trudged back to the ward. The attendant looked at me as if I too was crazy, then shrugged as I walked into the middle of the room. None of the women appeared to notice me or show any interest. I'd walked into a room full of zombies.

The voice in my head telling me I was crazy, insisting I couldn't do it, just made me more determined. I took one woman by the hand, moved her to what I hoped would be a circle, smiled, and told her to stay there. She did. I did the same with a few more of the women. Some waited, some wandered off. When I had about six women in something resembling a circle, I threw a ball to one of them. Although it rolled over her feet she showed no reaction. I rolled a ball to another woman. No reaction, but most of the women stayed in the circle. Why I thought this was some sort of success, I don't know, but I kept at it for about half an hour, rolling a ball to each woman before picking them up and putting the balls back in the sack. I gently thanked each woman before leading her to the place where I'd found her.

As they wandered off I sat on a bench watching them. Their lack of connection scared me. I'd never seen people so out of contact, but I decided, no matter what, I'd keep coming back just to see what might happen.

"How'd it go?" asked the attendant as I was leaving, not bothering to hide her amusement. I knew she'd seen me with the women and I couldn't tell what she thought of my efforts.

"Okay. If it's all right with you, I'll come by for a short time every day."

"Everyone's given up on the women in this ward, so don't get your hopes up. I'll understand if you decide not to return." All of a sudden it occurred to me that not having any regular supervision might turn out to be a good thing. I could pretty much do what I wanted as long as no one noticed.

I left and walked past building 6, where the violent women patients were housed. From the outside it looked no different from the building where I worked. Trying to imagine what people did that landed them in the violent wards, I stopped and looked up. A tall, beautiful black woman in an attendant's uniform stepped onto the porch. Her nametag read "Mrs. Cooper." "What are you doing here?" she asked. "You want something?"

"No. I'm the recreational therapist for building 5. I was just walking by."

She didn't even hesitate. "You willing to take out some of my people?"

Me? Work with violent people? "Am I allowed? Isn't there a recreational therapist assigned to your building?"

She laughed bitterly. "Look, Sweetie, around here you're a therapist. You got some power. You can pretty much do what you want as long as you don't cause trouble. And no, we don't a have a therapist. The woman who was assigned to this building quit."

"Why?"

She shrugged. "Guess you better ask her. Anyway, you willing to play games with some of my people? They sure would like to get out of the building. A few of them are pretty good athletes."

I was trying to get used to the idea that I had some power, and I was curious about the patients in this building, but still—violent women? I hesitated.

"You afraid of working with these women?"

I had no idea what I felt.

"I don't think so," I said, trying to look assured. "Are they that different from the women in building 5?"

"Sometimes. Sometimes not."

What have I gotten myself into? "What does that mean?"

"It means they have moods, just like the rest of us. You get the equipment. I'll bring out some women. She walked away before I could say anything.

What if they attack me? What if I'm not supposed to be working with women from another building? What if they fire me for transgression? The longer I waited the more anxious I felt. Did I really have the power to choose to work with violent patients?

I hoped my key wouldn't work, but it did. I got out the equipment and waited, troubled and nervous and scared, the large bag of balls and bats a heavy weight against my legs. When the women came out to meet me they didn't look any different from the women in building 5, except that most of them were black. I didn't remember seeing any black faces in building 5. Was there some kind of segregation going on? Even the thought made me uncomfortable.

"Thanks for taking us out," smiled a woman almost as wide as she was tall and bouncing with energy.

"Yeah. Did Coop tell you the other lady wouldn't come near us?" asked another. She looked me up and down. "You gonna play softball with us?"

"Sure," I answered, feeling a little less panicky. At least these women were eager to be out and excited about playing.

"Great. Let's go!" hollered the first woman. Despite her girth, she ran toward the field, the others following, with the attendant bringing up the rear. I was relieved that she didn't bark, "Two by two, ladies!"

The round woman, Rosa, gathered everyone together. "I'll be the captain of one team. Georgia, you be the other captain if no one minds." There was an agreeable silence and then a nodding of heads. "Okay, my team, let's hit the field. Georgia, you decide who bats first."

The get-up-and-go of these women was in stark contrast to those on Martelli's ward. They were more like Shirley, joyfully running around the bases, hitting the pitched balls as hard as they could, cheering each other on as they practiced, squealing with joy when someone hit to the outfield. To make the teams equal, and have enough to play the field, I offered to pitch. The attendant said she would catch. She was such a stunningly gorgeous woman she could have been a model. Why was she was working in this place? When I addressed her as Mrs. Cooper she told me to call her Coop. I was impressed that she knew everyone's names and used them; the patients called her Coop.

We had a great time. The women were good athletes and obviously delighted to be outside, playing. Whatever disagreements they had they quickly settled amongst themselves, refusing to let me or Coop intervene. Their seeming normality puzzled me. Why were they housed in the building for violent women? When it was time to pack up, Rosa asked, "Can we do this again?" I looked at Coop. Rosa and Georgia stared at Coop, then Rosa said, "We were good, weren't we?" Coop nodded. "So, can Miss Weinstein take us out again?"

"It's up to Miss Weinstein."

A chorus of women begged me to come back. They promised they'd be good, wouldn't fight, wouldn't run away—grown women pleading with me, a teenager, just to allow them outside and play a game. My heart hurt. I had no idea if I'd be allowed to come back. I guessed it would be best not to ask for permission. "Sure," I said, with more confidence than I felt.

Coop smiled approvingly. "Thank you so much, Miss Weinstein. You have no idea what this means to us."

"Call me Weinstein. Who needs the Miss?" We agreed to be Coop & Weinstein, catcher and pitcher.

I congratulated myself for surviving my second day after checking out and locking the last gate. When I discovered the Vespa wasn't where I'd left it I was upset, yet not surprised. Someone, maybe two or three someones, was playing a game I didn't like. The situation was beyond my control, sort of like my job at the hospital. Again the patients on the top floor yelled at me from their screened-in porch. This time I paid attention to their directions. This time I was able to drive it out of its hiding place. I waved my thanks and one of the patients yelled, "We're watching. We'll tell you where they put it."

I drove off, my mind replaying the day's events. I couldn't stop thinking about the contrast between the patients on Martelli's ward and those on Cooper's. When I got home I had no desire to read the newspaper, listen to the radio, or watch my family's tiny black-and-white TV. All I wanted to do was to sit on the porch, put my feet up, watch the birds, and sip iced tea.

When I had the energy to pick up the mail and saw Jake's familiar handwriting, I danced around the room, goofy with happiness. I hadn't had any letters from him since he'd left, even though I'd written to him at various American Express offices according to dates he said he'd be picking up mail.

I tore it open, my heart beating wildly.

Hey Rennie,

It's taken me a while to write because my plans suddenly opened up and I wasn't sure what I was going to do or where I was going. A guy I met in Paris suggested we travel together. He's a mountain climber and offered to teach me how to climb harder stuff than what you and I have done. I got really excited when he described what he wanted to do and so he showed me what equipment to buy. Fortunately, he has a car, which is so small our stuff barely fits in but at least it doesn't use much gas. I'll try to write when I can but if you don't hear from me, it's because I'm swinging from a rope on some huge cliff waiting to be rescued.

I think I'll still be going to Amsterdam on schedule so you can send letters there.

I hope you're enjoying driving the Vespa. I grin thinking of you riding it on the Queensboro Bridge because I'm sure by now you've figured out how to deal with the ridges.

See you in September. Take good care of yourself.

Love, Jake

After I read the letter a few times, it occurred to me that he never asked how I was or how my job was going. That didn't feel very good, but I told myself it was probably because he didn't know when he'd receive my letters. Still, the feeling was too strong for me to rationalize it away.

8

The next morning I drove the Vespa to the hospital in a downpour. Despite my waterproof rain gear, water dripped down my neck, soaking my blouse. It didn't help that I had to change a spark plug just blocks from the hospital. I arrived feeling miserable, looking worse. At least the weather might discourage the "scooter movers" from messing with my Vespa. I dried myself off as best I could in the administration building bathroom and then ran to building 5. I knew I couldn't take the women outside in the rain and there wasn't enough space to play any ball games on the ward, so I had to figure out what to do before facing Mrs. Martelli.

Much to my surprise and relief, she wasn't there. Instead, a white-haired woman with sparkling blue eyes greeted me. "Good morning, Miss Weinstein, I'm Marge Denby. I'll be taking Mrs. Martelli's place for a while."

"What happened to Mrs. Martelli?"

"She had an emergency appendectomy last night, but we've heard she's doing well. I brought a get-well card for her. Would you like to sign it?"

No. "Sure. I hope she's okay." *This woman seems nice. Wonder if it will make a difference to the patients.*

"What do you plan to do today? Sixty women is a large group."

Think, Rennie. "It's raining. We can't go out. Is there something you'd like me to do? There's no room on the ward to play games with everyone."

"Can you tell stories?"

Mrs. Martelli, I don't wish you ill, but I wouldn't mind if you took a whole lot of time off to fully recover. "Yes." I wasn't about to tell her Mr. Carson's reaction to my previous storytelling effort. She was in charge.

I thought of the parable of loaves and fishes as I watched Mrs. Denby organize the women, finding places for them to sit when there didn't appear to be enough room. Her firm, soft voice was melodious compared to Mrs. Martelli's, but the women paid attention. There seemed to be less extraneous movement and mindless chattering as the women settled down, less tension in the air. Even Liz and Maggie, who sat near where I was standing, seemed a bit softer, less guarded. It was too early to tell how long this would last, but if she could make a difference in such a short time maybe I could too. Maybe then I'd feel better about the work I was doing at the hospital.

"Miss Weinstein can't take you outside this morning because it's raining, so she's agreed to tell stories. I hope you will listen carefully and enjoy them."

"Mrs. Denby, can we tell stories too?" asked Liz, her voice rapier sharp.

Mrs. Denby didn't react. "That's up to Miss Weinstein."

Liz's familiar mocking look made my heart sink. What kind of story did she want to tell? Then again, why was I worried? Mrs. Denby was in charge. "Well, Miss Weinstein?" Liz challenged.

I looked at the sea of faces. Maggie had an amused expression, clearly enjoying my discomfort. Barbara, with her glasses perched on the tip of her nose, looked like a schoolmarm waiting to see whether her student would give the correct answer. I hated feeling caught. Mrs. Denby wasn't helping. I shrugged. "Sure, Liz. Why don't you start?"

She stood up, smiled at Maggie, Carol, and Barbara, then took a moment to gaze at her audience. When she began, her voice was deep and resonant. She sounded like a person used to speaking to large groups. "Once upon a time, a long time ago, there was a woman who had a bad temper. Nobody liked her. She was—"

"Stop," interrupted a woman, her voice full of anger. "No sad stories."

"Happy stories. No sad stories," echoed a woman sitting near Mrs. Denby.

Other women joined in, each shouting over the other.

Liz began trembling, her bravado and power ebbing away. I sensed trouble. "Liz, can I add to your story?" She nodded. Her body sagged as Maggie and Carol made space for her to sit next to them.

What the hell am I going to say? "She was upset because she was—"

"Hungry," shouted a woman. Others quickly chimed in.

"She wanted a big, juicy steak."

"Meatloaf with mashed potatoes and gravy."

"Spaghetti with lots of sauce."

"Fresh asparagus from the garden."

"Lima beans cooked with ham hocks like my grandma cooked them."

"A baguette like I had in Paris."

"What's a baguette?" asked the woman next to her.

"It's the best bread you ever tasted," she answered. "Better than you could ever imagine. Nothing like it here."

Mrs. Denby looked pleased, signaling me with her hands to keep going. Liz was crying quietly, trying to hide her tears. I continued, changing the focus. "When people realized she wasn't a bad person, and she wasn't angry at them, they began to bring her food. Lots of different delicious food."

"They brought her cake," said Carol, awkwardly patting Liz on the back. That set the group off once again. They called out mouthwatering desserts:

"Chocolate with walnuts and marshmallow icing."

"Lemon cake with blueberries."

"Orange chiffon with strawberries."

"Hot fudge sundae with whipped cream and cherries."

"Rice pudding with raspberries."

"Strawberry shortcake with peach ice cream."

"Apple pie with vanilla ice cream."

"No, pecan pie with coffee ice cream."

A few women got up and started moving, chanting their favorite food, their arms and legs flailing, waving, clapping. Soon almost everyone was on her feet, a kind of mass dance. I shuddered to think what Mrs. Martelli would say if she were here, but Mrs. Denby was enjoying the spectacle. So was I until I saw Liz get up and move unobtrusively to the far end of the room. I followed her as best I could, nodding and smiling and moving to the chants. She was leaning against the wall closest to the ward gate, her head in her hands. I hesitated. What did I have to offer her? "Liz? Can I help?"

She whirled around, her face contorted in fury. She spat out her words. "You want to help? Get me out of here!" Her rage shocked me and I took a step back. "You can't help. No one can."

"Would talking help? I'm happy to listen."

"Happy to listen," she mocked. "You're a kid, what do you know?" She turned away and leaned against the wall. I felt like putting my arm around her, but I didn't know if there was a rule about touching patients and I was afraid to make her even more upset. She was right. I was just a kid.

I turned around when I heard a tinkling sound; Mrs. Denby was ringing a small bell. The women quieted and most sat down. "What a wonderful way to celebrate a rainy day," she said.

"That's a poem. You're a poet," shouted a woman.

Mrs. Denby smiled. "So I'm a poet and don't know it?" The women laughed, nodding their heads. "Poetry aside, one of my favorite stories is Cinderella. Would you like to hear Miss Weinstein tell it to us?" A chorus of yeses. I couldn't bear to see Liz's misery and put my arm around her, praying I wasn't making things worse. Much to my surprise she allowed me to lead her back to where Maggie was sitting. She stood up and helped Liz sit, making a space for her. I wished I knew more about what I was supposed to be doing.

I have always enjoyed telling stories. I tell them to myself as much as to anyone listening. But this time I was telling the story to Liz. I emphasized Cinderella's despair, her suffering, her inability to make her stepmother and stepsisters like her. When the fairy godmother came to talk with her, Cinderella was so despondent that her fairy godmother had to convince her that she deserved better, that there was a way out of her wretched life, and that even a fairy godmother couldn't make it better it all by herself. Cinderella had to help. I knew there were no fairy godmothers in a mental hospital but it was all I had to offer. When I finished, there was a roar of approval and clapping. I felt a little better. I had no idea how Liz felt.

Natalie came up to me, surprisingly animated, her face glowing with happiness. "I never heard anyone tell Cinderella, I always read it. Hearing the story makes it come alive. I feel like Cinderella a lot of the time. I wish I had a fairy godmother." *So do I.*

Carol and Barbara joined Natalie. "Thanks for the way you told the story," said Barbara. "Even with the fairy godmother crap, there was something to it, not just a fairy-shmairy happy ending."

"I'm not much for fairy-shmairy anything," I said.

"How did you make it so real?" asked Carol.

"Whatever story I tell is real to me. I needed a happy ending."

"You?" challenged Carol. Natalie looked shocked.

Who do they think I am? I don't know what I'm doing. I think the world is going crazy. I'm working in a place with crazy people. "Just because I work here and can go home at night doesn't mean everything in my life is great," I shot back and then wished I'd kept my mouth shut.

Barbara seemed to know when Carol was ready to pounce. She turned to me. "You're young, lots of time to be unhappy. C'mon Carol, Natalie, Liz, we need to get ready for lunch."

Under the tree had become my lunch place, but because of the rain, Mrs. Denby invited me to eat in her office. She smiled companionably as we unwrapped our sandwiches. I fumbled for conversation. There were so many questions I wished I could ask her, but I didn't know how to begin. I wanted to know about the bell, about the difference between how she talked to the patients and the way Mrs. Martelli barked at them, about her calm and gracious manner. "Have you worked here long?" was the best I could come up with.

"Yes," she said. I waited, hoping she would say more about working at the hospital but she startled me when she changed the subject. "You've been taking some of the women in building 6 out to play."

"Yes," I mumbled, afraid I was in trouble.

"Good for you." She finished her sandwich, stood up, and said as she left, "See you tomorrow." The conversation left me uneasy, thinking the real dialogue had gone unspoken. I found it reassuring that she knew about me taking out the women from the violent wards and didn't tell me to stop, but why had she mentioned it? Maybe, if I ever saw Bruce again, he could tell me about her.

After lunch I went to ward 2, which I now thought of as the Zombies ward. The attendants greeted me in a friendly way, not bothering to hide their amusement. I walked patients into a circle again, not stopping the ones who drifted. Six women stayed. I threw a big rubber ball to them, one at a time, for several rounds. No one responded, but that didn't upset me. I had no expectations. It was an easy way to spend time.

There were wards in the building I still had to visit, but the women on Martelli's ward used up so much of my energy, I decided to take my time going to other wards. According to Bruce, as long as I didn't cause trouble or let Mr. Carson see me with my patients lounging under a tree, no one cared what I did. So far, it seemed he was right.

It had stopped raining, so I walked over to building 6, hoping Coop would see me and bring out the women. I hesitated to ring the bell, in case Coop wasn't available. A different attendant, on her way into the building, asked why I was there. Not wanting to cause any trouble for Coop, I told her I was a recreational therapist and wanted to take Rosa and Georgia, and any others who wanted to come, out to play ball. She nodded and said to wait.

In a few minutes she came back and said Rosa and Georgia couldn't come because they were going on a toot, but she would bring out a few others. I had no idea what a toot was. "Can you ask them to go on the toot some other day? And, if Mrs. Cooper is on duty, would you let her know I'm here?"

The attendant gave me a strange look and said, doubtfully, "All right. I'll ask them." A few minutes later she brought out Rosa, Georgia, and about ten others, some of whom I recognized from the previous day. "Mrs. Cooper is off today. I'll be with the patients."

As we went to get the equipment I asked Rosa, "What's a toot?"

"Oh, it's when we go crazy." She laughed when she saw the bewildered look on my face. "I can't explain it, so don't ask." *Were she and Georgia going to go crazy, whatever that meant, while they were with me? Maybe I shouldn't take them out. Maybe I should wait until Coop was back on duty.*

"Rosa, would you do me a favor?" I asked nervously. She nodded. "If you think you're going to go crazy would you let me know? Ahead of time?"

"Sure," she said, as calmly as if I'd asked her to let me know when she was tired. While Rosa and Georgia organized everyone, I kept thinking about them going on a toot and hoped they were right about being able to postpone it. They did seem to have extra energy. They talked louder and faster, ran more quickly, argued more, and reacted faster, but nobody complained. This attendant wasn't as good an athlete as Coop but she was willing to catch and did pretty well. I liked the way she yelled "gotcha" as she tagged someone out. When it was time to take the women back, they thanked me for letting them play and said they hoped I'd do it regularly.

When we were far enough from the patients, and they couldn't hear me, I asked the attendant about the therapist who had been assigned to the building. "She quit after a bunch of patients attacked her. Sent her to the hospital with broken bones. So far they haven't been able to replace her."

It took me a moment to find my voice. "Attacked her? Why?"

"I wasn't there so I don't really know. My guess is she was bossing them around in a way that made them mad. You got to be real careful how you act around these folks. They can be good as gold one minute and thrashing anyone in hitting distance the next. Don't take nothin' for granted."

At the end of the week, nervous and unsettled, I walked to Mr. Carson's office to pick up my paycheck. I hadn't seen him since he'd yelled at me the first day and fervently hoped he wouldn't remember me. As I was about to enter the building I heard a sarcastic male voice. "Where've you been, Miss Goody-Goody?" I turned around. Bruce was leaning against the porch post, his hands in his pockets, a knowing smirk on his face. "Hear you've been taking Cooper's people out to play. Building 5's not enough for you?" *How do you know?* "Guess you're too busy working two buildings to meet me for lunch."

"I…"

"I know, you're so involved with doing your job you forgot."

His demeanor and assumptions irritated me. "How come you think you know so much about what I do?"

"I grew up here. I know how this place works. I knew the first time I saw you that you'd never understand. You're too busy trying to make a difference in the lives of people who aren't your concern."

"If I'm hired to be a therapist, why aren't they my concern?"

"Your title's just a fancy name for a person whose job is to take people outside and play games with them. Therapy has nothing to do with it."

His words stung. "How I choose to do my job is none of your business."

I turned to go inside, but he took my hand and stopped me. "Hey, Rennie, don't be mad. I'm only telling you the truth. I thought we were friends. Didn't we have fun at the Armstrong concert?"

I nodded, pulling my hand away, not ready to tell him it had been more than fun, that it was like being in a world I didn't know existed. We walked into Mr. Carson's office together and I watched in amazement as Bruce said hello to everyone by first name, helped them find my check, then joked with them before following me outside. "Thanks," I said, churlishly, annoyed by his joie de vivre with the staff and his criticism of me.

He shrugged. "What bus do you take?"

"I don't. I drive a Vespa, if I can find it." He followed me as I walked to where I'd parked it that morning. I told him how I had to search for my scooter each afternoon after work.

"That's ridiculous. I'll find out who's doing it and get them to stop."

"Is there anything you can't find out?"

"Depends on what I want to know."

There wasn't much I could say to that. With the help of patients, we found my scooter. Bruce promised to do what he could to stop the people hiding it. When he asked for a ride, I could hardly say no. At least he wasn't heavy like Will. He put his arms around my waist, holding on lightly as we rode around the periphery. When I let him off, he asked so many questions about the Vespa I asked, "You thinking of buying one?"

"Don't have the courage."

I must have looked as surprised as I felt. "Courage?"

"Takes guts to ride. What if you hit something lying in the road?"

"I try not to think about stuff that might or might not happen."

"Then how do you keep yourself safe?"

Safe? I stared at him, puzzled. "What do you mean?"

Bruce ignored my question. "There's a coffee shop a few blocks from here. Could I buy you a cup of coffee? I'd like to hear how your week went."

That surprised me, too, given his criticisms. The ride was short, and as we approached the coffee shop delicious smells wafted through the open door into the street. "This doesn't smell like any coffee shop I've ever been to. What are they cooking?"

"It's not really a coffee shop. I only call it that because they serve great coffee and that's what I usually have, but I didn't eat lunch so I'm hungry. What about you?"

"Not really, though I wouldn't mind a cup of coffee."

Jake was on my mind, so I noticed when Bruce held the door open for me, something that would never have occurred to Jake. I couldn't help compare the two. Bruce wasn't at all like Jake or men to whom I had been attracted. Bruce was tall, at least six-one, and lanky. Jake was about five-ten and muscular. Jake exuded sexuality, Bruce didn't. When Jake looked at me it was as if we were the only two people in the world. Bruce seemed uncomfortable if by chance we made eye contact. Jake never talked about friendship—I think all his so-called friends were male classmates. What Bruce meant when he said we were friends, I didn't know.

Inside, we passed a counter with bar stools. A man wiping up a spill smiled and gestured for us to sit at one of the tables in the next room. The room was small and cozy. Every table was covered with a white tablecloth, set with heavy modern flatware and sparkling glasses. Each had a vase of fresh yellow and white flowers at its center. When I saw the paintings that covered the walls, I stood transfixed. Horrified. Jagged lines and garish colors collided with swathes of thickly applied black paint, exuding danger and menace. "Those paintings look as if they were done by a patient in the hospital," I muttered.

"They were," said Bruce, tersely. I waited for him to say more but he pulled out a chair for me, then, after I sat down, turned abruptly and walked back to the counter. I heard him say, "Could you bring us some food, please?" *No menus? That's odd.* I stared at the paintings. They reminded me of *Guernica*. I spent lots of time looking at it at the Museum of Modern Art and was fascinated by the way Picasso painted struggle and pain. But these paintings had reds so bright it hurt my eyes to look at them, shards of brilliant color like broken glass slashed with black. If the paintings had voices, they'd be screaming, vying with each other for attention.

"What do you think of them?" asked Bruce.

"I can't imagine why whoever owns this place would hang them in the dining room, where people want to relax and enjoy their food."

"I guess you have a limited imagination," retorted Bruce. Stung, I stood up, ready to walk out. "I'm sorry. Don't go," he said.

He looked so unhappy I sat back down.

"Tell me about the paintings."

"Let's eat first."

"I told you I wasn't hungry. Besides, the paintings took away any appetite I might have had." I didn't want to tell him I had a headache that was steadily getting worse.

"You're too sensitive."

"I don't even know what that means, but I'd sure rather be too sensitive than not sensitive enough to care about people's feelings." I stood up, furious. *And he wants to be friends?* He tried once again to apologize but I'd had enough. "Your apologies don't mean anything. I'm leaving. You can walk back to the hospital, it's only a few blocks."

"Rennie, wait! I painted them."

I froze.

Bruce? Painting with such passion and abandonment? Bruce—a mental patient?

I felt as if all the air in the room had been sucked out. Who was he? My head was throbbing. I wanted Bruce to disappear, along with his paintings.

"Are you all right?" he asked. "You look a little pale."

"I have a migraine. I need to go home while I can still drive."

"You can't drive a scooter with a migraine if they're as bad as mine." He took out a small vial of pills and offered me two. "They really work." By this time my head hurt so badly I would have taken poison just to stop the pain. He came back with a glass of water. I swallowed the pills without hesitating. "You should eat something. In my experience an empty stomach makes the pain worse. Yanni, the guy who owns this restaurant, is a great cook. I'll ask him to make you some rice, it's the only thing I can eat when I have a migraine. Go into the small office off to the left of the dining room. You can rest on the couch while I talk with him."

Feeling woozy from the pills, I was relieved to lie down on something soft. The next thing I knew it was two hours later and my headache was gone. Bruce was nowhere in sight. I found the bathroom and washed my face. The cool water cleared my brain but it didn't stop the questions. How could Bruce have made those paintings? And if he did, what made him paint them?

The dining room was almost full. I was grateful my headache was gone, otherwise the noise and smells, no matter how delicious, would have been impossible to bear. I tried to be unobtrusive as I walked between the tables, heading for the counter. An inveterate eavesdropper, I pretended not to listen to bits of conversation, some of which fascinated me, like the woman complaining to the man sitting opposite her. "What's the big deal about going to France by myself?" I couldn't stop to hear the answer, but I would have liked to. I hoped she told the man that she was going, no matter what. I hoped that if I were in that situation, I would go, no matter what.

9

I walked to the counter where a man with a mop of curly black hair that spilled out from the bandana looked up at me. His kind, deeply lined face and the furrows between his dark eyes suggested he was a man used to hard work and a difficult life. "Feeling better?" he asked. "I am Yanni. Welcome to my restaurant. Bruce told me about your headache. Come sit. I cooked you some rice, but if you are able to eat something more I would be pleased to have you taste a new dish I just made. Of course, if you still feel ill and don't want to eat, I understand. While you decide, I will call Bruce. He was most anxious about you."

Much to my surprise, the food smells emanating from the kitchen made me hungry. When Bruce came in and saw me he smiled. "You look a lot better. Did you have a good sleep?" I nodded, embarrassed. "Glad the pills helped you. It's the only thing that's ever helped me."

"What's the name of them? I'd like to get some."

Bruce hesitated. "I can't tell you."

"Why not?" He acted like he was wondering what or how much to say. "It's okay, I won't tell anyone."

"Rennie, I'm sorry, but I'm not allowed to say." He paused. Beads of sweat appeared on his forehead. "If I tell you something, will you promise not to tell anyone?"

"I guess it depends on what you're telling me."

"Don't worry, I haven't killed anyone. I just need someone to talk to. You seem like a person I can trust."

"What makes you think that? I mean I think I'm trustworthy, but we don't really know each other."

"I've heard about the way you take such good care of your patients. They need people like you."

"What did you hear? Who did you hear it from?"

"I told you, there are no secrets in this place, so be careful."

I would have questioned him more but Yanni came and put a dish of rice and a large bowl of something on the counter that smelled so good my mouth watered. I watched with fascination as he deftly portioned out the food, artistically arranging it on our plates. "Please, try to eat something," he urged before leaving and quickly returning with a basket of hot bread, a plate of dumplings, and two glasses of wine. I didn't think I should drink wine so he brought me sparkling water. Bruce ate as if he hadn't eaten in days, obviously enjoying the food. It tasted as wonderful as it smelled and reminded me of food I'd eaten in a Mediterranean restaurant, a kind of spicy stew with chicken and vegetables. I could feel myself relaxing as I ate. The bread, with its hot crisp crust and chewy insides, had just come from the oven—perfect for mopping up what I couldn't eat with my fork.

I couldn't help watching Bruce eat. With impeccable manners, he ate deftly, like a European, holding the fork in his left hand. When he had finished the last piece of bread, he said, "Wait till you taste Yanni's desserts. They're amazing."

"Right, but just coffee. I'm so full I can't eat another bite."

When I told Yanni how much I relished the food, his whole face lit up. He had a wonderful, irresistible smile and I smiled back, feeling as if a weight had been lifted from my shoulders, which made no sense. Nothing had changed. Life at the hospital was still frustrating and scary, and I had no idea what was going on with Bruce, but even he looked less tense. I was tempted to ask Yanni what he'd put in the food. When I told him I was too full to eat dessert, he said, "I will give you baklava to take home. Make you want to eat here again."

"I'll come back even without it. The food is marvelous." Yanni hummed what seemed to be a Middle Eastern melody as he cleared the dishes, promising to bring the coffee as soon as he brewed a fresh pot.

The restaurant was now full and noisy. We watched people stare at the paintings, trying to eavesdrop on their comments. At least people were really looking at them. Lots of times I've gone to restaurants and never noticed what was on the walls. I asked Bruce, "Did you really paint those paintings?"

"Yes, but it's a long story. Sort of complicated."

"Like not being able to tell me about the pills?" He nodded. I was curious. I also wondered why he wanted to tell me. I could see he was waiting for me to ask what happened, so I did.

"Let's talk in the back room. It's too awkward sitting at the counter." I followed him into the small room and we sat down. Bruce stared at the floor, tense, quiet in a way that felt noisy. I waited, relieved when he finally started to talk.

"In January a friend and I were making plans to go to Europe and I needed my birth certificate for the passport application. Whenever I asked my mother where I could find it, she'd say, 'Not now,' and leave the house. No matter how often I asked, she wouldn't tell me where it was. I finally lost patience and yelled at her, 'I need to have it. Now!' She screamed back at me that she didn't know where it was. Then she started drinking, steadily. She'd been on binges before, but this time my dad had to hospitalize her."

"He put her in the mental hospital?"

"No, he'd do anything to avoid scandal. He had a colleague hospitalize her in a place out on Long Island."

"Did you ask your father about your birth certificate?"

"Yes, but he said he didn't know where it was either, that my mother took care of 'those things,' and I had to wait until she came home." Bruce paused and stared at the wall above my head.

"And then?" I said. None of this was making much sense.

"At first, I was just upset and baffled by the whole situation. But something began to nag at me. I sort of remembered a man, not my father, playing with me when I was very young. I think we were coloring with crayons. Don't know why, but it took me days to work up the courage to ask my father about it. He laughed a fake-sounding laugh and said it was my imagination working overtime. He told me to pay more attention to getting good grades and dismissed the whole idea, but something didn't seem right. I stopped asking my mother where my birth certificate was and started searching for it myself."

This was more story than I'd bargained for. Bruce heard me sigh.

"Is this too much for you?" he asked. "I know you're tired."

"Seems like you need to talk."

"I do. The pressure in my head is building up again, like the last time." *What does that mean?* He paused and looked at one of the paintings. "I've seen the way you help the patients." *You have? When?* "You're not like the others, just there for the money." I was too tired to correct him. "The truth is, I don't have anyone else to talk to." *I know what that feels like.*

Bruce became even more upset and excused himself. I walked over to one of the paintings to look at it up close. The paint had been applied so thickly that the texture played with the light, creating interesting shadows. Up close, the paintings weren't as disturbing and I could look at them without feeling assaulted. The ridges, hills, and valleys of paint were so inviting I felt like touching them. I looked for where Bruce had signed it, but what should have been a signature was murky, as if it had been painted over.

"Go ahead," he said, "you can touch them. I like it when people do more than give them a quick look." I closed my eyes and gently moved my fingers over the sculptural surface. The edges were mostly rounded, a contrast with the razor-sharp quality of the shapes they contained, a soft inside and a jagged outside. Each painting had a NOT FOR SALE sign beside it.

We sipped coffee and I couldn't resist tasting a little of the desserts that were as delicious as he had promised. Eating gave us something to do as I listened and he talked. "When my father left for the weekend to visit my mother, I searched my mother's desk. In the bottom drawer I found a locked steel box, but couldn't find the key. I tried to think like my mother, which is no easy task. I remembered she had a bunch of keys on her car key ring and they were still hanging near the door to the garage. I was right. One of the keys opened the box." He paused for a bite of baklava and a sip of coffee.

"I found a birth certificate, but it wasn't mine. Right birth date, right first name, but my name is Bruce Miller and the name on the certificate was Bruce Andrew Lowenstein. I kept rummaging and found my mother's marriage license, but when I read it, the words made no sense. According to the certificate, she had married Seth Miller two years after I was born. I felt as if the ground underneath me had turned into quicksand."

"So who is your real father?" I felt sorry for Bruce, but I wasn't sure I wanted to hear all this. It had already been a long, strange day.

"The short answer is Andrew Lowenstein, but it took months before I pieced together most of the story. I think I would have been okay if my mother had been willing to tell me, but she preferred drinking booze to talking with me. When I finally worked up the courage to show my father the birth certificate and ask him who Bruce Andrew Lowenstein was, he lost his proverbial cool and cursed like I'd never heard before, then left the house without answering me."

"What was that like for you?"

Bruce hesitated. His jaw muscles tightened and his eyes narrowed. "If it hadn't been for Yanni I don't know what would have happened."

"Yanni? The one who made our dinner?" He nodded.

"After my father left I became hysterical, screaming, throwing things, smashing everything in sight. I even slashed my arms and legs with the broken end of a bottle. I don't remember much of what happened next. According to Yanni, who was working on one of the men's wards then, my father sedated me, called a colleague who ran a private mental health clinic, and arranged for Yanni to drive me there."

"Oh, Bruce, I'm so sorry. It must have been awful for you."

"I'm grateful you're still listening." Tired as I was, I knew I had to listen until he finished.

"After Yanni drove me to the clinic, he found an Andrew Lowenstein listed in the Manhattan phone book and called him. He confirmed that he was my father and that he'd been seeing me regularly until Seth Miller married my mother. After that, Seth Miller had forbidden him to visit or call or write, saying it was too much stress for my mother. Apparently, Andrew tried to see me anyway but it was so difficult he gave up."

Bruce looked away. I waited. He certainly wasn't the contained, know-it-all person I thought he was. "What happened after Yanni took you to the clinic?"

"The first few days were horrible. I was disoriented and confused, but the worst part was the rage. I thought I was going to explode. Then Yanni brought Andrew Lowenstein to visit me."

"What was that like?"

"The world was upside down. Neither of my parents came to see me, yet here were Yanni and a man I hadn't seen since I was two. I didn't know it at the time, but Yanni had persuaded him to come, picked him up at a Long Island railroad station, and told him what had happened. Andrew remembered that I had enjoyed drawing and asked Yanni to stop at a store where he could buy me art supplies. He brought acrylics and canvas and convinced the staff to let me paint whatever I wanted."

"You did all these paintings at the clinic?"

"No, I only had two canvases. I did the rest after I came home."

"How long were you at the clinic?"

"A couple of months. I had a really good psychiatrist who decided the stress of the discovery had triggered a psychological breakdown but that I was basically healthy and would be okay once I sorted out my feelings. I didn't want to go home. He strongly encouraged me to do it. He felt I was ready to face my parents and that it was time to decide how I wanted to live my life."

"Were you?" *Are you?*

"I didn't feel ready, but he helped me work out a way to tell my parents that I intended to keep meeting Andrew. He was not only my father but also an artist, and I wanted to study with him."

"What did they say?"

"My mother said I could do as I pleased, but I was not to bring Andrew into the house. My father reluctantly agreed."

"Did you do the other paintings with him?"

"Yes. He's a good teacher. He's also very kind. When he learned that Yanni had been a cook when he lived in Israel and dreamed of owning his own restaurant, he helped Yanni buy this place. I didn't want to hang my paintings here but Yanni and Andrew persisted. They've been up for about a month."

I pointed to the painting closest to me. "Did you sign that painting and then paint over the signature?"

"Good eyesight! Yes. When I finished the first two paintings, at the shrink's suggestion, I signed them, "Bruce Miller." But after I came home I was still so angry at my parents I decided I wasn't Bruce Miller, yet I didn't feel like Bruce Lowenstein either. That's why there's no artist's name on the sign. Maybe I'll just sign them Bruce, or make up a name. Any suggestions?"

I shook my head. In a mock-serious way, told him I would definitely think about it. I was amazed that Bruce could talk about such a devastating time and stunned that he wanted to tell me. "After all that's happened, how come you're still working at the hospital?"

"It's a way to earn money in a place where they're unlikely to fire me. My father would do anything to keep our family's troubles private. The good news is that Andrew took photos of my paintings and helped me apply to some art schools. I got accepted to Pratt. I'll be starting in the fall and I need to save money for tuition. Seth

Miller doesn't approve of my becoming an artist, but then nothing less than studying to be a doctor or lawyer would satisfy him."

Meaning, he won't pay for tuition. I looked at the paintings again. They seemed different after our talk, less violent, more complex. "I'd say you're already an artist."

Bruce murmured thanks and looked at his watch. "It's getting late. I'm sure you're exhausted. I'll drive you home. You can leave your scooter in Yanni's garage. I'll pick you up tomorrow at whatever time's good for you and bring you here."

I thought about saying it was too much trouble, but I was exhausted. It had been a long day. The week had felt like months and my brain was muddled from trying to make sense of so much that made no sense to me. Bruce had none of Jake's take charge, sexy quality, but there was a gentleness in him that I appreciated and it felt good to have someone notice how I was feeling even if I wasn't paying attention.

After Yanni gave me an enormous package of baklava to take home, Bruce drove me to my house, waited until I got inside, then left. If he'd been Jake he would have kissed me, hard if he was interested, a peck if he wasn't. That Bruce didn't was a relief. I was in no mood to be kissed and would have had no energy to respond. Still, I wondered if he found me attractive. Tired as I was, I couldn't sleep.

10

The next morning, while waiting for Bruce, I picked up the mail. My heart raced when I saw Jake's familiar handwriting. I tore open the letter, always happy to hear from him.

Rennie,

Went on my first big climb and I'd never tell Aaron, the guy I'm climbing with, but I was scared shitless. Only a rope and his confidence between me and a thousand-foot drop. My hands were so sweaty I could barely grip the handholds, but I felt exhilarated. When I reached the top he surprised me with a cold beer. Imagine, climbing with an insulated beer holder! The best beer I ever tasted. Belaying wasn't so bad. I remember teaching you how to do it. I hope we can do more climbing when I get back. He told me about some great places to climb not far from the city.

I told you that I'd pick up my scooter in September but my plans have changed and I'll be coming to get it in mid-August. I trust you'll have it ready for me to drive.

Hope life with the loonies isn't driving you crazy.

Love, Jake

Loonies? I reread the letter a few times with mixed emotions. His wanting to rock climb with me felt good but his use of the word loonies upset me, especially since I'd written him a long letter about what it was like working at the hospital. I decided he was just being funny—he did have a weird sense of humor. My thoughts were interrupted by the sound of a car pulling into the driveway.

Bruce's hello was warm and friendly and I didn't know how to respond when he said I looked upset. I told him I was fine, just a little tired. He gave me a long, hard look, then shrugged and said that if I didn't want to tell him, I should just say so. I felt trapped. There was no way could I talk with him about Jake.

We drove to Yanni's restaurant to pick up my scooter in an awkward silence. My limited capacity for small talk eluded me and I was afraid to ask if he was mad or disappointed or sorry he'd told me his story. When he parked the car, before I could open the door, he said he hoped I wasn't upset with him. Upset with him? I didn't have room to be upset with him; my upsetness at myself took up all the space inside me. I was trying to think of something not inane to say when he added, "I've learned it really helps to talk about what you're thinking and feeling." I nodded, murmured thanks for the ride, and got out of the car. That might have been the end of our time together except at that moment Yanni invited us to have coffee and pistachio pastries. They smelled so good I couldn't say no.

When we entered the restaurant the phone was ringing. Yanni ran to answer it. Although I couldn't hear what he was saying, I could see by his expression that the news wasn't good. He walked over to us, shaking his head. "My sous-chef is sick. And with a full house tonight." Both Bruce and I offered to help. Neither one of us considered ourselves great cooks, but we knew how to follow directions and how to dice, chop, and sauté. Bruce was especially adept at mincing garlic and cutting up onions. Seems he did the cooking when his mother was drinking, which was most of the time now. When I saw how much Yanni had to do in the next few hours, I told him if he needed more desserts, I made pretty good brownies and didn't need a recipe. He nodded, told us how grateful he was for our help, said he could always use desserts, and showed me where to find the ingredients.

Suddenly I was filled with anxiety. *What if I left out an ingredient? What if they weren't any good? What if the customers didn't like them?* The noise in my head was so loud, it was amazing no one heard it. I hated feeling so bad about myself but I didn't know how to stop the incessant inner voices that screamed, *"not good enough."* To quiet them, I focused on assembling the ingredients, chopping nuts, melting butter and chocolate, and preparing the pans. Yanni asked me to triple the amount of batter I usually make, but I made the recipe three times to make sure I didn't mess up.

When I took the first batch out of the oven, they smelled so good Yanni and Bruce decided the brownies needed to be tasted. I tried to control my nervousness as the brownies cooled and didn't realize I'd been holding my breath until Yanni pronounced them delicious. He asked if I knew how to bake cakes, saying that he was a little short.

That made me so happy I hugged him, then, blushing, pretended I needed to wipe off a counter. Bruce said he liked pound cake—could I make one? Yanni told me one cake wasn't enough, that I needed to make a few. He gave me a recipe to use and asked if I could make three cakes—same batter, but each slightly different. We decided I'd make one with walnuts, one with apples, and one with dried apricots.

When I'm baking I focus on what I'm doing—there's no time for questioning my ability or self-worth. Now the stakes were much higher. I was using Yanni's recipe and ingredients. The cakes would be on tonight's restaurant menu—if they came out well, that is.

While the cakes were baking, Bruce got a phone call from his father. His mother had collapsed and was being taken by ambulance to the hospital. Yanni put his arm around Bruce's shoulder and asked if there was anything he could do. Bruce shook his head. This was the third time his mother had been hospitalized in the past four months. Visiting her had become routine. The doctors would dry her out, she'd apologize and promise to quit drinking, and once she was home, the cycle would begin again. I felt sorry for Bruce. He'd been kind to me and I felt a need to do something for him. "If it would help, I'll be home after I finish here. You're welcome to come over. Or tomorrow—I have no plans." He didn't respond. Yanni walked Bruce to the car. At least there was one person in Bruce's life who cared about him, no questions asked.

Alone in the kitchen, where pots hung from the ceiling, knives were held by magnets on the wall. Blenders, coffee grinders, and other small appliances sat neatly on shelves next to a bookcase full of cookbooks. I was enveloped by the smells of onions and garlic sautéing, meat roasting, and cakes baking, and the voices in my head stilled. I felt a rare sense of inner quiet.

After wiping up the counters, I looked around to see if there was anything more I could do. I liked being in the kitchen. I liked having unambiguous tasks. Chopping, slicing, and dicing was satisfying work, with a clear beginning and end, unlike my work at the hospital where rules were more like landmines than guidelines. I wished I had enough skills to work as a cook or baker.

Yanni came back in looking worried, but when he smelled the cakes baking, his face brightened. He made a fresh pot of coffee, poured us each a cup, and gestured for me to sit at the little triangular table in the corner of the kitchen. I could tell he was thinking about Bruce. "You're worried about him, aren't you?" He nodded, quickly busying himself with cutting up potatoes. I checked the cakes. When the toothpicks I stuck in each one came out clean, I took them out of the oven and put them on racks. Yanni told me to let them cool in their pans, so all I could see were the tops, which, much to my relief, looked okay.

"What else can I do?" I asked. I wanted to stay. I wanted to know more about him. Maybe if I did, I'd understand why I felt so comforted in his presence.

"I think that's all. Two chef friends are coming in to help."

I hoped my disappointment wasn't obvious. Working in Yanni's kitchen made me feel useful and needed. "I could stay until they come," I offered, wishing he'd find more work for me.

"I'm sure you have better things to do than to work in a kitchen on your day off."

"Not really," I admitted, blushing in embarrassment.

He acted as if he hadn't heard. Instead, he gave me a loaf of fresh bread and thanked me for my help and for being Bruce's friend. Much as I didn't want to go, there was nothing to keep me from leaving. I could see he was busy, so I said goodbye.

I walked toward my scooter at a snail's pace, hoping Yanni would call me back. There was nowhere to go but home. About three blocks from my house, my scooter slowed way down, then stopped. I heard the familiar sound of a spark plug gone bad. At least I wasn't on a busy street or in the pouring rain at night. I changed the plug while a bunch of neighborhood kids watched. Their admiration for my skill felt great, but their nasty comments when I refused all requests for rides left me tense.

At home, I parked the scooter, put new spark plugs in the equipment pack, and went inside. I poured myself a glass of orange juice and went out to the porch. When I was away at school, Jake and I wrote letters to each other once or twice a week and I wore his Phi Beta Kappa key on a chain around my neck. I fingered it, remembering how we hugged the night he gave it to me. The memory made me feel so good I wrote a chatty letter and was about to sign it when I realized his use of the word loonies still bothered me. Trying to find the right tone to tell him this took a long time, and none of what I wrote satisfied me. I finally decided not to say anything.

Maybe it was a joke. I signed it with love and hugs the way I usually did, found a stamp, and walked to the mailbox.

Even after helping Yanni and mailing the letter, there were still too many hours to fill before I could go to bed. My parents had left a list of chores, stuff I usually disliked doing. Now I welcomed them; they gave me something to do. I cut our postage-stamp-sized lawn, weeded the flowers, and tended to the blueberry bushes my dad had just planted, but nothing distracted me. Bruce didn't call—not Saturday evening or Sunday. Having nowhere to go and no one around to talk to exacerbated my anxieties. I almost looked forward to going to work.

Monday morning arrived, providing a respite from my restlessness. At least at the hospital I had a role to play. Mrs. Denby greeted me with a smile and told me that since it was haircutting day, I could only take out patients whose hair had been cut. I was astonished to learn that every patient had to get her haircut—no exceptions. "But what if a patient doesn't need a haircut?" My shocked expression apparently touched a nerve in her. She spoke curtly. "Miss Weinstein, it is not your business to question hospital policy." When I protested that I wasn't questioning the policy, which I was, she shook her head and left. Two attendants I hadn't seen before took charge. One woman supervised the hair cutting, the other marked the patient's name off a list. I sat on a bench, waiting until I could take out fifteen patients. The hairdresser was a tough-looking middle-aged woman with short frizzled hair and a girdled body. She draped a sheetlike garment around the neck of each patient. Although the hairdresser didn't put a bowl on the patient's head, she might as well have. Each woman got the same haircut, whether the hair was straight or curly. I had to admit, she was quick and skilled.

When it was Carol's turn, she politely told the woman, "I'm going to be released tomorrow. I don't need to have my hair cut." Her light brown, curly hair framed her face and looked nice, so I was surprised when the hairdresser ignored Carol's comments, telling her to sit in the chair and to be quick about it. Carol repeated what she'd said, with the same result. Trying to be reasonable, she said, "Okay, if you have to cut my hair, could you just take off a little piece? My husband is coming to pick me up tomorrow and he likes the way my hair looks."

"A piece is not a haircut. Sit down and shut up."

"But I don't need a haircut."

"If you don't sit down right now, I'm calling for help."

Carol looked at me, silently pleading for help. The women on the ward, even those still waiting for haircuts, retreated.

I walked between Carol and the hairdresser. "No one will know if you don't cut her hair. It looks fine and she's going to be released tomorrow. I'll take her out with the other patients who've had their hair cut."

"I'm in charge and this is none of your business. Stop interfering with patient care!" she snapped at me. Then, turning to Carol she barked, "*Sit down, now!*"

Carol started to cry. "I don't need a haircut. Please!" There was nowhere for her to run or hide but she ran anyway. The hairdresser called for help. Two attendants grabbed Carol and forced her to sit in the chair. Carol kept struggling to get up, screaming that she didn't need her hair cut. A third attendant appeared with a straightjacket. It was a scene from a horror movie, only this was real. The attendants forced Carol into the straightjacket, the hairdresser chopped off her hair, then she was carried off, still yelling that she didn't need her hair cut.

As if nothing had happened, the hairdresser yelled, "Next!" A woman sat in the chair and the haircutting resumed.

Stunned. Frozen. Outraged. How could this happen? I was supposed to take patients out to play, but all I could see was Carol begging the woman not to cut her hair. Maggie, Liz, and Barbara were huddled together, crying. I didn't know what I could possibly say or do, but I forced myself to walk over to them, as much to have company in my misery as to try to comfort them. Liz snapped at me, "So, Miss Weinstein. Miss Therapist. Miss Let Me Help You. What now?" I felt guilty and ashamed.

Barbara looked up at me, her face a mask of despair. "They'll take her to 6. Who knows when she'll get out now. Why couldn't that stupid woman leave her hair alone?" She mimicked the hairdresser's tone of voice, "It's the rules. I'm only following the rules." She spat out, "Damn rules!"

I heard Mrs. Denby call, "Miss Weinstein, I need to talk with you. *Now!*"

Barbara stopped me. "Tell her what happened. Maybe she can help." She started crying. "Never mind. Once you're in 6, you're in there for months." Liz and Maggie huddled close, shielding Barbara from the watching women.

I walked over to Mrs. Denby, still in a state of shock and disbelief. Her friendly demeanor had gone. In its place was a stern and disapproving look. "Miss Weinstein, I understand you have interfered in normal ward procedure." I was so taken aback I just stood there staring at her. "Well?" she asked, like a prosecuting attorney. I told her what happened. She listened without interruption; I'll give her that. When I finished, she snapped, "Do not, ever, interfere with patient care again. It is not your place. It is not your job. It is not your business. Now, do what you have been hired to do and take your patients outside."

Coop was wrong. I have no power. If I can't help Carol, who can I help? Moving like an automaton I asked women if they wanted to go out. To my surprise, Maggie, Liz, and Barbara volunteered. Everyone was subdued. I kept seeing Carol struggling with the attendants, hearing her pleading. When we were outside, and away from the building, Liz asked, "Could we just walk?" I nodded. Even the attendant offered no resistance when I opened the gate to the outer area. Like a funeral procession, we walked slowly and silently around the perimeter. No one looked at anyone. No one reacted to the flowers or the birds or the blue sky. What had happened to Carol could happen to any one of them. Even me. If whatever sense of safety I had was gone, how must the patients feel? How did anyone ever get well in this place?

The haircutter's treatment of Carol felt like a kind of mental-hospital McCarthyism; just as people might be labeled Communists with no proof, being rational in this hospital was no protection from mistreatment. I was so demoralized I wanted to drop the patients off and leave, but I needed to stay until they were all accounted for. When Liz, Barbara, and Maggie walked by me I barely looked at them, mutely despondent. Maggie didn't miss a beat. "Cheer up, Cherub, this is life at Concordia. Happens all the time." Her sarcasm was completely at odds with her hopeless look.

"Maybe it does, but it shouldn't. I just wish I could have helped Carol."

Liz muttered, surprising me. "Well, at least you tried, that's something."

I walked to the place where I usually ate lunch but was too depressed to eat and too upset to sit. I took a walk, hoping the sound of the birds and the smell of freshly mowed grass would lift my spirits.

"Hey Rennie, what's the matter?" asked Bruce, sauntering toward me, eating an apple. When I told him about Carol, he was neither sympathetic nor comforting. "Happens all the time. I told you at the beginning, the place runs on rules. Break a rule, you pay the price. She should have let the hairdresser cut her hair, especially since she was to due to be released tomorrow."

"Oh, so when you get upset and make a mess of your kitchen, and yourself, you're not put into a straightjacket and sent off to the violent ward. Oh, no! Not you. Not Doctor Seth Miller's son! You're driven to a private hospital by a kind and caring man. He brings your birth father, who gives you paints and canvases. Doctors talk with you. Listen to you. Help you get well. They even encourage you to paint your feelings. Seems you get to play by a different set of rules than Carol. Tell me, what makes you so much better than her?"

He blanched and stepped back. "That's not fair."

"No? Well what happened to Carol isn't fair. You know how it feels to be treated unreasonably. You of all people should understand. What is it about these damn rules, anyway? Do they help people get well? Make them feel safe? As far as I'm concerned they're just an excuse to hurt people who can't defend themselves." I turned away and started walking, fast. What was the point of working in a place where I was powerless to help patients resist an uncaring, unfair, and unjust system—where I was part of the system?

He caught up with me. "Rennie, please. I thought we were friends. Don't be mad at me for telling the truth." I was dumbstruck. "You're new here. You don't understand. The rules do keep people safe. If she'd let the hairdresser cut her hair she'd have been out of here. Maybe she wasn't ready to be released."

I glared at him. "And maybe it's you who don't care about her. Maybe she was ready to be released. Maybe she was just pushed past her breaking point. We all have them. Oh, forgive me. You're one of the exceptions. You count on being treated well. You're Seth Miller's son!" I started to walk away. He grabbed my hand.

"Why are we fighting? Carol has nothing to do with us. Besides, it isn't worth your getting fired." *Fired? For telling a hairdresser a patient didn't need a haircut?* "I'll be at the meeting this afternoon. You might need me to intervene—one of the advantages of being Seth Miller's son. And, by the way, I doubt you'll have any more trouble with your scooter being moved."

I was so astonished that I might be fired for telling the woman cutting hair that Carol didn't need a haircut, I couldn't think about my scooter. Bruce tried to ease the tension between us by inviting me to have lunch with him, but even if I'd been able to eat, there was no way I'd go back. When I told him I'd brought my lunch but was too upset to eat it, he looked concerned and started telling me what a bad idea it was to be too friendly with the patients, that I needed to keep clear limits. This was too much. I hurled my fury at him. "And you, of course, know all about boundaries and how to behave, given that you're protected by the chief psychiatrist of the hospital." He cringed, as if I'd punched him. "What I really need is for you to leave me alone."

"Please, come with me tonight. The Modern Jazz Quartet is playing. I think you'll love them."

Before I could answer, a tall, well-dressed man approached. His harsh expression and the rigid way he walked made me hope I'd never have to deal with him. He stared at me, then turned to Bruce. "How about introducing me to your girlfriend." Without waiting for Bruce to respond he said, "I'm Dr. Miller, Bruce's father." For a psychiatrist, I thought he was remarkably clueless, assuming, wrongly, that I was Bruce's girlfriend. Bruce blushed and mumbled something about me being just a friend. "How did the two of you meet?" he asked, ignoring Bruce's comment and proffering a smile that didn't include his eyes.

"I'm a summer therapist. I work with patients in building 5." I took a chance, just in case he had as much power as Bruce implied. "Sometimes building 6."

"You're too young and too pretty to be working here, much less with violent inmates." His flattery offended me. Bruce looked embarrassed. Still, one day this man might keep me from being fired so I forced myself to mutter a pleasant thank you.

"Bruce, you need to come with me. I'm going to visit your mother. She's been asking for you."

Bruce reacted as if he'd been attacked. "I'd like to, but I have the meeting with Langstrom this afternoon. She let me know how upset she was that I missed the first one. Says it sets a bad example for the other summer therapists."

"Since when did you start caring what she thinks or says?" The tone of Dr. Miller's voice was chilling. Before I could think of an excuse to leave, he asked Bruce, "Don't you want to see your mother? Don't you care about her wellbeing?"

A panoply of emotions flitted over Bruce's face. He spoke slowly, searching for the right words. "I doubt that she's been asking for me. When I went to see her Saturday she refused to talk to me. In fact, she screamed for me to go away in such a loud voice the nurses ordered me to leave." He hesitated, looking at the grass, avoiding his father's stare. "In my experience, it takes at least a week before she's more or less herself. I have a job, you know. I should think you'd be the first one to want me to meet my responsibilities to my patients."

Bruce turned to me, looking for a way out. "Rennie, we better go see if your equipment key works. If not, it might have been changed and you'll have to get a new one." He finally looked directly at his father. "When you see my mother, please tell her I'll visit when she wants to see me—when I'm not working."

With a curt goodbye nod to his father, Bruce started walking toward building 5. I followed, shuddering to think what it was like to live with an alcoholic mother and such a judgmental father. When we were out of sight, Bruce sighed. "So, that's Seth Miller, my stepfather."

"I never heard you refer to him as your stepfather. He even introduced himself as your father."

"I know, but since I seem to have two fathers, I've decided to call Andrew Lowenstein my father and Seth Miller my stepfather." When we got to building 5, he asked again if I would come with him to the concert. I said I'd think about it and let him know at the meeting. We agreed to meet outside of the administration building and walk into the room together. Maybe seeing me with Bruce would temper Mrs. Langstrom's comments. I wasn't sure I liked Bruce, but we'd had fun at the Satchmo concert and I hoped he would help me if I got in trouble at the hospital.

I walked to my Zombies ward, welcoming their lack of communication. There was something soothing about bringing each woman into the center to form a circle. This time more than half stayed where I placed them. As before, I threw the ball to a woman, waited a bit, then retrieved it, and threw it to the next. At one point I thought I saw a glimmer of a smile on one woman's face. Perhaps it was a grimace. It seemed that some of them were watching even if they weren't responding. Despite the condescending attendants, who teased me in a good-natured way, I sensed something was changing. Even if I was wrong, I intended to keep doing it.

11

I walked to building 6 with a heavy heart. Carol was in there, somewhere. *How was she? Had they taken off the straightjacket? Was anyone helping her?* I kept imagining her crying, unkempt, struggling, feeling desperate and alone, trying to explain what had happened while attendants refused to listen. I had no idea how to find Coop, since she had originally found me. There was a bell at the front door but I didn't have the courage to use it. Even though Mrs. Denby, and now Dr. Miller, knew and neither of them had told me to stop, that didn't mean I was authorized to work with these patients. What finally gave me the nerve to press the bell was imagining Barbara asking me what I'd found out.

I heard the bell ring. No one answered. I stood, waiting, hoping, afraid to ring it again. The longer I stood, the more helpless and angry I felt. I pressed the bell again, twice. The attendant who opened the door asked brusquely, "What do you want?"

"I'm here to take out patients from Mrs. Cooper's ward."

"Why didn't you use your key? You think we have nothing better to do than answer doorbells?"

I didn't know who she was. I didn't want to tell her I had no key. And I was still so angry about what had happened to Carol, I took it out on the woman. "Just tell Mrs. Cooper I'm here. She's expecting me." I spoke harshly, not caring what she felt.

She went inside, and shut the door behind her. I waited. If Coop didn't come out, at least I'd be able to tell Barbara I'd tried. After a few minutes I was too hot to wait in the sun so I walked over to a large maple tree near the front door and saw a spider spinning a web. I'd never seen a web being spun and watched, mesmerized, as the spider moved slowly up, then dropped down to make a new string. As I stared at the web an insect flew into it. The web shook as the creature struggled to free itself. Fascinated and horrified, I saw Carol and the hairdresser. My sense of unease was compounded by Mrs. Denby's reaction, her not caring about Carol's reasonable request. I felt vulnerable and afraid—not of the patients, but of the administration and staff, the people who were supposed to help, not hurt.

I was so entranced watching the spider and the fly I forgot about time. When I looked at my watch and saw that more than fifteen minutes had passed, I couldn't make myself go back to building 5 and ring the bell again, so I walked to the administration building. Good thing I did. No one told me there was a summer therapist bulletin board. I gasped when I read:

All Monday supervisory meetings will begin at 3 pm.

If I hadn't seen it I would have been an hour late. I shuddered to think what Mrs. Langstrom's response would have been. Another notice caught my eye:

This season's men's softball team is being formed. Male attendants are asked to suggest men who play well and are healthy enough to leave the hospital to play other men's hospital softball teams.

There was no mention of a women's softball team. If men could leave the hospital to play other hospital teams, why couldn't women? I knew I couldn't take patients from building 6, but maybe enough women from building 5 would be interested enough to want to practice and play on a team.

The meeting was due to start in about twenty minutes, but it was sweltering and I didn't want to wait outside. Opening a door, I discovered the small employees' lounge—an uninviting room with two shabby, faded brown sofas and four chairs upholstered in a nondescript beige fabric. The overflowing ashtrays disgusted me. The air reeked of stale cigarettes and old coffee. A coffee machine and a stack of paper cups stood in one corner on a scratched red Formica counter. I poured myself a cup just to have something to do, but the coffee smelled bad and tasted worse. I dumped it into the sink, threw away the cup, and walked outside to a large oak tree. Remembering the comfort I used to feel when I climbed trees as a kid, I began climbing up the well-spaced branches and quickly reached a place where I could sit contentedly, about halfway up the tree. The solidity of the tree was in sharp contrast to my sense that life was precarious no matter how careful I was or how hard I tried to avoid trouble.

When life was too much for me I often climbed trees. High above the ground I felt safe, but now my sense of safety was gone. Even being in a wonderful, large, old tree, fanned by a breeze, made no difference. Remembering what happened to Carol upset me all over again. I could feel tears building up, stuck inside wherever they came from. The last time I remembered crying was when I was twelve. Every girl in my class had been invited to a classmate's birthday party—except me. I only found out about it because one girl, a newcomer in the neighborhood, asked what gift I was bringing. I knew enough to pretend that I didn't care about not being invited, but when I got home and told my father what happened, I started crying, hot wracking sobs. He sternly told me the girls weren't worth my tears, that crying never solved anything, and if they didn't want me at their party, it was their loss. My weeping disappointed him, he said, which only added to my misery. To please him, I stopped crying. Since then, my tears seemed to have disappeared.

I tried to pull myself together. I tried to tell myself that what happened to Carol was part of working in a mental hospital, that I had done the best I could to help her, but the thought lodged halfway between my mouth and stomach, an undigested, foul-tasting lump. Since I didn't want to be late for the meeting, I slowly climbed down, careful not to tear my skirt on the sharp bits of broken branches. Before jumping from the lowest branch, I looked to see if anyone was coming, but I couldn't see behind the trunk.

"Miss Weinstein, what are you doing?"

Mrs. Langstrom was staring up at me with a shocked expression. I was too tired and discouraged to lie. "It's been a difficult day. Sometimes climbing a tree makes me feel better." I waited for her to tell me I was fired. The truth was, at that point, I'd have felt a huge sense of relief. My sense of failure would have kicked in later. Instead, she reached up and helped me down, a smile of remembering on her face.

"I used to climb trees when I was a girl. Back of our house was a huge old maple. My dad had coiled a rope around a thick branch so we could climb up to the first strong limb. My brother and I built a treehouse in the middle of the tree. When we didn't want company we'd haul up the rope and have ourselves a great time eating cookies and drinking lemonade we'd taken from the kitchen."

Mrs. Langstrom, the ogre? Mrs. Denby, the kind one? Seems as soon as I decide who they are, they act differently. Working in this hospital is like riding a roller coaster in a seat with no straps. I'll be lucky if I can just catch my breath. Falling is another matter.

To be polite, I asked where she grew up. As we walked to the meeting, she told me about living on a small farm in Iowa and all the chores she had to do before and after school. She laughed as she told me about having to walk three miles to school each day and said no one believed her, but I did. Something had made her tough. What else it made her, I couldn't tell. I hoped the pleasant feeling between us would continue. I needed her goodwill. I needed her to give me the benefit of the doubt. I needed her to be nice to me.

We were the first ones to arrive. She asked me to set up the chairs in a three-quarter circle rather than the rows of last week, to open windows, and to plug in a large coffee pot she'd taken out of a cupboard. Unlike the lounge, this room, sort of a conference room, was large, clean, and smelled fresh. There were no ashtrays, and the breeze coming in through the windows was revitalizing. I sat in the end seat so I could see everyone without turning my head. The other recreational therapists came in together, talking and laughing. I felt a pang of envy at their easy camaraderie and tried not to stare. Judging from their conversation, they had worked here before. Much to my dismay, there was no sign of Bruce.

Mrs. Langstrom clapped her hands to quiet us, saying it was time to begin the meeting. She asked us to introduce ourselves, to say where we were working, and what we were doing. One woman talked about wanting to be a psychiatrist, which evoked peals of laughter from people sitting around her. I wished I knew why everyone thought this was so funny. When it was my turn I merely said my name and that I worked in building 5. Even if we were all doing the same job, hired for the summer, I felt like an outsider—younger, anxious, inexperienced—and just that morning had done the unthinkable, supposedly interfered in the treatment of a patient.

I noticed that no one was assigned to building 6 and I asked why. Mrs. Langstrom repeated what Coop told me, that the therapist working there had been attacked and quit. When I asked why, she reprimanded me. "Miss Weinstein, there is no why. They are violent women and cannot be trusted to behave." I shivered. Maybe she was right, but that hadn't been my experience. Looking at me, she added that the administration hadn't been able to find a qualified replacement because they were looking for a woman with experience.

My guess was that no one with experience would work for the same salary I was getting, but maybe the word violent was too scary for a "summer" therapist. During the meeting people asked questions but none of them had to do with patient care. I kept waiting for Mrs. Langstrom to make reference to what had happened with Carol, and I mentally debated what I would say when she did. The meeting was just about over, and I was breathing easier, when she said, "Miss Weinstein, tell us what you learned this morning."

I was caught off guard. The stares of the therapists unnerved me. *Where was Bruce? He promised he would be here.* I think there's an imp who lives inside my brain and takes advantage of my conflicting thoughts by blurting out what I'm thinking but not ready or supposed to say. "What I learned is that patients have no rights." I could feel my face turning red. I saw Mrs. Langstrom waiting for me to continue, but I had nothing more to say. There was no way I would defend the hairdresser's actions, nor would I condemn what Carol did.

"Miss Weinstein, what else did you learn?"

My cowardly self was overshadowed by a blazing sense of injustice. "I learned that a patient who defends her right not to have a haircut when she doesn't need one, and is scheduled to be released the next day, can be treated so," the words poured out. "Badly, terribly horribly—"

Mrs. Langstrom's tone was withering. "It is not your place to judge a patient's treatment. We will discuss this after the meeting."

As if to defuse the tension, one of the men asked when they could start recruiting for the softball team. I noticed he didn't say men's team. This wasn't the best time to ask about starting a women's team, and, maybe Mrs. Langstrom wasn't the right person to ask, but who was? I kept thinking about what a women's softball team might do for the patients' spirits, as well as the practice they would need to be deemed good enough to play another hospital's women's team, if there was such a thing.

I tried to steel myself for what Mrs. Langstrom would say to me after the meeting, and prepare what I might say in defense of Carol, but the tongue lashing she gave me felt so unjustified I gave up. There was no point in saying anything. She told me I could be fired for what I'd done, but she didn't fire me. Maybe Bruce had talked to his father or stepfather or whatever the hell he called him. When she finished by asking me if I understood how inappropriately I'd behaved,

I stared at her, unable to even nod. I wanted to ask her how a person who played in a treehouse, and sympathized with me climbing a tree, could be so unsympathetic about a horrible miscarriage of justice. She took my silence as assent and said, "Remember, Miss Weinstein, you are here to take patients out, play games with them, and bring them back. *That is all.*"

She strode out, the door slamming behind her. I stared at it, waiting until there was no chance I'd meet up with her. Outside, the air was still hot and humid. Heavy. I sat on the grass and replayed the morning's events, thinking I should have done more. But what? Nothing I thought of ended in a good way, with Carol's hair intact, with Carol ready to meet her husband the next day. I felt overwhelmed by pain and outrage and grief. What made it worse was that I knew there was no one I could go to. Both Mrs. Denby and Mrs. Langstrom had made it clear that the little I had done was "interfering" with patient care. Mr. Carson would certainly agree. I desperately needed to do something and there was nothing to be done. I felt helpless. Hopeless. Alone. At least I didn't have to look for my scooter. Whatever Bruce had done, worked. No one hid it. If that had happened yesterday, I would have been overjoyed and relieved. Today, it was just part of my day at the hospital.

12

I wasn't ready to go home to my silent house. Never before had I faced the emptiness of my life so directly. I needed to talk about what had happened, so I drove to Yanni's restaurant hoping I'd feel better after a cup of his wonderful coffee and a piece of something delicious. My heart sank when I saw the sign: CLOSED MONDAY. I was just leaving when Yanni drove up. "Rennie, good to see you. Come in for coffee and some of your cake. I froze two pieces so you could taste what you made." His kindness undid me. Much to my shock and embarrassment, the tears I'd thought were forever locked up inside me, flowed. I cried—hot, huge tears.

Yanni saw me struggling to wheel the scooter off the road and helped me put it behind the restaurant. I tried to stop crying but couldn't. He gave me a handkerchief from his jacket and led me inside. While he turned off the alarm and turned on the lights, I went to the bathroom to wash my face. I hardly recognized myself: face drawn, hair messy, eyes red and haunted. I combed my hair, put on a bit of lipstick and dabbed some on my cheeks.

The kitchen was less welcoming without the pots of broth on the stove, bread and pastries baking, herbs and onions ready to be chopped and diced, but Yanni's look of concern, and the smell of coffee brewing, lifted my spirits. He put the slices of cake into a small warming oven and sat across from me. "You look upset, Rennie. Did something happen at work?"

I hesitated. I'd come without thinking. He was Bruce's friend, not mine, but I was too upset to care. I sank into a chair, silent for an uncomfortably long time before I could tell him about Carol, how awful it was to work at the hospital, how patients had no rights, that no one in the administration seemed to care. Even in my misery I noticed that, although he listened attentively, the lines in his face were deeper than I remembered. I was ashamed that I had needed to talk so badly, that I ignored his fatigue, but I couldn't stop myself. "On top of everything that's happened, in order to work at the hospital

I signed a loyalty oath, which is against the Constitution and my principles."

"That's not the end of the world, Rennie. Besides, look at the people you're helping. You couldn't do this if you had refused to sign the oath."

"Well, I will never do it again. Nothing is worth feeling so bad about myself."

He didn't respond. I waited for him to say something. The silence was uncomfortable. "You look tired, Yanni. Is something wrong?"

He seemed about to talk, but when he didn't I poured two mugs of coffee, and brought them and the plates of cake to the table. Still waiting, I sat down and held the hot cup of coffee against my cheek, hoping he would say something. The silence felt so awkward I blurted out, "It's okay, you don't have to tell me."

"Taste your cake, Rennie. I got lots of compliments. One couple even asked if they could buy a whole cake." I felt hurt that he wouldn't tell me what was wrong, especially after I'd said so much about myself and wasn't in the mood to eat. Still, I was curious to know how the cake tasted, so I ate a piece. The moist, rich, buttery taste complemented the crunch of nuts. Maybe I could find a job at a bakery. Any job seemed better than the one I had.

Inside me was a growing sense of embarrassment about crying and spilling out my miseries to a man I hardly knew. So I apologized, but Yanni waved away my words. "I know it's good to talk and I'm honored to listen, but I just can't talk about what's on my mind right now." Honored seemed a strange word. What was honorable about me talking but not him? Was there something wrong with me? Mortified, I thanked him for listening, got up, and was ready to go when he asked if I wanted to help him make piecrusts. The offer sounded so ludicrous I worried that he suggested it out of pity. Yanni ignored my obvious astonishment. "I always make piecrusts on Monday and then freeze them. It would be nice to have company, and you are a good baker. I will pay you for your help."

"You don't need to pay me. Helping you would make me feel better."

"Okay, I will pay you in dinners. Where did you learn to bake so good?"

"It's a silly story."

"Tell me," he said, assembling ingredients for the piecrusts. "I like stories."

"I guess I was about twelve and my sister was six. Our mother was out and my sister said she was hungry. When I asked what she wanted to eat, she said, 'Apple pie.' I'd only baked cookies for her before but there was something about making a pie that intrigued me. 'Okay,' I said, 'We have apples, let's make a pie.' I put my sister on the counter and told her to read the directions. What a mess we made. There was flour everywhere—on our faces, clothes, the floor. Even though the pie looked a little lopsided when I put it in the oven, it smelled pretty good baking and tasted even better. Ever since, if I feel like eating a cookie or a cake, I make it."

Yanni smiled appreciatively as we mixed and kneaded the dough, then fitted it into pastry shells. We worked well together. It was so satisfying and enjoyable that as we cleaned up, I said, "I think I'll quit my job at the hospital and find work as a baker. You know anyone who'd be willing to hire me?"

Yanni's tone was sharp, his response quick. "Don't."

"Why not?" I asked, feeling sorry for myself.

"You couldn't help Carol, that's true, but she'll remember that you tried, and so will the patients who saw you. They need your caring no matter what happens. Believe me, I know."

"How do you know?" I asked in an accusatory tone.

He shook his head. "We can talk about it another time. It's getting late and we both have to work tomorrow." He ladled stew into two bowls, cut slices of heated French bread, and put them on the table before sitting down across from me.

To ease my tension, I teased, "What, no wine with this delicious meal?"

"You have to drive home. No wine!" At least he smiled.

After eating I helped clean up—anything to avoid going home. It puzzled me how I felt I could be myself, whoever that was, in his presence. With almost everyone else I watched and waited, needing to figure out what the other person wanted, and then how to be what they wanted. Bruce told me Yanni had come to the US from Israel, where he'd been a cook, but wanted to change his life so he applied for a scholarship to study international law. He finished his degree but missed cooking. When the restaurant he was working in closed, he took the job at the hospital, which is where Bruce met him. There was a lot more I wanted to know about him, but I felt shy about asking. All I knew about him came from Bruce. Yanni hadn't told me enough about himself for me to ask why he'd come to the US or what it was like for him to live here. At least I was able to say, "I really enjoy working with you in the kitchen. It's not only what we make, which I like a lot, but," I hesitated, then blurted out, "being around you somehow makes my worries seem less troublesome. Why is that?"

"If your heart is open it's possible to feel someone's pain. If not, you don't care and you don't listen."

"You care. You listen." I didn't dare look at him when I said, "But you don't let me listen to you and I care." *About you.*

"You're young, Rennie. Some things are better not spoken."

"What has age got to do with anything? Did my being young keep me from helping Carol? Does my age mean I can't feel when someone is hurting?" Ashamed of my outburst, I mumbled an apology and started to walk out the door.

"Wait, Rennie, I know you care. And you're right; it's not your age. Some things I just can't talk about. Please, don't be mad at me. I like you. You're a good girl."

What did that mean? At school, a good girl was someone who never had sex before marriage. That certainly wasn't me. At least he said he liked me. That was something. I stood in the doorway, unwilling to say goodbye, but after reassuring me I was welcome to come back anytime, Yanni shooed me out, wishing me a good night's sleep. I didn't tell him that falling asleep was almost as difficult as working at the hospital. No matter how tired I was, the minute I turned off the light, the day's events replayed in my mind until nightmares took over. No one knew I'd gotten so desperate that I'd gone to a doctor at school who'd given me a prescription for sleeping pills. I didn't have enough to last me until September so I hoarded them, deciding each night whether I felt upset enough to take one. Tonight there'd be no question.

13

The next morning Mrs. Denby's pleasant greeting was disconcerting. I thought there'd be some reference to Carol, if only a brief commiseration. Nothing. I didn't want to pretend everything was okay, nor did I want to play ball, but it was a gorgeous morning in the mid70s, the air fresh from a cleansing rain the night before. I decided to take everyone in the ward out for a walk. This didn't sound like an outrageous idea to me, but many women grumbled and probably wouldn't have gone if they had a choice. At first, Mrs. Denby doubted the wisdom of the idea, but given the bright sunshine, she reluctantly relented. Her primary worry was that we would be breaking the rule: one attendant for every ten patients taken out. She had only three attendants to spare for the more than sixty women on the ward. I assured her this would be no problem, since I was only going to walk around the inside perimeter. As Mrs. Denby lined up the women, I was surprised to hear them complain:

"I don't want to."

"I don't feel good."

"I can't walk so far."

"It's too hot."

"It's too cold."

She ignored their comments and told me to do the same, despite the lead attendant's equally vocal complaints. "Why force people to walk outside, even if it is a nice summer day? Why make people walk up and down stairs?" According to her, no therapist before me had ever cleared the wards and required everyone to walk outside—why was I so determined to do it? Didn't I care about the women's feelings? Was I too young to consider their ages, that some of them were old? The last comment stung but I pretended I didn't hear it.

I thanked her for her help, deliberately returning her dirty look with a smile. The patients' and attendants' grumbles made me laugh. Why would anyone want to be cooped up in a smelly ward when they could be outside enjoying the fresh air and the smell of roses? It took quite a while for the group to walk outside—a cortege would have moved faster—but eventually we made it through the gates and into the inner courtyard, where we walked around the perimeter. I told the women they could stop if they wanted to sit in the grass or smell the flowers, but the attendants would have none of this. Without quite countermanding my suggestions, they periodically said, "Two by two, ladies. Let's keep moving." The attendants turned out to be right, for the wrong reason. It took such a long time for the women to walk the full perimeter we arrived late, barely making it in time for them to get ready for lunch.

As we entered the building, many of the women said, "Thank you, Miss, that was lovely." A few even suggested we do it again. Mrs. Denby made no mention of my returning the group behind schedule. I guess Mrs. Martelli was right, there were rules and then there were rules. I just had to learn when some didn't matter.

After our lunch together, I waited for Mrs. Denby to suggest we do it again, since she still seemed friendly despite the incident with Carol, yet after thanking me for taking the patients for the walk, she went to her office and closed the door. I was disappointed, but there was nothing I could do so I headed for my lunch tree. I leaned against it, closed my eyes, and was dozing when I head a familiar voice, "Mind if I join you?"

"Bruce! Where have you been? How come you weren't at the meeting Monday?"

His clenched jaw and hard eyes made his sarcasm even sharper. "Whoa! How about: 'Nice to see you. How are you?'"

When I stood up and dusted off my skirt, I noticed how exhausted he looked. "I'm sorry, but you startled me. Is something wrong?"

"Too much. The short answer is that my mother had a stroke going through detox. To make matters worse, while I was visiting her, the eminent and wise Dr. Miller got to the mailbox before I did, found a letter that Andrew Lowenstein had written to me, and decided to read it to my mother, using the excuse that he was acting in my best interests."

"Oh no! What did the letter say?"

"I don't know. He returned the letter to the envelope, sealed it, wrote address unknown, and sent it back to Andrew Lowenstein."

"How did you find out? Why would he do such a thing? Isn't it some kind of federal crime to open someone else's mail?"

Bruce managed a wry smile. "I told you, in some ways this is a very small world. Nothing goes unnoticed, although what people choose to do about it is another matter." He sighed. "Sometimes I think being a patient isn't the worst thing that can happen. Obey the rules, ask no questions, and all your needs are taken care of."

"Stop it! You don't believe that for one minute."

"I need to get out of here. We've still got half an hour, maybe more if you'd stop being Miss Goodytwoshoes. I could use a great cup of coffee."

"I can't."

"You mean you won't."

"I'm hired to do a job and that's what I intend to do." *You're the son of the chief psychiatrist. No one will fire you.*

"I thought we were friends."

What does that mean? "Let's go for coffee after work."

Bruce nodded, started to say something, then waved and walked away. From the back he looked like a defeated old man with barely enough energy to put one foot in front of the other. I thought about the many times he'd said, "I thought we were friends." For me, our so-called friendship had mostly to do with how he could help me. I had no idea what he felt or thought about me. From the little I knew about him we didn't have much in common. When I told him how upset I was about signing the loyalty oath he had shrugged and said, "You want to work here, you sign the oath. End of story." Besides, his talking so freely about his feelings unsettled me. He had asked me to tell him about my life several times, but aside from my relationship with Jake, which I didn't want to talk about, my life wasn't full of drama like his.

I went back to building 5, looking forward to working with the Zombies. Arranging the women in a circle and throwing balls to them was relaxing and, in a funny way, enjoyable—no pressure, no expectation. By now the attendants were used to my coming and going and had stopped teasing or trying to convince me that I was wasting my time. Occasionally, I thought I saw a glimmer of reaction in one or two of the women, but I never mentioned it to anyone.

Afterward, I walked to building 6, hoping Coop might come out. I stood in front for a few minutes, working up the courage to ring the bell. I knew attendants disliked having to answer it because it usually meant they had to deal with a problem. After ringing I waited and waited and waited. I was just about to walk away when an attendant came to the door. I asked if Coop was on duty. She nodded and agreed to tell her I'd come to take out some patients.

There was something about Coop that made me feel better about working at the hospital. She exuded joy, a rare attribute, especially for attendants working with violent patients. When she saw me, her face lit up. "Weinstein! Great to see you. The women have been asking when you were coming back." I told her about my difficulties ringing the bell and asked if we could make a schedule so my visits would be routine. She nodded, "Good idea. I'll get the women ready while you get the gear. We can talk about it while they're playing."

The women ran to the field like kids let out of school for summer vacation. They ran and shouted and argued and cheered, releasing pent up energy, laughing when someone hit a home run. While the women changed sides and took a break, I told her about Carol and asked if she'd seen her. Coop took a moment, as if reviewing all the women on her ward, then shook her head. "No, but I'll keep an eye out for her." Just before I walked to the pitching mound she said, "You can't let stuff like that get you down, otherwise you're no good to anyone."

"I can't help it. I felt so helpless. Watching what happened was awful: it keeps replaying in my mind."

"Change the movie!" she said, throwing the ball to Rosa, who was playing first base. I wished I knew how.

As we walked the women back to the building I told Coop about wanting to start a women's softball team. She thought it was a great idea and wished some of her women could play on it, knowing there was no chance this could happen. She also warned me: "Changing precedent is almost impossible in this place. And, if you do, by some miracle, have the team approved, people will be upset."

"Why? It's only a softball team for goodness sake."

"No one likes to see someone do the impossible. They'll be jealous and angry and resentful that you, a summer therapist, would try to change the status quo, so think twice before you do anything." I shook my head. What she said made no sense. How could anyone be upset about a women's softball team?

Bruce was waiting for me when I walked to the admin office. "Don't you ever work?" I teased.

"Dr. Miller decided it wasn't a good idea for me to work with patients so I'm working with the landscapers. He may have thought I'd resent having to mow and weed and plant, but it's a whole lot better than playing sports I hate. The guys I work with know a lot about gardening. One of them suggested I go into landscaping."

"Sounds like you'd be really good at it. Like making art with plants."

"First I'd like to try making art, but who knows, maybe I'll consider it. Let's go to Yanni's for coffee. Seems someone asked about buying a painting, even though the sign says they are not for sale."

"That's great. Put a really high price on it and you won't have to worry about paying for art school."

"I'll let you be my agent. I'm horrible when it comes to money."

"What makes you think I'd be any better?"

"You're tough. You know what you want. I envy you."

I laughed. I was as far from his description of me as I could be, but it was interesting to think about his point of view. While we were talking, Dr. Miller strode up to us. He was glaring at Bruce, not me, yet I shivered. "What are you doing?" he snapped.

Bruce looked assaulted. "Rennie and I are—"

"You are supposed to see your mother after work and I don't imagine you were planning to take Rennie with you." It was as if the air inside Bruce whooshed out and only his bones prevented him from collapsing. I felt so sorry for him I put my arm around him to steady him, but Dr. Miller took it another way. "Rennie, you may be my son's fiancée, but both his mother and I feel you're not part of our family until you're married."

Fiancée?

Behind Dr. Miller's back Bruce silently pleaded with me not to say anything. Stunned, I stared at Bruce's father or stepfather, still not sure what to call him, aware that even if he wasn't my boss, one day he might have something to say about my employment. Since I needed to stay on his good side, if there was one, I lied. "I asked Bruce to meet me after work so he could tell me about the men's softball team. I'd like to start a women's team."

"Bruce knows nothing about softball and we don't have a women's team because the women have no interest in participating." *Did anyone ever ask any women if they wanted to form a team?*

His peremptory tone made me feel sorry for any patients who had to see Dr. Miller for therapy. "Does that mean if I found fifteen women who were good ball players, I could form a team and we could play other hospitals?"

"Discuss this with your supervisor. Bruce, let's go. Your visits are the highlight of your mother's day and an important part of her recovery."

I watched, astonished, as Dr. Miller put his arm around Bruce's shoulder, almost a hug, and kept it there as the two walked off. Bruce didn't pull away. If anything, he leaned into the older man's body. I sensed their relationship was a lot more complicated than Bruce made it out to be.

At loose ends, not ready to go home, trying to avoid the temptation to go to Yanni's, I walked over to Mrs. Langstrom's office. Just before I knocked, she opened the door, surprised to see me. "Miss Weinstein, is something wrong?" I had second thoughts about talking with her. What if I couldn't find fifteen women who played well and were healthy enough to leave the hospital grounds? My thoughts were so jumbled, what came out was nothing I intended to say. "No, but I was wondering if there might be time during our meeting for the summer therapists to share what they're doing and to talk about any problems they might be having. It seems they have more experience than I do."

"A lot more, my dear. You're the only new therapist hired this summer. What do you want to know?" Unable to think of anything I was willing to say, she unwittingly came to my rescue. "I hear you've been taking out women from building 6." I nodded, waiting. "You weren't hired to work with violent women."

I mumbled, "I know."

"Mrs. Cooper tells me you're very good with them and that there has been no trouble." I nodded. "You do know that the woman we hired to work with them was attacked by a group of patients so severely she was hospitalized for several weeks?" I nodded again, not knowing the attack had been so bad, worried that she might tell me not to do it, or that I was breaking rules, or that I was fired. "You have no experience working with such difficult patients. What made you do it?"

I didn't want to involve Coop, so I lied. "I saw some patients walking around the inner courtyard. Seems they knew I was the recreational therapist for building 5 and they asked if I would play softball with them. They were no trouble. In fact, they were happy to be able to play." I didn't want to tell her the women in building 6 seemed normal to me, whatever normal meant. I certainly wouldn't mention Rosa and Georgia postponing toots or that I felt sorry for the women cooped up in a ward with no regular outlet for their energy and frustration.

Mrs. Langstron stared at me as if I were a specimen under a microscope, then she shook her head. "Miss Weinstein, I don't know what to make of you. You have no experience working with mentally ill people, and yet, in just a short time you have interfered with the treatment of a patient and voluntarily worked with the most dangerously ill people in the hospital. Why?"

I shrugged. "They said they wanted to play so I helped them play." I knew it would do no good but I couldn't stop. "Carol didn't need a haircut and she was willing to have a tiny bit snipped off just to satisfy the rules. I tried—"

Mrs. Langstrom cut me off. "Haircuts and the treatment of patients are none of your business." I expected her to add that taking out building 6 patients was none of my business as well, but she didn't.

"Miss Weinstein, it is in your best interest, as well as that of your patients, to follow all hospital rules. They exist for a reason." I nodded, waiting for her to end the meeting. Then, something shifted—the way she looked at me suddenly softened. "Thank you for coming," she said, closing the door, clearly dismissing me.

What was that about? I stood in front of the closed door, unable to stop thinking about the woman who climbed trees as a girl, who turned into a woman who had more interest in following rules than caring for people. Too depressed to go home, and keenly aware that I had no other place to go, I thought about stopping at Yanni's restaurant, which was on my way home, but I told myself he was busy with food preparation. His restaurant was a business, not a haven for a female in trouble with her employer. I knew I should go straight home. I didn't. It was only after I drove into the parking lot that I asked myself what I wanted from Yanni. Why did I feel so good when I was with him? All the questions pointed to an uncomfortable answer.

The realization that I was attracted to Yanni was so unsettling I immediately drove home, but once I'd admitted it to myself I couldn't stop thinking about him. I took a long walk, trying to sort out my inner turmoil. I trusted him. I even found myself able to talk openly with him, sharing my feelings without censoring myself, although why and how that had happened eluded me.

I was still thinking about Yanni when I picked up the mail. Amidst the letters for my parents were a check and birthday card from them and my sister, wishing me a happy birthday, hoping I had plans to celebrate my twentieth birthday. My father had added a note saying he was breathing a sigh of relief knowing I had made it safely out of my teens. It felt good to know they remembered my birthday even though they were in Mexico. This year it fell on a Saturday, so I wouldn't be working. Maybe I could go to a concert at Lewissohn Stadium. I enjoyed sitting in the bleachers listening to classical music. In years past when I worked at a camp, we celebrated campers' and counselors' birthdays with a birthday cake at dinner. Now there'd be no celebration at the hospital and certainly no cake. When I was younger, turning twenty had seemed like a big deal. Now what mattered was that I'd no longer be a teenager working at the hospital. Twenty seemed older, a little more dignified.

There was also a letter from Jake, which I opened, expecting more instructions about the scooter.

Dearest Rennie,

I've been thinking about you a lot, missing you more than I could have imagined. I realize I was so caught up in the thrill of rock climbing I forgot to ask you how work is going. Please write and tell me how you are.

I don't know when you'll receive this letter, but even if it arrives after your birthday, I don't want you to think I forgot it. I'm planning ways we can celebrate when I come back. Please write and tell me that you love me, that you miss me.

Much love, Jake

14

I didn't know it was possible to feel grief, about Carol, and elation, from reading Jake's letter, simultaneously. The conflicting emotions pushing against each other made it impossible to stay in the house, so I left and ran to a park a mile away. What about my feelings for Yanni? Too wrought up to deal with streets and traffic lights, I inadvertently took a trail that I normally avoided in the evening.

I walked faster than usual, my thoughts fueling my pace. When I saw three guys emerge from the shadows and stop in front of me, I glared at them. "Don't know what you're up to, but you've got the wrong woman." Without waiting for a response, I pushed through a space between them and walked on, even faster than before. There was no more room inside me for new feelings, not even fear. I zoomed around the trail several more times until I felt tired enough to walk home.

The letter was lying on the table in the foyer where I'd dropped it. When I reread it, I noticed Jake hadn't mention his scooter, which made me think he might be concerned about my feelings for him. According to the trip schedule he'd given me, it would be at least two weeks before he arrived at a place where he could pick up mail. That gave me time to think about what I wanted to write, if I wrote. I knew from previous experience, when he'd misunderstood something I'd written, that writing letters wasn't the best way to express feelings. Letters could cross, statements could be misinterpreted, words might not fully describe what I was thinking. Not that talking in person was so great. I dreaded the times when Jake got angry. I hated my reaction—silence, waiting for his anger to pass—which left many issues between us unresolved. Sometimes I tried to defend myself, but most of the time I quickly gave in to end my discomfort, leaving me feeling depressed. There was also the question of whether to tell him how much the word loonies still bothered me. I took a chance and wrote that my patients were people, not loonies, to please not use that word again. Normally our letters were pretty short but once I started writing about Carol, my feelings of shock and horror and fear filled three pages. It was the longest and most honest letter I'd ever written to him.

When the phone rang, I hoped it was Yanni and had to hide my disappointment when I heard Bruce say, "I know it's late, but I just got home from the hospital. I need to talk with you. Can we meet for lunch tomorrow, please?" The desperation and fatigue in his voice was so obvious I told him I would. It wasn't the time to ask why he'd told his father I was his fiancée.

Later, as I was washing the dishes, I burst out laughing. Not only did I have a boyfriend, I was another man's fiancée, and the only man I wanted to be with was Yanni. How was I supposed to make any sense of this?

Lying in bed, unable to sleep, I thought more about what it might take to start a softball team. Was there a reason no one had formed a women's team? Apparently, the men had had one for years. Then again, given the lack of enthusiasm for playing, maybe the women didn't care about a team and had no interest in practicing. Should I? Shouldn't I? I finally fell asleep envisioning a triumphant women's softball team being greeted by Mr. Carson, who was holding flowers for each team member.

The next morning I was greeted by Mrs. Denby, who looked at me with an ironic smile. "Miss Weinstein, I don't know what to do about you." *Was she going to fire me? I was afraid to ask what was wrong so I just looked at her.* "I knew word travels fast in this place but..." She stopped, shook her head, "Your apparent gift for storytelling has reached the attention of the psychiatrist in charge of our new children's unit. It's in an experimental stage—only seven or eight children, and the staff has been having a difficult time with them." *What does this have to do with me?* "They've asked if you could go over there and tell the children a story. They think it might help them settle down."

"Me?"

"You."

"When?"

"Now!"

What?

Dazed, stunned, anxious and bewildered, I tried to focus on her directions to the unit. She wished me well. *What was that supposed to mean?* I made my way to the children's unit full of trepidation. How was a story supposed to calm down kids who were out of control if their doctor couldn't do it? It didn't help that I was greeted by a tense attendant, who said to follow her. "Can you tell me something about the children?" No response. "Can I talk with their doctor first?" No response. Once again no one thought it necessary to tell me anything. The patients might be crazy, but being given no instructions or information seemed insane. She led me to a door, told me the children were waiting for me, and left.

I stood outside the door listening to the screaming and shouting and yelling. *What am I doing here? I took one course in child psychology. I don't know anything about mentally ill children.* I couldn't make myself open the door. A nurse rushed out of the room, looked at my nametag, and said, "Thank God you're here." She practically pushed me inside, then closed the door behind her.

The large room had padded floors and walls. Eight kids were fighting, hitting, biting, scratching, and making so much noise there was no way I could say anything they could hear. Too shocked to move, I leaned on the door, then slumped to the floor. I don't know how long I sat there but eventually one of the older boys noticed me and stopped. Slowly the rest of them quieted down, standing where they were, like statues. "Who are you?" he asked.

"My name's Rennie."

"If that's your first name, what's your Miss name? We're not allowed to call staff by their first names."

"Miss Weinstein."

"What do you want?" asked the taller of the two girls.

What I want is to go back to building 5. "I'm supposed to tell you a story."

"Are you a doctor?" asked a red-haired boy with freckles across his nose.

"No."

"Then who are you?"

Since they didn't appear to be afraid of me, I asked if they would like me to come into the room and we could sit on the rug and talk to each other.

"You gonna sit on the rug? Like us?" asked the other little girl.

"Where else should I sit?" I was beginning to relax. So far, they didn't seem all that different from elementary school kids I'd taught.

"Everyone's afraid of us," said the boy who'd spoken first. "Are you?"

"I don't know you well enough to be afraid of you. Should I be?" They thought that was extremely funny and laughed, a comforting sign although the hysterical tinge made me edgy.

I slowly stood up, walked even more slowly to where they were standing, slowly sat down in the middle of the room and then, speaking in the calmest voice I could manage, invited them to join me. I watched as each one made the decision to sit near me—close, but not too close. I asked them to tell me their names.

"Why do you need to know our names?" asked Freckleface. "You're just here to tell us stories."

"You know my name, I'd like to know yours."

The freckle-faced boy nodded. "I'm Peter." One by one, the others told me their names, some so softly I could barely hear. "Jenny, Molly, Jeffrey, Richard, Paul, Michael, David." I repeated them a few times.

"I think I've got them as long as you don't move." I meant it as a joke but they took it differently, immediately changing places, defying my ability to know their names. I sat, waiting for them to sit back down. No one sat next to anyone. Some turned their backs to me. They looked as if they had no interest in hearing a story and I wasn't about to force one on them.

I was visibly surprised when Jeffrey, seemingly the oldest, challenged me. "When are you going to tell us the story? It's almost time for snacks."

"Tell us 'Jack and the Beanstalk,'" pleaded David, the smallest.

"That's a baby story," jeered Richard, solemn-faced, with piercing dark eyes.

"I like 'Cinderella,'" offered Jenny, with blonde pigtails.

"That's for girls," jeered Paul, skinny with a jagged scar across his face.

"I like to tell stories that I make up. Is that all right with you?" I asked. They wanted to know what kind of stories I made up, several of them offering ideas, others turning their backs or spinning around. Their restlessness irritated me. I felt like leaving. At least I could talk to the women in building 5. What made anyone think I could help these kids?

I saw Molly's pleading look and decided to just start. "Once upon a time there was a group of children whose parents worked in a circus." They immediately interrupted, bombarding me with questions: What kind of circus? How many kids? What did their parents do in the circus? Did the kids have to go to school? Who took care of them when their parents were working?

Stumped, I told them, "Why don't you tell me what you think." They shouted out their answers simultaneously. I couldn't understand anything they said. Annoyed, I asked them, "What if we go around the room and each of you can tell a little bit of the story? Richard, why don't you start?"

Much to my surprise, he did. When he had no more to say, he pointed to Peter, who added a few words. When he finished, he pointed to Jenny. The last one to talk was Molly, who said to me, "You finish."

I picked up on their theme of loneliness—of not fitting in with the circus performers and seldom seeing their parents, and ended with, "Each night, when the circus performers line up to make their entrances, the children gather together in a circle around a campfire and tell stories to each other."

Before we could talk about the story or their participation, three attendants strode into the room without knocking or paying attention to what we'd been doing, ignored me, and told the children to stand up and wash their hands to get ready for snacks. They stood between the children and me, preventing any possible communication. I tried to make eye contact but the children reacted to the sudden intrusion by running around, yelling and screaming as they had before. All I could do was stare in disbelief at the shockingly sudden change in them.

The attendants told me to leave as they herded the children out of the room. I walked out, so absorbed in thought that I jumped when I heard a voice from behind. "Miss Weinstein, I'd like a word with you." I turned around to see a tall, slightly stooped white-haired man with a deeply lined face walking toward me. "I'm Dr. Glassman, the psychiatrist assigned to the children. Let's go to my office where we can talk. Mrs. Denby knows you'll be a bit late." Puzzled, I followed him, stopping for a second when I saw the notice on a bulletin board.

This season's men's softball team is being formed. Male attendants are asked to suggest men who play well and are healthy enough to leave the hospital to play other men's hospital softball teams.

It had the same infuriating effect on me as when I first read it. No mention of a women's team. Why hadn't anyone started one? Were there no women who were good players and well enough to leave the hospital to play other women's teams?

I was still thinking about the notice when Dr. Glassman ushered me into his pleasant, spacious office. Framed children's paintings covered one wall. Flowering plants in window boxes perfumed the air. He offered me a chair and asked whether I'd like coffee or tea. "Coffee, please." He nodded, poured me a cup, then sat in a chair next to mine rather than behind his desk.

"Miss Weinstein, although the staff has been trained to work with mentally ill children, they are often more difficult to deal with than adults since they have little or no experience of what it means to be mentally healthy. Most children like to hear stories, and when Mrs. Denby told me about your storytelling ability I wondered how these children would react to being told a story. I knew you had never worked with mentally ill children before, so I watched you in the one-way glass mirror in their room just in case you got into trouble and needed help."

He watched me?

"You did well. I can't say the same for the attendants." I nodded, still shocked by the way they had barged into the room. "If it's all right with Mrs. Denby, would you be willing to come two or three times a week, for half an hour or so, to tell stories to the children?"

Me? I don't know anything about working with these kids. What happened was pure luck. "Okay, if you and Mrs. Denby think I can help."

"Good. I'll speak with Mrs. Denby to arrange the schedule. Thank you very much, my dear." He ushered me out graciously, as if we had signed some kind of treaty. An attendant, waiting outside the door, unlocked the doors and led me to the outside door. The ominous click as the door closed was not comforting.

15

I walked back to building 5 feeling depressed, angry, bewildered. When Mrs. Denby told me the hospital had plans to build a 400-bed unit for kids, I was astonished. How were they going to treat four hundred when they didn't seem to know how to deal with the eight kids currently being treated? I was still thinking about the storytelling when Barbara, Maggie, and Liz greeted me, ready to go out.

They must have sensed my upsetness because they asked what was going on. I didn't think it was proper to tell them about what had happened with the children, so I muttered something about wishing the world were more fair. Liz, as always, was ready with a quip. "Well, well, Sweetpea, welcome to the world. Fairness in a mental hospital is an oxymoron."

She looked at me as if to see whether I knew the meaning of the word. I did, but I was in no mood for her sarcasm or for any platitudes that might be forthcoming from Barbara. Without considering the possible consequences of talking to patients about something for which I had no authorization, and for which there was no precedent, I blurted out, "I'm thinking about starting a women's softball team, and I want it to be so good Mr. Carson will agree to let the women's team go with the men's softball team when they go out to play other hospital teams."

"A women's softball team?" They sounded like a Greek chorus, repeating it as if they'd never heard the words. Well, maybe they hadn't. I nodded, and once I got going, my enthusiasm took over as I explained my plan, hoping they would help. Only after I stopped talking and noticed their incredulous excitement did I realize what a huge mistake it was to talk about something for which I had no permission. I didn't even know if starting a team was possible. Worse yet, I had no idea how they would react if I got their hopes up and then nothing happened. I cursed my impulsiveness and big mouth.

"How good do we have to be?" demanded Liz.

"Better than the men's team, of course," I managed to quip. We laughed, a rarity, which made me feel better. Maybe starting a women's team was a good idea. I had to work hard to persuade them to agree to not say anything to the others until Mrs. Denby gave her permission and we had enough women who wanted to practice and were healthy enough to play. Although they agreed to keep quiet, I reminded them that I could get into trouble if they said anything to the other patients, since there had never been a women's softball team and there might never be one. They each assured me they would keep quiet. I hoped I could get a team going before Mrs. Martelli came back, but I had learned one lesson: There was no knowing how any attendant would react—there were too many variables.

Much to my horror and chagrin, in spite of what they promised, Liz, Barbara, and Maggie immediately spread the word. Women began volunteering to go out. There was nothing I could do about it, so I took the first twenty and asked the attendant who looked athletic, if she'd come with us. Unlike previous sessions, when it seemed to take as long to get the women to the field as it did for them to play, they made it down the stairs and out to the ball field in record time. Liz and Rita, a woman I hadn't noticed before, had decided that they would be captains and quickly divided the group into two teams. Before we could start, the women peppered me with questions: How will you choose the women to play? How much practice can we get? How are you going to decide what position we play? When will the first game be? I cursed my enthusiasm. When I reminded them I had no permission to start a team, Liz cut me off. "Too much talk, let's get going."

Liz and Rita took charge of everything, deciding who would play and where. They refused to let the attendant and me catch or pitch. I was allowed to referee, but the one time there was a disagreement, the women ignored my suggestion and quickly resolved the matter among themselves. Any doubts I might have had about starting a team dissolved as I watched the change in the women. Having a stake in what happened to them had transformed their passivity into involvement and their apathy into enthusiasm. Even the attendant noticed the difference in their attitude and energy. What if I hadn't thought about starting a women's team? What if I'd taken Bruce's advice and just done the minimum, whatever that was? When I told Barbara I'd asked about Carol but the attendant hadn't seen her, she said, "Thank you for asking. Knowing you care keeps me going on days when it's hard to remember I once had a life." I felt as if I'd been punched in the stomach—a reminder that everyone in the hospital had lived lives where they weren't patients, perhaps with families and jobs, worries about making mortgages, problems with boyfriends or children.

The women didn't want to stop playing. I had to promise I'd select the ones who wanted to play softball and let them play every day, which meant I had to take the others out in the afternoons when I wasn't with the women from building 6. Even though I repeatedly told them I didn't know if I could convince the administration to allow the women to have a team, this had absolutely no effect on their interaction. They nodded as if they understood, then went right back to talking strategy. Nothing I said dampened their enthusiasm or their hopes. What had I gotten myself into? What had I done to them?

When I brought the women back, Mrs. Denby noticed the difference. "They seem so much happier than when they left. What happened?" She kept probing until I reluctantly told her the truth. When she spoke, after a moment of silence, the anger in her voice made it clear she was not paying me a compliment. "Miss Weinstein, you certainly are a remarkable young woman. With no experience to use as a guide, and no permission to act, not only have you taken it upon yourself to work with violent patients, you have assumed authority to start a program that will never happen, one that goes well beyond your job description. Who do you think you are?"

My excitement and enthusiasm dissolved into despair. I defended myself as best I could. "The men have a team. I thought the women should have one too."

"And who are you to decide that? Without knowing if you'd be allowed to start a team, much less travel to another hospital, you have raised the hopes of patients who are extremely suggestible and whose mental health is, at best, fragile. The sensible thing to do, as well as the appropriate and correct approach, is to ask first." *She's right, but I didn't say it would happen, I only said I was thinking about it.* "If you want to continue working here you will have to be much more careful about what you say to your patients. You have to think before you speak." I nodded, already worried that I'd promised the women more than I could deliver. Mrs. Denby's warning about the emotional fragility of the women hit me hard. In the moment, too often, I forgot just how true this was.

"Since the women are so excited about having a women's softball team, who do I ask for permission?"

"Mr. Carson."

My spirits sank. "He's the only one who can give it?"

"Yes." She turned and joined a group of women, helping them get ready for lunch. I watched her interacting with them, smiling, speaking to them by name. I could see she cared about them. She wasn't my enemy, any more than Mrs. Martelli had been. I needed to stop judging and start learning what I could from them. I stayed behind, watching the women as they lined up, two by two, slowly leaving the ward. Empty of women, the ward loomed large, bare, and inhospitable. Benches with backs lined the walls. No cozy sitting arrangements where people could talk in small groups, no pillows to soften the benches. The dormitory smelled of unwashed bodies, filled with too many beds, and, as far as I could see, no place where a woman could keep private mementos. I pushed down the misery rising within me and left to meet Bruce.

He was waiting for me, sitting against the tree where I usually ate my lunch. His gaunt appearance and glazed eyes shocked me. I sat down next to him and asked how he was. "My mother died last night."

"Oh, Bruce." I put my hand on his shoulder. He pulled away.

"She was in the hospital. Died of an overdose—some kind of pills." He glared at me. "How could she save so many pills and the nurses not know? Where did she hide them?" He put his head in his hands.

My stomach growled. I was hungry. I wanted to eat my lunch, but it seemed callous given his grief. "The funeral's tomorrow. I asked my stepfather to arrange for you to have the afternoon off so you could attend." *Me? Without asking?*

"Bruce, I am not your fiancée."

He looked up, his face a mask of misery. "I know."

"So why did you tell your father, I mean stepfather, we're engaged?"

"It's a long story. I don't want to talk about it now." He stood up, using the tree for support. *You lied. How can it be such a long story?* "I'll meet you at the admin building at one. We'll be in the first car. You don't need to wear black but something dark would be good. Afterward, there'll be a reception at my aunt's house." He took a jewelry box out of his jacket and thrust it into my hand. "Wear this tomorrow."

Inside was a heavy gold ring with a large oval diamond. It looked old and expensive. "Bruce! I can't wear this. I am not your fiancée." Stupidly I said, "We haven't even kissed." I closed the box and gave it back to him.

He put his hands on my shoulders, lightly touched his lips to my cheek, and thrust the box into my hand. "There. Now you can wear the ring. It was my grandmother's. She gave it to my mother and now I'm giving it to you." "Just wear it tomorrow. All my relatives will be there. Please!"

"Why should I wear a ring that says we're engaged when we're not?"

Bruce didn't hide his anger. "I'm simply asking you to do me a big favor for a few hours."

"It's not that simple." I put the box in his jacket pocket and slumped down against the tree. My stomach growled again. "I'm hungry. I'm going to eat my lunch." But when I saw his despair, I told him, "I'm willing to go to the funeral, but why should I pretend to be your fiancée?"

"Why is not important. People get engaged and then break it off all the time. Besides, it's only for one day—not even for a whole day." He tried to put the ring on my finger.

I pulled my hand away. "I'm not people and I already have a boyfriend. How much plainer can I say it?"

"I thought you were my friend."

I glared at him. "Friends do not ask friends to lie. Friendship has nothing to do with what you're asking me to do."

"Please. Just for tomorrow."

"Look, I'm sorry your mother died, and I'm sorry if you're feeling pressure from someone to have a fiancée, but I can't be what I'm not."

"Maybe I should just do what my mother did and be done with it."

Right. That will solve everything. I stared at him, speechless. I was in over my head. "Let's sit down. We can share my sandwich. After work, we'll go see Yanni. He helped you before."

"Yanni's no miracle worker. All he did was drive me to the hospital."

"He cares about you. He arranged for your father to visit you. That's something."

"You could be a miracle worker if you wanted."

I've told plenty of lies, but this one felt like a one-way road to trouble. I sat down and took out my sandwich. "Here, have half. It's turkey."

"What are you, some kind of Jewish mother? You think food is the answer to everything?"

Anger usually scares me, but Bruce's anger felt like desperation. I didn't respond. Instead, I ate my lunch while he sat slumped against the tree. When it was time to work with the Zombies I told him I had to leave but he wouldn't look at me. Feeling more irritated than compassionate, I said I'd meet him at the front gate after work. He didn't respond. I didn't repeat the offer. I put two cookies into his hand and left, wishing I could talk to Yanni. Maybe he would know what to do.

Any thought about having an enjoyable time with the Zombies was dispelled by the specter of Mrs. Denby waiting for me at the entrance of building 5. "Miss Weinstein, I know you usually work with patients on ward 2 after lunch but I'm short staffed. I need you to help with the showers." I stared at her uncomprehendingly, still thinking about Bruce's talk of suicide. The last thing I wanted to do was look at a bunch of naked women, but, having no choice, I followed her into a lower level. Attendants were helping patients take off their clothes, then leading them into a large room with too many showerheads to count. I was struck by the passivity of the women waiting for their turns. I dreaded seeing Liz, Barbara, and Maggie. Not that I wanted to see any patients undressed, but I wouldn't be able to avoid looking at them and I could only imagine our awkwardness the next time we met.

I hung back, wishing there was something else I could do besides take off patients' clothing, but Mrs. Denby saw me and pointed to a group of women. By the expression on her face I could tell she was not pleased. Reluctantly, I walked over to a group, trying not to look at their flabby breasts and sagging stomachs. After a while, I found myself admiring the endless variety of female curves and shapes. There was a kind of beauty in the way the women walked, unselfconsciously, with surprising dignity. I turned to help the next woman and recoiled. Liz! The one woman I most didn't want to see.

Mrs. Denby was watching so I whispered, "I'm so sorry," as I helped her undress, folding her clothes, placing them neatly on top of her shoes. She glared at me, tears in her eyes, as she walked resolutely into the shower. I wondered how she could walk with such self-possession, given her situation. Watching her, I felt embarrassed and ashamed that I was dressed and she was naked; it didn't seem right. I even felt ashamed that I was thankful not to have to wash the women's bodies or shampoo their hair. Helping the patients dry themselves wasn't quite as bad, but I was uncomfortable and they probably felt it. I kept reminding myself to focus on the job, handing patients towels and drying what they couldn't reach, rather than on my feelings about what I was doing. By the time I had to help Barbara and Maggie dry off I was numb. They acted as if they didn't know me and I took my cue from them. It was a long, long, long afternoon.

16

We finished the bathing half an hour before I was due to leave. It was too early to go and not enough time to take a group out. I was about to ask Mrs. Denby if I could leave, that I had a personal emergency, when she said, "Miss Weinstein, Dr. Glassman told me you did a fine job telling a story to the children. How about telling the women a story in the time we have left?"

Although I was pleased and surprised by his account, I worried about Bruce and wished I could just leave. However, her question wasn't really a question. I hoped she didn't hear my sigh. "Okay. Any particular kind of story?"

"A good one, of course," she laughed.

I was in no mood to tell a story. My brain was jumbled with worries, taking up any imagination I might have had. All the folk and fairy tales I knew disappeared as if a gate had opened and everything inside had run out. While I was stewing, trying to think of a story, Mrs. Denby gathered the women together, once again finding places for everyone to sit. The patients looked up at me expectantly. I felt even worse when I saw Liz staring at me, a scornful smile on her face, daring me to say something that would interest her. Barbara and Maggie were huddled together; neither one looked at me.

"We're ready for your story, Miss Weinstein," said Mrs. Denby, her voice a command rather than a request. Beads of perspiration wet my face and I had no tissue.

"Use your sleeve," suggested a woman sitting near my feet, pointing to my sweaty forehead.

Trying not to panic, I stood in front of the group, desperate to think of something I could turn into a story. I saw Mrs. Denby fidgeting and knew I had to start, somehow.

"Once upon a time, long ago, in a place far away..." I hesitated, allowing the powerful words to penetrate the jumble in my mind. Much to my relief, I remembered an old German folk tale I could use as a base, "there was once a king who traveled far from his kingdom, and in that faraway place he ate the best chocolate chip cookies he had ever tasted. He tried everything he knew to persuade the baker to return with him, but to no avail. The baker refused to leave. When the king returned home, he immediately hired the finest bakers he could find, but none of them could bake chocolate chip cookies as good as he'd eaten in the kingdom far from his."

"You're making me hungry," someone commented.

"He should have hired me," retorted another. "Everyone says mine are the best."

By now I was somewhat used to the interjections of the women. Rather than finding them annoying, I was grateful for them and also surprised that some had the courage to speak loud enough to make their voices heard in such a large group. "So what do you think he should do?" I asked.

"He should marry a woman who knows how to bake great chocolate chip cookies," shouted a woman sitting in the back. "I made delicious cookies for my kids."

"Well, that's exactly what he thought," I responded. "He decided it was time for him to marry, and not only would his wife be wise and beautiful, she would know how to bake scrumptious chocolate chip cookies, just the kind he craved."

"She has to be wise and beautiful and bake great cookies?" asked a woman who stood up to respond. "What is he, some sort of paragon? What's so great about him?"

I laughed, feeling a lot better than I had just a few minutes before. "I guess, since he was the king, he thought he had a right to choose the perfect woman to be his queen."

"Darling, let me tell you, she doesn't exist," commented the woman, laughing knowingly. I glanced at Liz, whose expression was less hostile. Mrs. Denby seemed to approve of my so-called storytelling.

I continued the story, telling how the king had found a wise and beautiful princess but she couldn't bake chocolate chip cookies, only cupcakes. The next princess he found was beautiful, if not so wise, and she hated chocolate chip cookies, but claimed she baked delicious gingersnaps. The king disliked gingersnaps so he kept looking. The next princess he found was not beautiful but she was wise. She told the king, "Not only do I not bake chocolate chip cookies, the man I marry has to be kind and cheerful and play the flute." The king was taken aback. He might be kind, perhaps cheerful, but he couldn't play any musical instrument. Although he liked her the best of all the princesses he'd met, he sadly told her goodbye.

"Why doesn't he give up the cookie business, already?" hooted a woman who jabbed her neighbor, looking for agreement. "She can't bake, he can't play—it's a perfect match." The women nodded in agreement.

"Well," I said, "after visiting with the princess he liked best, he went home and told his advisors what had happened, describing all the princesses he'd been meeting. They noticed he kept talking about the one who wanted her husband to be kind and cheerful and play the flute. In truth, he had no musical talent and no interest in playing the flute. Still, he decided to pay her another visit. Since she was wise, perhaps she would think of a solution."

"Just like a man, always expecting the woman to figure things out," complained Barbara with mock seriousness. Everyone laughed—even Liz. Telling a story wasn't easy with all the interruptions, but stories seemed to help patients feel better. Maybe I needed to tell stories more often. Maybe Dr. Glassman was right. Maybe telling stories could help the children.

"When the king met the princess again, he was sure she was the one he wanted to marry, so he asked her, 'What shall we do? You can't bake chocolate chip cookies and I can't play the flute.' The princess, who liked the king very much, suggested that since he was kind, and she was wise, they could marry and promise never to mention chocolate chip cookies or flutes. The king thought this was an excellent solution and so they were married on a beautiful day with all the courtiers and villagers cheering them on.

"When the couple had been happily married for a year and a day, they decided to celebrate their anniversary by going on a picnic. But the morning of the picnic, the queen awoke with a terrible headache. The king was grumpy because it was raining. When they met for breakfast the eggs were cold, the toast was burned, and instead of orange juice, they'd been served grapefruit juice. The king was so mad he said to the queen, 'None of this would have happened if you had just learned to bake chocolate chip cookies.'

"The queen countered, 'Well, if you had learned to play the flute, I wouldn't have such a terrible headache.' They glared at each other and stormed out of the dining room. They refused to talk to anyone, not even their advisors. When they didn't come to the dining room for lunch, the cooks left food outside their doors and scampered away before they could be yelled at, or worse."

"I knew it, they got a divorce. Can't have a good marriage based on a bad bargain," laughed Maggie. This time the whole group laughed and their laughter was contagious. They were making me feel a lot better than before I began the story. "So, what happened? Tell us," she said, still laughing.

"Well, the king got to thinking. 'I'm supposed to be kind and it wasn't very kind of me to mention chocolate chip cookies.' The queen also spent time thinking, and she thought to herself, 'I'm supposed to be wise and it wasn't very wise of me to say that hearing the flute would ease my headache.'

"After that, for many days, the king and queen disappeared. No one saw them, but when servants passed the king's quarters, they held their noses to avoid smelling a horrible burning odor. From the queen's quarters they heard dreadful squawks and squeaks. The courtiers and villagers couldn't imagine what was happening, but, after a while the smells began to change. Now when the cooks and courtiers passed the king's quarters, their mouths watered, yet there was no sign of the king. At the same time, although no one saw the queen, the squeals and screeches became melodic and tuneful, yet there was no sign of the queen."

"I know what happened. The king hired a baker and the queen hired a musician," quipped Maggie, "and they all lived happily ever after." The group, apparently satisfied, laughed and clapped, as if this were the ending.

I held up my hands to quiet them. "Not quite!"

Barbara joked. "I know, the villagers got so upset with the noise and smells, they found a beautiful maiden who could bake chocolate chip cookies and a handsome man to play the flute, so all was well."

Once again everyone laughed but I managed to say, "Nope! Any other ideas? " It felt really good to see the women enjoying themselves.

"So tell us what happened already." A chorus of voices joined in, wanting to know the end of the story.

"What happened was this. One morning, after all the bad smells and horrible sounds had stopped, the king and queen met for breakfast. Gone were the bad tempers and mean words. Both were smiling. The king said to the queen, 'My love, I decided, the kind thing to do was to learn to bake my own chocolate chip cookies.' He clapped his hands and the cook brought out a tray of warm cookies just out of the oven. He looked so pleased with himself the queen gave him a hug, ate two chocolate chip cookies, and pronounced them delectable."

"Oh, this is a fairy tale," said the woman sitting closest to me. "I love happy endings."

"What about the queen?" asked a few of the women.

"The queen decided the wise thing to do was to learn to play the flute. So, after she ate the cookies she said to the king, 'I too have a surprise.' With that, she took a flute out of its case and played a lovely tune. The king listened, a delighted smile on his face, entranced by the wonderful melody and the happiness of his queen."

"And now they lived happily ever after," yelled a woman sitting far in the back.

"I can't tell you that, but I think it's fair to say they never again argued about chocolate chip cookies and flute music."

"Good story," shouted some of the women. They looked a lot more relaxed and I felt less tense.

Mrs. Denby shook her head and walked up to me. *Did I tell a bad story? I was already worried about Bruce. Now I began to panic.* "Miss Weinstein, your story was wonderful and the way you make room for the women to comment is simply splendid. Thank you."

Simply splendid? Wow! For a moment I forgot about Bruce. All the hopelessness I'd felt working at the hospital disappeared. I even had hopes of helping the children. Practically skipping to the front gate, my happiness soared until I saw Bruce slumped against the wall, looking even worse than when I'd seen him at lunch. Everything about him was gray—his face, his shirt, his pants. It looked like he was lost inside himself and I had no idea how to help him, if I even could. "Ready for coffee at Yanni's?" I asked. He didn't respond. Exasperated, I spoke louder. "Bruce, do you want to go for coffee?" No answer. "I'm going. Are you coming with me?"

He barely eked out, "I guess." My scooter was parked a few blocks from the gate so I told him I'd go get it. He nodded. Just looking at him made me tired. I wanted to tell him to fight back, that it wasn't his fault he'd had an alcoholic mother and a tyrant for a stepfather. But what did I know about the miseries of dealing with them? I wished

I could just drive to Yanni's, have a cup of coffee, and go home. How did I get so involved in Bruce's life?

He saw me drive up, got on the back of the scooter, put his arms lightly around my waist, and we drove off. Yanni heard us drive into the parking lot and came out to meet us. He nodded to me and helped Bruce off the scooter and into the restaurant. I almost got back on and drove off, but I wanted to see Yanni. A lot. Too much.

I followed them but stopped when they walked toward the back room, talking quietly. The food smells were so rich and inviting I wanted to bottle them. Two men in white hats and coats were in the kitchen preparing the evening's meals. Hesitating, unsure of what to do, I walked to the dining area, festive with a variety of fresh flower arrangements and interesting, different place settings on each white cloth-covered table, ready for the diners who would start coming in an hour and a half. Every bit of me wanted to get back on the scooter and go home, but I thought I should at least say goodbye. Then, Yanni came out, closed the door, and whispered, "Rennie, thank you for helping Bruce. He needs friends right now. I'll make a fresh pot of coffee. See if you can get him to talk. If he doesn't let out some of what's inside, I'm afraid of what he'll do." *And how exactly am I supposed to do this? He won't even look at me.*

I walked in. Bruce was slumped against the arm of the small sofa. His eyes were closed. "Bruce, you told me how much talking helps you. I'm..."

The bitterness in his voice stunned me. "Maybe you're willing to listen, but you're not willing to help. I've said everything I have to say to you."

"What? The only way to help you is pretend I'm your fiancée?"

"I don't know why you're making such a big fuss out of such a little nothing. It's only for a few hours. It's not like I'm asking you to hurt someone or do something illegal."

"If it's such a little nothing why ask me to be your fiancée for a day?"

"An afternoon, not a day!"

"You didn't answer my question."

"It's none of your business," he snapped.

"It is my business. I'm the one who'll be lying. If you won't tell me, I'm leaving." Just then Yanni entered, set a pot of coffee down on the table, and quickly returned with mugs and a basket of hot pastries that smelled too good to ignore. "Hey you two, come eat. Tomaso made a batch of scones and I need you to tell me if we should add them to our upcoming Sunday brunch menu." Bruce hesitated, but even he, upset as he was, couldn't pass them up. Like children who've had a fight and not yet made up, we sat in silence while Yanni poured coffee. Tomaso brought a tray with plates, knives, napkins, spoons, three pots of different kinds of jam, and a bowl of whipped cream.

They hovered over us, Tomaso making sure we sampled all the pastries he'd made: chocolate, raspberry, and orange walnut. "We start serving in a week and we plan to have muffins, scones, brioche, and a variety of breads. So, what do you think?"

I quickly told him that the scones were delicious and absolutely deserved to be on the menu. Their excitement was contagious and I blurted out, "Yanni, if you don't have a waitress yet, could I be the server?" I had no experience waitressing, but how hard could it be? His troubled look told me I shouldn't have asked. I felt stupid. To cover my embarrassment, I said, "That's okay. I was only kidding," then picked up one of the raspberry-filled scones. "This is my favorite."

"I like them all," said Bruce. "What about cranberry scones? I had some once that were utterly divine." *Utterly divine? Who talks like that?* "Tomaso, maybe you could make some for the gathering after the funeral tomorrow?" He nodded, writing down suggestions from the three of us.

The more I thought about the funeral, the less I wanted to go. The idea of calling in sick appealed to me. I said goodbye and left in a hurry, feeling as if I'd narrowly escaped an unknown disaster. When I put my hand into my jacket pocket to get my scooter keys, I gasped. Without my knowing, Bruce had managed to put his grandmother's diamond ring in my pocket.

17

Furious, yet not wanting to go back in and create a scene, I drove home, the ring burning a hole in my pocket and my imagination. How could Bruce do such a thing? If it really had been his grandmother's, it was not only valuable, it was also sentimentally irreplaceable. I put the ring on the table in the foyer, but it looked so vulnerable I picked it up and tried to find a place that seemed safer. Then, I don't know why, everything in my brain told me not to—I put it on my ring finger. It fit perfectly. My mind screamed to take it off but my body paid no attention. I wore it for the rest of the evening, even to bed. I hated realizing that having a ring on my finger was comforting, better than wearing Jake's Phi Beta Kappa key around my neck.

Nightmares and dreams kept me awake most of the night. In the scariest of the nightmares, Bruce kept multiplying, surrounding me, making it impossible to get away from him. All the Bruces shoved me toward the funeral gathering, shouting, "You have to help me. I'll die if you don't." Terrified, I got up and turned on the light. The facets of the diamond gleamed like evil eyes. I tore the ring off my finger, wrapped it in tissue paper, stuck it back in the box, put the box in an envelope, sealed the envelope and put it in my purse. One way or another I would manage to give it back to him.

I made a cup of tea and toasted a bialy, my favorite comfort food, and slathered it with butter. I kept telling myself that Bruce couldn't make me do anything I didn't want to do. I was not responsible for him, no matter what he said. After I finished eating I felt better and decided not to call in sick. I didn't want to give anyone any excuse to fire me.

In the morning, I had to figure out what to wear, clothes suitable for a funeral or the more casual clothes I'd taken to wearing. I put on and took off a lot of clothes as the *yes, go,* voice collided with the *no, don't go* voice. I didn't want to go and was afraid not to. I settled for a blue dress and sandals. If I went, it would be good enough. Then, when I looked at myself in the mirror I looked so awful that I went into my parents' bedroom and searched for makeup my mother might have left behind. I don't usually wear anything but lipstick, and even this I often forget to use. I found mascara, eyeliner, and some rouge, but I used too much. The effect was ghastly rather than enhancing so I washed my face and started over. I looked a little better when I finished, but getting most of it off took more time than I planned.

Knowing the ring was in my purse made me nervous. I not only put the box with the ring in a pouch in my saddlebag, but I also tied the saddlebag to the scooter. Instead of having time to collect my thoughts before going to the ward, I barely made it to work on time, supremely grateful that the spark plugs did not require changing en route.

Before I had decided whether to go to the funeral, Mrs. Denby told me she'd been notified that I would only be working half a day. She offered her condolences and asked if I felt up to taking patients out. Sitting around, waiting to attend an event I didn't want to go to was the last thing I needed. Besides, word had spread about the softball team, and my attempts to remind the patients I had no authorization fell on deaf ears. The women wanted to have a team. They were so excited about having an opportunity to play other hospital teams like the men they let me know they were willing to do whatever they could to improve their playing. Their enthusiasm surprised Mrs. Denby, who told me she'd never seen them so excited about anything other than going home. "You better get permission to form a team or these women will be extremely upset. The sooner the better." I knew she was right but I didn't look forward to asking for it. "Mr. Carson will be at the funeral. He likes good publicity," she said, before leaving to get patients ready to go with me. I stared at her receding figure. *What is that supposed to mean?*

I didn't know what to do with my purse. Normally, I put it in a desk drawer in Mrs. Denby's office, but I was worried about the ring. I couldn't take the purse with me and I didn't trust the shallow pocket on my dress. I opened the envelope and tried wearing it on my right third finger, but it didn't fit as well as on my left ring finger, where I definitely was not going to wear it. I could hear the patients calling me. Desperate, I put the ring on my left finger, turned the diamond around, and hoped no one would notice.

What the patients first noticed was my distraction. Barbara asked me twice if I'd gotten permission, and when I didn't answer her right away, she asked what was wrong. Embarrassed, I shrugged. "Still thinking about the best way to ask. Let's play ball." They asked if we could practice throwing, catching, and pitching, as well as playing in the outfield, which they used to consider a place to dream. I was impressed with their determination to improve.

Just as I was getting ready to try a new strategy, Liz asked, "Why are you so dressed..." and then she saw the ring. "What's that? You got engaged and didn't tell us?" She yelled, "Rennie's engaged. Look at her gorgeous ring." I cursed under my breath. It just got worse. Barbara wanted to know how my boyfriend had asked me to marry him. Given the size of the ring, Maggie wanted to know all about my fiancé. Their questions encouraged others until there was no stopping the women. They bombarded me, wanting more and more details. And I wasn't supposed to get personal with them? Obviously they hadn't heard of Mr. Carson's rules.

There was no way I could tell them the truth. I couldn't even think up a story that would explain why there was a ring on my finger today that would be gone by tomorrow. The situation was so bizarre it defied explanation. "It's not really mine," I finally said.

"So whose is it, and why are you wearing it?" demanded Liz, ignoring my obvious discomfort, assuming the role of speaker for the group.

"All I can tell you is that tomorrow I won't be wearing it."

"Now there's a story to tell us next time," quipped Barbara, disbelieving me.

Frustrated, I pleaded with them, "Can we please stop talking and start playing?"

"When are you going to ask for permission?" asked Maggie. "We should have the right to play other hospital teams if the men can." Relieved to be talking about softball rather than engagement rings, I told them I planned to speak with Mr. Carson that afternoon if possible. As soon as I said it, I regretted my inability to think before I spoke. I hadn't even decided to go to the funeral. "And if not this afternoon, as soon as I can get an appointment to see him," I added.

There was nothing wrong with Maggie's brain. "So how do you plan to speak to him this afternoon if you don't have an appointment?"

Why can't I keep my big mouth shut? Disgusted, I blurted out, "I'm going to a funeral. He'll be there and I might have a chance to ask him then."

"Why would you do that?" asked Barbara. "Who wants to talk business at a funeral? Anyway, who died?"

"A friend's mother."

"How did she die?"

"Stop with the questions! If we want Mr. Carson to let us form a team, we have to show him that the women from this hospital can beat women from other hospitals." Without waiting for their response, I organized drills. For once I was grateful they were used to obeying orders.

I brought the women back a few minutes early so I had time to write a note to Bruce saying I was sorry for his loss and for his need to have a fiancée, but not only couldn't I the wear the ring, I wasn't able to go to the funeral. I planned to give the ring to Mr. Carson's secretary and then leave since I'd been given the afternoon off. If asked, I'd say I didn't feel well and went home.

There's a Jewish saying: "Man proposes, God disposes." I recoiled in disbelief and shock when I saw Bruce and Dr. Miller waiting for me on the ward, talking with Mrs. Denby. I tried to take the ring off before they saw me, but Bruce was quicker than I was. He rushed up to me, his gratitude making me cringe. "Thank you so much, Rennie. I knew you'd help me." Ignoring my look of incredulity, he said it again. "I knew you'd help me."

Dr. Miller followed him, his face taut with grief. "I'm so sorry to be welcoming you into the family on such a sad occasion."

I stared at the two of them, stunned. Mrs. Denby put her arm around me. "If you need to take tomorrow off, call the office, before five tonight if possible." *I want to take the afternoon off. I am not Bruce's fiancée. I do not want to go to the funeral.*

I lost my will to act. I allowed Bruce and Dr. Miller to shepherd me into a waiting black limousine, longer than any I had ever seen. They sat me between them and introduced me to people sitting in the other seats. I tried not to wince when the congratulations began. Two women recognized the ring and told Bruce how wonderful it was that he had given me his grandmother's ring. In response, Bruce started to put his arm around my shoulder. I muttered, "Don't touch me." He patted my hand before I could pull it away.

At the funeral home we were ushered into a small room where a buffet had been set up for people coming from out of town. I was standing far away from the food, too tense and upset to eat, when Dr. Miller brought a couple to meet me, introducing me as Bruce's fiancée. They didn't hide their surprise. Neither did three women, friends of his mother, when Bruce brought them to meet me. Their reactions only increased my bewilderment. Why did everyone seem so shocked? I was desperate to get away from the room, the crowd, the smells of the food, the reek of perfume, the stares no one bothered to hide. As I walked toward the door, Bruce asked where I was going. *None of your business.* "To the ladies' room." He looked so worried that it occurred to me he thought I was leaving. I wasn't sure how to find my way back to the hospital and my scooter, but it started me thinking.

While I was lingering in the stall, dreading having to return, I heard a woman speak. "Can you believe? Bruce? With a fiancée? Giving her his grandmother's ring? It's worth a fortune."

There was a laugh, not very pleasant. A second woman responded, "I wonder how long they've been engaged. I can't imagine it lasting very long."

"Maybe it's his way of dealing with Dorothy's death."

"Or her life."

"Marly, that's not fair."

"May not be fair but it's true. You know how worried she was about Bruce never having any girlfriends."

"That's not what turned her into an alcoholic and you know it. She didn't drink much of anything before she married Dr. Uptight and traded love for security."

"What's worse, it didn't take her long to discover she couldn't keep the bargain."

Their talked stopped suddenly when the door opened. "Hi Sheila," said one of them. I waited until I heard the door open again and then, hoping they'd gone, emerged from the stall, needing a few minutes to myself. I washed my hands, trying to decide what to do. No part of me wanted to go back into the room with the buffet or attend the funeral or wear the ring. I was already nervous about losing it; knowing that it was so valuable made me even more so. I left the ladies' room, saw that the hallway was empty, walked out a side door that had been left ajar, and hurried away, choosing to leave from the side of the funeral home with no windows.

I kept walking. Nothing was familiar. I kept looking for a street with lots of traffic where I might find a taxi. When I heard someone yell, "Rennie, Rennie!" I couldn't help turning around. Yanni was driving slowly toward me. He pulled to the curb and stopped the car. "What are you doing out here?" He got out, came around, and opened the passenger door for me. "Get in. I'll drive you back to the funeral home."

"I don't want to go to the funeral. And, in case Bruce told you I was his fiancée, I'm not. But I'm worried about the ring so I'd appreciate it if you'd give it back to him. It belonged to his grandmother and it's worth a lot of money." I told him what had happened, hoping he would explain my absence to Bruce. "They kidnapped me. I know, he's upset about his mother's death, but..." I stopped. Yanni looked unsympathetic, which hurt my feelings. I took the ring off my finger and gave it to him, but he put it back in my hand.

"Put it on and come with me. I'll take you back after the service. Bruce needs you to be there. You're his friend."

He held the car door for me, but I refused to get in. Something inside me stiffened. It was much harder to say no to Yanni than to Bruce. "Yanni, I am not going. If Bruce wants to know where I am, tell him anything you want."

"Rennie, listen to me." He put his arm around my shoulder. I didn't like how good it felt and it took all my will power not to lean against him. "I'm not at liberty to talk about why your presence matters so much, but if ever I can, I will. I promise."

I suddenly remembered Mrs. Denby telling me Jack Carson would be at the funeral. I could ask him for permission to start a women's softball team. Maybe being at a funeral would distract him enough that he'd just say yes. I looked at Yanni's pleading expression, felt the warmth of his body close to mine, and once again, lost my willpower. "All right, I'll come with you." *At least I have a reason to go, I'm not just giving in.* This did not make me feel better.

"Thank you, Rennie. You won't be sorry." He looked at his watch. "We need to hurry, the service will be starting in a few minutes." When I got into his car, which smelled of his aftershave, I wanted to be with him, go anywhere with him—except to this funeral. *Think about the women. Focus on what to say to Jack Carson.*

18

Cars were parked everywhere. A surprising number of people had come to pay their last respects to Bruce's mother. Or was it because she'd been married to Dr. Miller? Didn't sound as if she had had much of a life besides drinking, but maybe her life had been different before she was married. What made her marry him? Did she really start drinking because of him?

As we approached the funeral home, Yanni squeezed my hand. I squeezed his hand back, already missing it when he let go to park and open the door. Inside was a cliché come true; the silence was deafening. So many people, so little sound. As we walked into the room where the service was to be held, I saw Bruce, looking agitated, standing close to a tall, lanky man with a well-trimmed beard. He was wearing a black suit, his light brown hair tickling his collarless black shirt. They were facing a grim-faced Dr. Miller and a rabbi whose hand rested lightly on Dr. Miller's shoulder. I heard Yanni mutter, "Uh-oh."

I stared at him and mouthed, "What?"

He whispered, "That's Andrew Lowenstein."

"What's he doing here?" Yanni shrugged as we made our way to the flower-draped casket, which, to my relief, was closed. I don't know what I expected, but Bruce's mother had a lot of friends. They paused before the casket, tears in their eyes, murmuring words I couldn't hear. Some of them reached out to me, patting my shoulder, gently taking my hand in theirs. One whispered, "Dorothy would have loved to meet you. You're just what she hoped for and thought would never happen." That made no sense to me, so I smiled politely, grateful when she moved on.

Yanni and I took seats assigned to us in the front, too close for me. We could hear the rabbi telling Dr. Miller, "It will be all right. Don't upset yourself even more." People were moving restlessly in their seats; the service had been scheduled to start at one o'clock and it was now well after that. Bruce edged closer to Andrew Lowenstein, who put his arm around Bruce's shoulder and then, nodding to Dr. Miller and the rabbi, walked him to the seat next to me. Bruce introduced me as his fiancée. Andrew Lowenstein smiled, offered his congratulations, said he looked forward to talking with me at the reception, then walked to the back of the room. Looking relieved, Bruce sat down. He whispered, "Thank you." I turned away from him and stared at the variety of flowers that filled the room with overpowering scents. I began to feel dizzy. When Dr. Miller finally sat down next to Bruce, signaling the rabbi to begin, I was relieved. The sooner it ended, the sooner I could leave.

The service was mercifully brief. A woman with a beautiful alto voice, accompanied by a cello, sang songs from Schubert's *Song Cycle*, then the rabbi talked about Dorothy Miller as a person and an artist, never mentioning how she died. A friend read a short story she said Mrs. Miller had written shortly after her marriage. I wondered if this was the only story she'd written or the friend had another reason for reading it. It was about a rare bird with stunning plumage and a song so beautiful the other birds listened in silent rapture when it sang. Then a hunter, entranced by its beauty and the power of its song, captured the bird, brought it home, and built a magnificent cage for it. The bird never sang again.

Bruce started to cry. Dr. Miller tried to put his arm around Bruce, but Bruce shook him off and took a handkerchief out of his pocket to wipe his eyes. The pocket of his jacket was so close to me, I could easily have slipped the ring into it. *Why didn't I?*

A few people got up and talked briefly about Dorothy Miller— what a wonderful artist she was, what a good friend she'd been. No one mentioned her drinking or her suicide. I felt I was part of a conspiracy, where everyone pretended that her death had been natural, not a suicide. No one mentioned that she'd died young, only forty-two. One of her friends told me when the service ended, "We Jews believe that we are born into life with a certain amount of time, and, tragically, Dorothy had used up her time." *What the hell does that mean? To use up her time?*

Bruce and Dr. Miller joined the rabbi to form a receiving line. I watched people wipe away tears as they slowly made their way through the line to the reception. I couldn't pretend to be upset by Mrs. Miller's death so I went to the ladies' room, splashed water on my face, and stared at myself in the mirror, not liking how I felt.

The whole afternoon seemed surreal. At my aunt's funeral, after she had been killed by a drunk driver, people mourned her dying at thirty-seven, but no one talked about her time being up. Instead, people expressed their anger at the driver, their rage at the injustice of the fact that he lived and she died. When people shared stories about her, they talked about the woman they knew. They didn't make her out to be a saint.

As I left the ladies' room and saw all the people crowding around Jack Carson, I decided that talking to him at the funeral was a bad idea. The room where the reception was being held was soon filled with people eating and drinking. I stood at the doorway searching for Bruce. When I finally saw him standing in the far corner, next to Andrew Lowenstein and Yanni, it wasn't easy to make my way through the crowd. A few women stopped to congratulate me. I nodded and kept moving, not wanting to make eye contact. I could feel my resolve wavering, so when I got to Bruce, I took off the ring, put it in his hand, and muttered, "I'm going," then left without waiting for him, Yanni, or Andrew Lowenstein to respond.

Yanni followed me, murmuring, "Rennie, wait," but I kept moving, trying to be polite as I pushed between groups of people laughing and crying. When I got outside, Yanni caught up with me. "Rennie, please go back."

"Why is it so important that I pretend to be Bruce's fiancée?"

"It's not my place to tell you."

"Well, it's not my place to pretend. I should have said no firmly, and meant it, the first time he asked." Without looking back I started walking away, hoping that Yanni would offer to drive me to a bus stop or train station. He didn't. I was angry at myself for caving, at Bruce for asking me to pretend, and at Yanni for being so attractive. The pleading look on his face had been hard to resist, but this time, determined to do what was good for me, I kept walking. I figured sooner or later I'd come to a main street and a store where I could ask for directions. Each step I took I felt lighter and freer. The day was warm, but not hot. The cool breeze playing with my hair felt good. I wasn't proud of the way I'd let myself be manipulated, but at least I'd finally said no. That had to count for something. Eventually. Maybe.

I couldn't find a bus that went to the hospital and it was too far to walk, so I took a cab, the first I'd ever taken. I barely had enough money to pay for it and vowed to keep at least ten dollars in my wallet from now on. Thanks to Bruce, I no longer had to worry about searching for my scooter; it was right where I parked it. By the time I got home I was exhausted and puzzled and upset. I found an old bottle of bath salts and took a long hot bath, luxuriating in the lavender-scented water. I thought about overhearing the woman's odd remark—his mother worrying that he never had any girlfriends. As far as I knew, he didn't have any boy friends either.

Poor Bruce. His mother is dead. He has a father he likes but isn't supposed to see, and a stepfather who seems more concerned about appearances than about Bruce. Did Bruce ask me to be his friend because he thought we had loneliness in common?

The next morning I drove to the hospital earlier than usual, hoping to talk with Jack Carson. The door to his office was closed. His secretary, Miss Hempner, said he was busy and asked what I wanted. I didn't have a good feeling about her. Her face was made up like a circus clown; her perfectly coiffed hair and tailored blue suit seemed out of place in a mental hospital, even in administration. I tried to avoid answering but she asked again, in a no-nonsense tone of voice that demanded an answer. Reluctantly, I told her that I wanted to start a women's softball team that would play away-games just like the men's team did.

"Really!" Her surprised response held no criticism. "Do you have enough women who could play? Remember, they have to be well enough to leave the hospital."

"I think so, but Mrs. Denby says I need to have Mr. Carson's permission before we can hold any special practice." She looked interested, so I pressed on. "The men have a team. Why shouldn't the women?"

"I agree," she said, looking a lot warmer and kinder than when I walked in. "The best time to talk with him is right after lunch; he's usually in a good mood then." She gave me an appointment and wished me luck. I felt bad that I had so misjudged her.

A group of women were waiting for me when I walked into the ward, all wanting to know if I'd gotten authorization to form a team. My heart sank. I never imagined that playing on a softball team would turn out to be so important to the patients. I told them about my appointment and tried to downplay participation, but they refused to listen.

"Why should the men have a team if we can't?"

"What's it to him if we play other women?"

"It's not like it's gonna cost him anything, they already have a bus for the men."

They stopped talking and began backing away when they saw Mrs. Denby approach. She asked about the funeral. I was mumbling that it was fine and that the funeral service was moving, when she interrupted to tell me Mrs. Martelli would be back on Monday. "I've enjoyed working with you. It's refreshing to see a summer employee who cares about the patients. I just hope you've learned to think before you speak, much less act." She softened her tone. "Were you able to speak with Jack Carson yesterday?" I told her about my appointment after lunch. "Leave a little early so you're there well before time. He hates to wait." Since she was being so friendly I asked if she had any advice. "Don't emphasize fairness—men have a team so the women should have one too—he doesn't care about that."

"But that's the truth. If he doesn't care about that, what does he care about?"

Mrs. Denby sighed. "Around here, truth is, shall we say, fluid, and, you'll get nowhere if you argue with him. What he likes is good advertising. Tell him that having a winning women's softball team will bring the hospital favorable publicity, something that's dear to his heart."

"I never thought about that. But what if the women lose? That's a lot of pressure to put on them."

"They can't lose. It's that simple. If you start a women's team, and they play other teams, they have to win. I know Jack Carson. He likes winners. If the women lose, they won't be allowed to continue to play as a team."

"The men's team always wins?"

"Just about." She laughed at my look of incredulity and explained that when the men's team seems to be losing, attendants, who are always chosen to accompany them because they're good ballplayers, substitute for the patients."

"But that's cheating!"

"Jack Carson likes winners." She turned away and left to organize the women who were going out with me.

Without my knowing, Liz and Rita had selected women they thought could play well enough to form a team, plus enough other women to make two teams. As soon as we picked up the equipment and got to the field, the patients took pre-arranged positions and began to warm up. I continued to be astounded at the difference even the possibility of playing as a team had made. Apathy, gone. Waiting for me to tell them what to do, gone. Complaining and bad moods, gone. If I hadn't known better, I would have thought this was a different group of women. Barbara, who'd told Liz and Rita that she wasn't very good at playing softball but wanted to be involved, acted as coach and referee, telling women where to move and how to watch for possible base stealers. Who could have guessed she knew so much about softball? Made me realize, once again, how little I knew about these women.

When we took a break I asked Liz what was going on. In true Liz fashion she mocked my amazement. "In case you didn't know it, Miss Weinstein, we were people before we got sent to this place. Just because we've been labeled mentally ill doesn't mean we're completely worthless or totally crazy. Some of us even held jobs that mattered. " I blushed. She laughed mirthlessly. "We thought if you could see how much it means to us to play as a team, it might help you convince Mr. Carson to allow us to form a team and play other hospitals. Even thinking about getting away from this place for an afternoon makes me feel better." The women who'd gathered around us nodded in agreement. Their obvious yearning increased my apprehension but I assured them I'd do my best when I saw him. Afterward, as we headed back to the ward, they offered suggestions as to what I should say and made me promise to come back and tell them what he said.

Too tense to eat my lunch, I sat in the crook of a huge oak tree and leaned against the thick branches. The light breeze that rippled through the leaves felt like a caress against my face. At twelve-thirty I got down and hurried to the administration building, imagining various ways to approach Mr. Carson, wishing I felt more hopeful. I knew I was early but I wanted to be there when he returned from wherever he ate.

I didn't have long to wait. About five minutes after I sat down, he came in, smiling, clearly happy to see me. "Miss Weinstein! I hear you're Bruce's fiancée. Must say I'm a little surprised, but good for him—and for you of course." *Oy! Now what do I say?*

I looked at Miss Hempner, silently pleading for her to help me broach the subject. She smiled approvingly but then went back to typing. I took a very deep breath. "Mr. Carson, I'd like to talk with you about starting a women's softball team that would travel with the men's team when they play other hospitals."

"A woman's softball team? Now why on earth would we want that?" Not a promising beginning, but I ploughed on. "There are a lot of good athletes in building 5 who would like to have the opportunity to do what the men have been doing for years." I stopped, remembering Mrs. Denby's advice, and changed my approach. "Their winning games would be great publicity for the hospital." He hadn't interrupted me, so I kept going, trying to make the best case possible. "Too many people think that every person in this hospital is crazy, but most of the women in my building are normal people with emotional problems." I didn't know if this was true but it sounded good. "I think they would work hard and bring honor to Concordia. Maybe knowing about the men's and women's teams winning games against other hospitals would help change people's views about Concordia."

I paused. He hadn't cut me off so I told him something I thought Bruce had mentioned. "Every Christmas, Concordia has a big gala and the staff invites people from outside to watch patients perform. Maybe we could have a celebration to honor the winning men's and women's softball teams." *Please, let me find the words to persuade him to say yes.*

Mr. Carson looked amused. Miss Hempner nodded approvingly, even as she continued to type. "How do you know the women's team will win?"

Thank you, Mrs. Denby. "They're already very good players and they're sure that with practice they will play well against any team."

"Well, let me think about it."

Oh no, you need to say yes, now. Desperate, I tried a different tactic. "Mr. Carson, I made a big mistake." He raised an eyebrow. "I made the mistake of talking with my patients about how nice it would be if the women had a softball team and could travel with the men. I didn't say it would happen, it was just me thinking out loud, but they got so excited they organized two teams to play against each other. Before I mentioned the possibility, they had no energy or interest in anything, but afterward, even though I kept telling them I had to talk with you, they couldn't wait to get outside." Despite Mrs. Denby's warning I kept blabbering. "They've been practicing hard. The truth is, they're waiting for me to tell them that you've given your permission for them to form a team and play women from other hospitals." *I mentally crossed my fingers and toes and eyes and whatever else I could cross.*

He stared at me. Through me. "You did indeed make a mistake, Miss Weinstein, a very serious mistake. Raising hope for no reason is dangerous for patients. They need to learn to deal with reality, not wishful thinking." *He's going to say no. Now what am I going to do?*

Miss Hempner stopped typing and looked thoughtful. "Mr. Carson, I believe representatives from the Board of Health are coming to visit next week. They might enjoy watching the women's softball team practice. If I remember correctly, one of the issues they raised was the quality of summer recreation." *Bless you, Miss Hempner. May you live a hundred years.*

"That's true, they might." I held my breath. "How soon can you form a quality team that would be worth watching?" *Yikes. From nothing to perfect? In one week?*

"We'll start today. I'm sure the women will do their best to play well for the visitors." *What have I gotten myself into? Even worse, what have I gotten them into?*

"Very well, you have my permission to form a team and, if I consider them good enough, they may ride on the bus with the men, if the hospital where the men are playing has a women's team." He turned to his secretary and asked about his next appointment. I looked at Miss Hempner, who winked at me, thanked Mr. Carson, and left. He'd given his permission, but with so many ifs, who knew what it really meant. There was nothing to do but tell the women the truth and hope for the best.

19

This time I needed the Zombies more than they needed me. Working with them was like trying to repair something that had been broken a long time ago, with no manual to go by and, according to the staff, no hope of change. I had no expectation that I could fix their lack of connection, but what I did seemed purposeful, at least for me. The half hour I spent with them was my only tension-free time working at the hospital.

As soon as I walked into the ward, Mrs. Denby called me into her office and asked about my meeting with Mr. Carson. Her reaction was similar to mine: "So many ifs. Do you really think the women are good enough to play other teams?"

I shrugged. "Who knows? But, if Mr. Carson is bringing people to watch the women play, we need to use the best athletes we have." She nodded. I took a chance. "Some of the women in building 6 are really good ballplayers."

She gave me a withering look. "There is absolutely no way on earth women from building 6 will get permission to play off the grounds."

"I know, but I was thinking that Mr. Carson probably doesn't know which women are in which building so if we had women from buildings 5 and 6 playing, it would be a good game and great practice for the women we are able to take."

Mrs. Denby shook her head. "Miss Weinstein, you have no idea what you're suggesting. The women in building 6 are violent. Unpredictable. Dangerous. What if they act up? That would completely ruin your chances of forming a team. Consider the effect it will have on our patients. You really need to think about the consequences of your 'good ideas.'"

She had a point, but I had faith in the building 6 women I had met. Hadn't two of them postponed their toots that day in order to play? "I could ask Mrs. Cooper if she thought there were any women who could be relied upon to play without causing problems. Some of the women I took out were really good ball players."

"You know that if something happens you'll be fired, don't you? You might be fired anyway if the administration found out. Do you think it's worth it?"

"If we don't have a good game, there's no chance Mr. Carson will let our women form a team, and I don't know whether we have twenty-two women in building 5 who play well enough to form two good teams."

She looked at me thoughtfully. "As far as I'm concerned, we haven't had this conversation. You decide how you want to proceed. Just be aware that there can be unintended consequences." *I don't need the warning. I'm already worried about losing control.* "By the way, congratulations on your engagement to Bruce Miller. He's an interesting young man." I stared at her, wondering how she knew, who told her. She laughed. "No secrets around this place, so be careful what you say and do." I hoped my fury didn't show. I had to find Bruce and get him to clean up this mess. "You better go, the women know you're here. They've been waiting anxiously to find out what Jack Carson told you."

The women crowded around me. "Let's go out and we'll talk on the field," I said. They got ready in record time, showering me with questions. Some looked hopeful, others disgusted, convinced he'd turned them down. After I explained what he said, there were immediate and strong reactions—cursing, cheering, questioning. I cut them off. "Let's play! We need every minute we have to practice."

Twenty-five women had come out, so we arranged two teams and let those not playing act as coaches and referees. The women, usually docile and passive, had transformed. No one wanted me to play, coach, or referee. The contrast from before the possibility of a team to now, when they were playing with purpose and energy, settling their disputes by themselves and relying on each other, was miraculous. Liz and Rita had done such a good job of organizing and playing that everyone agreed they would be the captains. What I thought might be contentious was easily settled.

When I brought the women back, Mrs. Denby said Dr. Glassman had called to ask if I could tell the children a story and she had told him I would.

"When?"

"Now. Only for half an hour, maybe less. Their attention span isn't very long." Of course I had to agree to go, but I felt apprehensive and resentful. It wasn't my job and I knew less about mentally ill kids than I did about the women. At least I could talk with them—most of the time.

On my way to the children's unit I walked to building 6, hoping to talk with Coop. Contacting her always depended on the willingness of an attendant to answer the bell—sometimes they ignored it. This time I was lucky; Coop came down to meet me. When I told her my plan she was aghast, totally opposed, and shocked that I had even considered such foolhardiness. "I know you mean well, Rennie, but this is a place where there are rules and lines that can never, ever be crossed."

I was stunned by her vehemence, as well as disappointed. I thought for sure she'd be an ally. "But what about the women who postponed their toots?"

"You were lucky. I never heard of that happening before."

"Maybe no one ever asked them to do it before," I said, more bitterly than I intended.

"You haven't been here long enough to know what they've been asked to do," she said, as angry as I'd ever seen her. Coop was adamant. "There will be no building 6 women playing with building 5 women. Period." She asked if this would keep me from taking her women out to play ball. I told her one thing had nothing to do with the other, that I would continue to follow the schedule we'd made.

Her face softened and she spoke more kindly. "Work with the women from building 5. They could surprise you. Patients around here don't have much to look forward to. Even release dates, as you well know, are subject to change."

Like what happened to Carol? "Have you met Carol, the woman..." I couldn't bring myself to finish the sentence.

"I've heard about her. Seems she's extremely depressed. Won't talk to anyone." I asked about her prognosis, but Coop didn't know. I asked if she thought it would help if she gave Carol a message from me or her friends in building 5. She thought for a moment. "I know the head attendant on her ward. Want me to ask?"

I nodded. Thinking about Carol upset me all over again. "Is there any chance I could see her?" Coop stared at me. "I mean, as a recreational therapist..."

"Rennie, this is a hospital. With very sick people. Good intentions are not enough. In fact, sometimes they cause damage. You have to know what you're doing. You have to know what you can do." I knew she was right, but I felt let down. I didn't realize how much I was hoping I could see her.

"I hear you've been telling stories to the children. Good for you."

"What?"

"Rennie, everyone knows. People talk. You could say it's our form of recreation." I nodded, still a bit shocked at how quickly word traveled. "I'm glad. They need someone like you."

After she left I walked to the children's unit, needing to make sense of what was happening. Suddenly I was not only the recreational therapist for building 5, I was also the storyteller for the children's unit. Did that make me a storyteller therapist as well? The idea was ridiculous and discomforting.

The door to the children's unit was locked, and I had to wait for an attendant to let me in. "I'll see that you get a key," she said. *One more key on a belt that's already too heavy.* "I'd be careful if I were you. The doctor gave them tetanus shots and they're a bit upset." *More than last time?*

I had trouble making myself walk into the room. They were screaming and running and pushing each other and crying. I wanted to leave and never come back but that didn't seem to be a choice, so I stood just inside the door, too afraid to breathe.

Molly saw me and shrieked. "What do you want?"

I was about to say Dr. Glassman told me to come but decided that might not endear me to them. "I thought you might like to hear another story."

"Go away!" shouted David, his little body pulsing with energy. "We hate you."

"How come?" At least they quieted down. That felt like progress.

Jeffrey spoke for the group. "We don't want to hear stories. We want to go outside and no one will take us."

"Why not?" It was a lovely summer day—not a day to be cooped up inside.

Peter, his freckled face red and sweaty, said, "We run away and then they have to run after us and then they get mad and they won't let us out."

"Oh, they'll let us out all right, if we wear leashes," added Jeffrey, bitterly.

"Leashes?" *Like dogs?*

"Will you take us out?" he asked. "If we promise we won't run away?" He sounded like Natalie, using the same pleading tone of voice that hurt my heart.

"I'm supposed to tell you a story. I don't have permission to take you out."

"But if you take us out and we don't run away and we come back, no one will know," argued Jeffrey.

"Coop's words echoed in my mind. "Yes, they will. There are no secrets in this place. *Besides, I could get fired even if you don't run away. And if you do…* Suddenly they were all begging me to take them out, promising to be good.

"I have no keys to open and close the doors."

"Ask for a key," said Jenny, her blonde pigtails shaking with excitement.

"Look, there's no way I can take you out right now, so let's sit in a circle and talk."

"We don't want to talk, we want to go out," said Richard, his dark eyes filled with anger. "We just want to run in the grass." He got up and started yelling, "We want to go out. We want to go out." The others quickly joined them, except for David who ran to me, hugging my body, shaking in terror.

"I want to go home. I don't like it here." The louder they yelled, the harder David held on to me. His tears wet my blouse.

Too frustrated to think rationally, I screamed at the screaming children, "Stop! Stop it now! If you want me to help you, you've got to help me. What you're doing is making everything worse."

"We just want to go outside," cried Molly. "What's so bad about that?"

These are children. They may be mentally ill but they are children. They want to play. They just want to play. "Okay. I know you want to go outside but there's no way I can take you out right now. If you're willing to sit in a circle on the floor, I'm willing to talk with you about going outside. That's the best I can do right now."

"Why do we have to sit on the floor? Why can't we sit on chairs like we do with everyone else?" complained Peter.

"I'm not like everyone else. Sitting on the floor is cozy. Anyway, if you want to talk with me, sit on the floor in a circle." David took my hand as I led him to the center of the room. He refused to let go of my hand as we sat down. At least the screaming had stopped. I looked at my watch. "I can only stay fifteen minutes more, so you decide how you want to spend the time."

"Where do you have to go?" asked Jenny. I told her a little about what I do.

"Could you bring some balls and play with us?" asked Paul, the scar on his face bright red from screaming.

"I don't know. Dr. Glassman has to give me permission."

"Go talk to him now," said Molly. "Maybe next time you come you can take us out." The others agreed.

"If that's what you want, I'll go see if he's in his office." I felt their stares as I walked toward the door. Before I rang the bell for someone to open it, I turned and waved. They surprised me by waving back. *What have I gotten myself into?*

Dr. Glassman's office door was open. When I knocked he looked up and motioned for me to come in. "Miss Weinstein, aren't you supposed to be telling stories to the children?"

"Yes, but they don't want to hear a story. They want to go outside."

"That's not your job." *No, it isn't, but neither is telling them stories.* "Mrs. Denby agreed to release you for half an hour a few times a week, to tell them stories. What the children prefer is not your province."

"But they're children. It's summer. Why can't they play outside?"

"You're right. Children like to play outside, but we're short staffed right now and we don't have enough attendants to make sure they don't run away..." He paused, then added with emphasis, "Which they have done every time we've taken them out."

"They told me they wouldn't run away if I took them out."

"And you believe them?" I nodded, feeling Coop's snort of derision. "What makes you think they will behave properly with you when they've never listened to any of the staff?"

"Somebody has to believe them." I knew this was a lame response, but I did believe them. "Don't they have to have a chance to prove they can keep their promise?"

"Miss Weinstein, they are mentally ill children. Even if they mean what they say at any given moment, they aren't always able to control their behavior. You don't know anything about treating mentally ill children." *True. I don't know anything about treating mentally ill people period.* He stood up, thanked me for coming, showed me to the door and closed it. My idea of what was possible for these children might not seem doable to Dr. Glassman, yet I'd seen the change in the building 5 women. I knew that forming a softball team had energized the players and given them a sense of power. Even the Zombies had changed. I was sure of that even if no one else saw it. I didn't know how I would do it, but just as I was determined to make sure Mr. Carson and his guests had an exciting game to watch, with or without women from building 6, I was going to figure out a way to take the children outside.

I didn't expect Bruce to be sitting under the tree waiting for me. Filled with frustration from my talk with Dr. Glassman, I snarled, "Why are you telling everyone we're engaged?"

"Thank you for asking how I am," he retorted sarcastically.

"You need to stop telling people we're engaged."

"It's not me, it's my stepfather. I tried to get him to stop, but—"

"I'm not interested in 'buts.'"

"It's hard to talk about."

"Talk anyway. I'm tired of hints and innuendos."

He looked away. "When I was six or seven my mother found me playing doctor with a kid named Jimmy. She told us to get dressed immediately and never do it again. She refused to talk about it. The boy was never allowed to play with me after that."

"So? Lots of kids play doctor."

"Does everyone's mother then decide her son only likes boys?"

I shrugged. "How would I know?"

"The last time my stepfather saw her alive, he told her you were my girlfriend. He said she felt relieved and happy. Relieved and happy! But," he added bitterly, "not so relieved and happy, apparently, that she wanted to live." He paused, staring into space. "Seems she told a lot of her friends about her fears, so maybe my stepfather wanted to let them know I was, 'Okay.' 'Normal.'"

"So that's the big secret? That some people think you like boys?"

He mimicked me. "How would I know?" He looked away. "The truth is, you're the only friend I've had since Jimmy, and I'm not even sure we're friends."

"Well, you seem normal to me, whatever that means."

"Thanks."

"Have you ever dated anyone?" He shook his head. I couldn't help myself, "Why not?"

"I've lived on the hospital grounds ever since my mother married Bruce Miller. There were no kids my age who lived here. In school, they called me "Crazyboy," "Wacko" and a whole lot of other names. I tried to explain it was because my mother married a man who worked here, but after they heard he was a psychiatrist, the name-calling got worse. To make myself feel better I pretended their words were a foreign language. I didn't have any friends. Who was I supposed to ask out on a date?"

"Bruce, I'm sorry you've had such a hard time, but one thing has nothing to do with the other. You have to tell people we are not engaged."

"You're right. It's just that—"

"What?"

"It... It feels nice to be engaged to you. I like people congratulating me."

"Well I don't. It embarrasses me."

"Okay, I'll tell Hempner this afternoon. Once she knows, everyone will know." *Miss Hempner? Mr. Carson's secretary?* He laughed at my bewildered expression. "If you want information, she's the one to ask. As long as she likes you, that is." He sighed, looking so dejected I almost hugged him. "You didn't ask why I'm here, but I'll tell you. I'm leaving." My shock was palpable. "My stepfather was furious that I invited Andrew Lowenstein to the funeral. Afterward, we had a terrible fight. What he said made it impossible for me to keep living with him, so I called my father and told him what happened. He was kind enough to invite me to stay with him. It's a big relief to have somewhere else to live."

"When are you going?"

"I'm not sure. Since I signed a contract, my stepfather requested that I finish out the summer working here no matter where I live. Less explaining for him," he added resentfully.

He'll still be able to help me if I need it. "I suppose it's ridiculous to ask how you are, but I'll ask anyway."

"I think I feel every emotion it's possible to feel simultaneously. Mostly I'm numb." He looked at his watch. "We both have to go, but there's something I want to ask." He didn't wait for me to respond. "Could we say you're my girl friend, not my girlfriend? It was so nice to have you share the concert with me. I'd really like it if you'd go with me again. I know the best places to hear great jazz."

I reminded him I had a boyfriend, but this didn't seem to bother him—or me. "I'll make a deal with you. You tell Miss Hempner we're not engaged and I'll say yes." His face lit up like he'd gotten the best birthday present, ever. He promised he'd do it before going back to the ward, thanked me, and left with more energy in his walk than I could remember seeing since the whole mess began.

20

Word that the women in building 5 had formed a softball team quickly spread to every part of the hospital. We even began to have visitors who cheered when a woman made a good play. Although Coop wouldn't bring any of her patients, she sometimes came, offering suggestions I wouldn't have known to make. I didn't press her to tell me about Carol, but she knew I was waiting for news. One morning, she walked to the field and I sensed something was wrong. She wasn't smiling, she walked slowly, and her body looked like she was carrying a heavy load. As I walked over to her, I thought, *it's about Carol.* I could see Liz, Maggie, and Barbara watching, as they did every time Coop visited, hoping for news. This time they backed off, as if they knew what she told us wouldn't be good. It wasn't. "Carol doesn't talk," she said. "She doesn't bathe voluntarily, and when attendants try to clean her, she struggles so violently they have to put her in a straightjacket." I shuddered, remembering Carol's bright smile, the happiness she felt because she was going home the next day.

"Isn't there anything anyone can do?"

"Like what?" Coop's tone was unusually harsh, a sure sign she was upset. She'd reminded me more than once there was nothing I could do, but I asked about visiting Carol anyway. Coop shook her head. "Rennie, if she'd broken her leg, doctors would know how to fix it. No one knows how to fix broken minds."

"Why not? What am I doing here if I'm not helping? If it isn't possible to help?" Coop strode back to the women before I could thank her for letting me know. Everything seemed pointless. I forced myself to smile and put energy into my voice as I coached the pitcher, dreading the moment when I had to tell Liz, Maggie, and Barbara about Carol. I waited until we were heading back, not wanting to spoil the practice. They listened intently. Liz cursed. Maggie backed away. Barbara cried. All the joy of playing dissolved into grief.

Bruce kept his word. When Mrs. Denby mentioned the broken engagement and offered her sympathy, I kept a straight face. A few days later she told me that Mrs. Martelli's health had deteriorated, and she had been given a six-month leave of absence. This meant I wouldn't have to deal with her before I left, a big relief. When she asked, "The game is tomorrow—are the women ready?" I shrugged. We both knew the women were emotionally erratic. How they played depended on the way they were feeling at any given moment, but I had faith their hard work and determination would pay off. "Well," she said, "whatever happens, the opportunity to form a team has energized them more than I could have believed possible. Let's keep our fingers crossed." *Fingers and toes.*

Although I never knew how Mrs. Denby would react, I felt she cared about the patients and that comforted me. Maybe Mrs. Martelli did as well, but her reputation and my interaction with her kept me feeling as if she were a landmine, always ready to explode. When I told Mrs. Denby about my daily visits to the patients on ward 2, I didn't dare call them Zombies; she'd given me a quixotic smile and told me to go ahead, if that was my choice. I might not have her blessing but I also didn't have her objection. That was worth a lot.

In the afternoon, when I threw a ball to one of the Zombies, I thought I saw a smile on her face as the ball came toward her. Probably my imagination, but the women staying in the circle without wandering off was not something I imagined. So when I picked up the ball I smiled at the woman, lightly touched the ball to her hand, and then threw it to another woman. I felt the first woman watching me. Either I was hallucinating or there was definitely a positive change in her behavior. I felt euphoric—too strong a reaction for such a small response, I knew, but I'd been told there was no possibility of change and the attendants had done their best to discourage me from trying.

Bruce met me after work and I drove us to Yanni's. We hadn't been there in a while and we both missed him. I felt a jolt of electricity when Yanni gave me a welcoming hug. Bruce didn't seem to notice that I never hugged him, but then, he never hugged me either. I watched the two of them together—bantering and joking, easy with each other, but nothing sexual as far as I could tell. Then again, what was I looking for?

Tired of trying to understand something that eluded me, I walked over to one of Bruce's paintings. Two had been sold. Somehow they no longer looked threatening, but I couldn't account for the change. Yanni's restaurant was doing well and he'd been able to hire more kitchen help, so he had a bit of time to sit with us. While Bruce and I devoured the fruit- and chocolate-filled pastries his new pastry chef had made, he told Yanni what had happened between him and his stepfather since the funeral. I stood up to leave, but both of them urged me to stay. When Yanni put his hand on my arm, I sat back down. Bruce told us that since his mother's death he had been openly referring to Andrew Lowenstein as his father, which had provoked a series of long and nasty arguments with Dr. Miller. In a voice devoid of emotion, Bruce said Dr. Miller had accused him of being ungrateful, enumerating all that he had done for him in the twenty years he'd considered himself Bruce's father. He emphasized how he'd taken care of Bruce's mother through all her bouts of illness and alcoholism. When Bruce accused him of stifling his mother's career as a painter, Dr. Miller got so angry he grabbed Bruce, shook him violently, and threatened to lock him out of the house. That was when Bruce called Andrew Lowenstein and asked if he could stay with him.

Bruce looked as if he was about to cry. Yanni put his arm around Bruce's shoulders and told him he could also stay with him and his brother. I needed to break the tension. "At least when you live with your father you'll be able to paint whenever you want." Bruce seemed to brighten a bit. "Have you decided when you're going to leave?"

"Tomorrow. I'll commute to work from Manhattan. Living with Seth Miller is impossible. Today, when I went back to my house to change my shirt, I found him boxing up my mother's paintings, ready to give them away. I told him I wanted all of them, as well as her jewelry. He got really angry and said that he could do what he wanted with her things, that she had given him power of attorney, that he was the husband and everything had been left to him."

"Is that true?" I asked, incredulous that a psychiatrist, who considered himself Bruce's father, could be so mean to Bruce, who was grieving his mother's life and death. "Don't children have any rights?"

"I don't know. Andrew asked me if the will had been read after the funeral." Bruce looked as if he was about to cry. "I don't even know if my mother left a will." He stood up, excused himself, and walked toward the men's room.

There was an awkward silence. All this emotion was too much for my overloaded nervous system. "I have to go home. Tell Bruce the big game is tomorrow morning, in case he wants to bring some patients to watch." Yanni walked me to the door, lightly kissed my cheek, and left. I felt bereft as I got on my scooter and headed home. Yanni was older, established in his career, and for all I knew had a wife or girlfriend, but I couldn't convince my body to stop reacting.

When I walked into my dark house I felt unaccountably lonely. Apparently Bruce felt he could talk with me, but I didn't feel the same way about him. He was too quick to judge, and even though he apologized, his first reaction was often sarcasm. To distract myself I turned on the news, then quickly turned it off. All the election talk about Eisenhower and Stevenson was interesting, and I wanted Stevenson to win because he seemed smart and thoughtful, but since I had to wait one more year to vote, and three more years before I could vote for a president, I didn't care as much as I probably should have.

I could feel depression hovering, waiting to strike. To try to forestall it, I went outside and trimmed the hedge, started my parents' car, and pinched off the dead roses while I let the motor run to make sure the battery stayed charged. There was nothing else that needed doing, and my thoughts were racing in too many directions, so I took a long walk around the neighborhood. TV screens glared behind picture windows. No one was outside. Did everyone just come home, eat, and watch television? Suddenly my loneliness felt much bigger than me. What did people do with their loneliness?

I was feeling down when I picked up the mail. Opening the letter from Jake didn't help. He'd written about his latest adventures—new foods he'd eaten, people he'd met—but no questions about how I was or what working at the hospital was like. It was satisfying to read that he looked forward to my next letter because he missed hearing from me, but writing to him was a problem. I didn't know what I felt for him anymore. My attraction to Yanni was too powerful and unsettling to ignore, even though he'd never given me reason to think he felt similarly. Maybe I'd be clearer when Jake and I were face to face. The letter I finally wrote was all about tomorrow's game and how I hoped the women would show Mr. Carson they deserved to have a team that played other hospital teams. Before I sealed it I added some questions about his travels. I didn't ask if he was seeing other women.

It was a long night.

21

The next morning I was up before six and ready long before it was time to leave for the hospital. Over coffee and an English muffin, I thought about what encouraging, calming words I might say to the women, as well as how to approach Mr. Carson. I didn't know how many guests he would be bringing or who they were, but I intended to focus on them, stressing how the hope of playing on a team had energized the women.

I arrived at the hospital about half an hour too early, so I went to the ward to see if we could get ready sooner than usual. Filled with excitement, the women gathered around me. Even those who had no interest in playing talked about the game, and many asked if they could come watch. The energy of the players seemed to be contagious. Only a few women were sitting apathetically on benches, babbling, moving repetitively, or staring out the windows. Even the attendants responded enthusiastically when I suggested that all the women who wanted to watch the game be allowed to go outside. I was so wound up Mrs. Denby took me aside and told me to take a deep breath, to remember that she was the one who chose the women who would go out. I could feel her deepening disapproval of me.

"One more thing, Miss Weinstein. Your tension is contagious. This is not good for the women. Any of the women. You must learn to control your feelings. You need to calm down."

I blushed. She was right. I wished I knew how to control my feelings—not only while working at the hospital. I wished I could ask her to tell me how to control what I felt. I wished I had no feelings. Seemed life would be a whole lot easier without them.

I planned to take just the players out to practice, with the other patients following later, but Mrs. Denby wanted everyone to leave at the same time. It felt as if it took hours to get the women organized, but my watch indicated it had only been fifteen minutes, a much shorter time than usual. They walked down the stairs and out to the field in record time. Those not playing happily found places to sit. For once the attendants didn't complain when patients spread out. Mrs. Denby had arranged the chairs for the guests in a semicircle. I counted them. Nine. Anxiety replaced my excitement. I decided the only way to deal with it was to organize hitting and fielding practice. Yelling at players to move faster or to different parts of the field calmed me down. If the players noticed my nervousness, they ignored it and focused on their practice. Bruce didn't come, which bothered me because I had counted on him to help me persuade Mr. Carson that forming a team to play other hospitals would be great publicity for Concordia. Since he knew so much about hospital news, maybe the outcome of the game didn't really matter.

By the time Mr. Carson and his guests arrived, the women had been playing hard for almost an hour and I worried they might be too tired to play their best. Liz and Rita were coaching their players with an intensity that belied their status as mental patients. When the women sitting overheard some of the guests commenting on the players' energy and focus, they shouted encouragement to the women on the field. I called the two teams over to where the guests were sitting and was about to introduce them when Liz spoke up. "Thank you for coming, Mr. Carson, and for bringing guests. We've been practicing really hard." She looked at me with a wry smile. "Miss Weinstein's a great coach. We hope you enjoy the game."

Rita, not to be outdone, spoke up as well. "We appreciate this opportunity and," she added, "your confidence in us." Then, as if to demonstrate the women's ability to organize and take responsibility, she turned to her teammates and said, "Okay, Liz, teams, let's play!" As they took to the field, I spoke a few words of welcome, trying not to stare at Mr. Carson before running off to stand near home plate. I was just there for moral support since the women refused to let me play any active part. Among themselves they had designated patients to be the umpire behind home plate and the referees in case of arguments. All I could do was watch and wait and hope.

Maggie told me the women were so determined to succeed, they had decided ahead of time how they would settle disputes. Barbara was chosen as final arbitrator. Everyone had agreed that if problems arose that a referee couldn't deal with, she would decide what to do and they would all accept her verdict with no question and, to them, most importantly, with good humor.

It was hot. There was no shade. Mrs. Denby had arranged for drinks for Mr. Carson and his guests, but not for the women watching. I asked her where I could get water for the women. She thanked me for thinking about them and told two of the attendants to bring water and cups. I worried that some might have a reaction to the sun since I had been told a few were taking Thorazine, but so far everyone looked okay. The game was exciting. Perhaps it was the energy of the players or their determination to prove they could play well, without tantrums or outbursts, or their realization we were only playing five innings and had less time to prove their ability, but they played with fierce concentration.

At the beginning of the fifth inning, Rita's team was batting; the score was 2-2, with two outs and women on first and second bases. Linda, the woman up at bat, had hit a home run in the first inning, so the tension was pretty high. I could see Mr. Carson and some of the guests watching as Liz signaled to the pitcher to do something; neither of the captains had talked with me about their private strategies. The guests seemed as intrigued as I was. The pitcher nodded, turned to the catcher, nodded again, then looked at Liz before throwing the pitch. The batter swung and missed the first two times. The third time she hit a line ball that the first baseman caught. She tapped first base and threw the ball to the third baseman to make sure the woman on second base didn't try to make it home.

Liz's team rushed off the field and gathered in a huddle. We could see heads nodding, then the first batter, a wild card, stepped up to the plate. Sometimes Carrie hit the ball so hard no one wanted to catch it, other times she missed easy pitches. Not this time. She swung at the first pitch, hit the ball out of the ball field, and easily ran around the bases for a home run. The game was over. Liz's team was euphoric.

The women watching jumped up and down with excitement. I was feeling terrific, and then, in an instant, everything changed. As Rita was running toward Liz to congratulate her, as they had practiced, she slumped to the ground. The ballplayers rushed over, circling Rita, protecting her from the view of Mr. Carson and his guests. When I got to her she was foaming at the mouth and the women looked scared; no one knew what to do. I remembered seeing photos of people having epileptic seizures from health class and knew I needed to put something into her mouth to keep her from hurting her tongue. All I could think to use was the bandana I had wrapped around my head that was wet with perspiration. Afraid to do nothing, I rolled it up and stuck it between her lips. When an attendant came with a tongue depressor and took charge, I was relieved. The seizure didn't last long, but it took Rita a few minutes to recognize where she was. As we helped her stand up, I noticed Mr. Carson and his guests had gone. Had they seen what happened? Would it affect his decision?

Rita, supported by two attendants, was crying as she and the women, subdued rather than joyful, walked quietly back to the ward. Liz asked me what I thought would happen. "We played such a good game," she said. I agreed. "Rita can't help having seizures. She didn't do anything wrong." *No, and neither did Carol.* Although it was time for lunch, the attendants half-heartedly gathered the women, not bothering to remind them to wash up. I wasn't surprised the ballplayers were upset, but seeing so many of the women on the ward move so listlessly made me realize that having a team had an even greater importance and impact than I envisioned. All eyes were on me as I left the ward. There was no point in waiting; I walked to Mr. Carson's office, prepared to do whatever I could to get his permission.

Miss Hempner greeted me with a big smile. "Congratulations! I hear your patients put on a great show." I felt a stirring of hope as I told her how much playing on the team meant to the whole ward. She didn't mention a patient having a seizure. Maybe Mr. Carson hadn't seen it. Or, if he had, maybe he was impressed by how caringly the patients responded. I was driving myself crazy, so I asked if I could talk with Mr. Carson. "I'm sorry, he's at the luncheon with his guests. He didn't say when he'd be back." Too disappointed and frustrated to move, I asked if he'd said anything to her about the team playing other hospital teams. "Officially? No."

My heart started beating fast. "And unofficially?"

"The guests were so impressed by the enthusiasm and energy of your patients, I think they convinced Mr. Carson to allow the women to play. But you better not say anything to the women until he tells you himself." I knew she was right, so I thanked her and left. It was almost time to visit my Zombies.

I felt they were waiting for me even though I knew the staff would say this was impossible. I was sure that a few of them looked at the ball when I threw it. And then, one of them smiled. A real smile. I smiled back at her and threw the ball to her feet. Although she didn't pick it up, she giggled. This time I knew I wasn't imagining anything. It was only a tiny change, nothing to tell the attendants, but I was too excited to let this moment pass unnoticed, so I told the women how happy I was to be playing with them. They didn't respond, but I felt they were more present; their eyes didn't look so glazed over. I stayed longer than usual, hoping one of them would pick up the ball. It didn't happen, but I wasn't discouraged. Something was definitely shifting.

In them.

In me.

Before I took this job, what people thought about me mattered more than what I thought or felt about myself. I paid attention to the rules. If my boss had said I was a fool to work with non-responsive people I would have stopped, or not started. I would never have voluntarily worked with patients from building 6 without formal authorization. I certainly would not have questioned Dr. Glassman about the children's need to play outside. Perhaps it was the absence of written rules and the prevalence of unwritten rules (many of which I continued to trip over) that made my previous way of being untenable. I wanted to think I was more aware of what it was like to have no power. I had counted on Bruce to keep me from being fired. Now, given his estrangement from Dr. Miller, I no longer had that comfort. I wasn't sure when or how it had happened, but the welfare of my patients had become more important to me than keeping my job, even though I didn't relish being fired. When I saw the women's excitement, how hard they worked to put on a good show for Mr. Carson, and how they protected Rita from prying eyes, and when I heard Barbara thank me for inquiring about Carol's welfare, I knew that the little I had done mattered to them. I could see changes in my patients as well. Liz's edges weren't as sharp. Maggie interacted more. And others, whose names I had yet to remember, thanked me for taking them on ward-clearing walks and telling stories in a way that was not condescending. I didn't fool myself. The changes were small and might be temporary, but by paying close attention to their responses I was learning how I could help them, given their status and my limitations. It was as if I were looking at the world with new eyes.

I walked to the weekly supervisory meeting, still thinking about the changes in my patients and me. When I saw Mrs. Langstrom standing at the door, I waved. The apprehension I usually felt about attending the meetings had been replaced by curiosity. The past few sessions she had asked us to talk about our experiences, but I had remained silent, mindful that I was working with patients from building 6 without being authorized to do so. I wasn't sure what to say about being asked to tell stories to the children, much less about advocating for them to be allowed to play outside. I wasn't ready to talk about what might be happening with the Zombies, and I was definitely afraid to mention anything about starting a women's softball team.

Mrs. Langstrom greeted me warmly. I greeted her warily, mumbling something about getting a cup of coffee before we started. Most of the therapists were waiting in line, talking about their lives, ignoring me. Just as I was about to pour myself a cup, a tall blonde with startling green eyes approached and said, "I hear you're engaged to Bruce Miller. How'd you pull that off?"

"I'm not. It was just a rumor." She immediately lost interest and left to sit with the other therapists. They were older and more experienced than I was but we had our work in common, so I wondered why they rebuffed all of my attempts to talk with them. The coffee was awful and smelled burnt. I threw it down the sink, although I wanted to throw it in the blonde's face, and was about to sit down in the back of the room when I felt a hand on my shoulder.

"Hey Rennie, how's it going?" Bruce looked different. Older. More assured. Before I could respond, several of the other summer therapists greeted him. The tall blonde sidled up, put her arms around him, and whispered something in his ear that made him blush. Annoyed by her interruption, I found a seat far away from them. The room was stifling. No one had bothered to turn on the fans. For once I was glad when Mrs. Langstrom began the meeting. I tuned out her announcements, thinking about the blonde's ease in approaching Bruce and was lost in thought so I didn't hear the announcement until the woman sitting a seat away from me leaned over and asked why I was doing it. *Doing what?* I looked up to see Mrs. Langstrom and the other therapists staring at me.

"We're waiting, Miss Weinstein." I had no idea what she was waiting for. One of the male summer therapists inadvertently came to my aid when he asked why women always had to push their way into men's activities.

I didn't know what he was talking about but I had to respond, so I asked, "Why shouldn't women have the same rights as men?"

His comeback was quick and whiny. "Carson won't spring for a separate bus. They'll have to share the seats. It'll be crowded and uncomfortable. The men aren't going to like it."

Carson? A separate bus? He must have given his approval. Of all the times to space out! Mrs. Langstrom's voice cut through my fog. "Miss Weinstein, will you please tell us why you decided, when no one else found it necessary to do so, that your patients needed to form a softball team? One that plays other hospitals' women's teams—if there are any?" *There must be some.* I looked around at the bored faces of the summer therapists and the amused smile on Bruce's face. They didn't care why or what I did, so I briefly told them about the women's enthusiasm and how much they wanted to play games away from the hospital. I sat down, hoping she'd go on to something else. "Miss Weinstein, you are only here for the summer. Why on earth would you start something you can't finish?" I had no answer. Or, for that matter, any idea of what would happen to the Zombies or the children when I left. Did that mean I shouldn't try? What was the point of being a therapist if I wasn't supposed to help my patients? And why hadn't someone started a women's team?

Trying to control my anger, I retorted, "I think it's only fair that if the men have a team, the women have one too." I saw one therapist roll his eyes. Bruce shook his head disapprovingly. "The women are really excited about playing," I added defensively.

"Excitement is not the measure of what is appropriate for our patients," retorted Mrs. Langstrom. "In fact, it could be extremely detrimental to their mental health and welfare, something the hospital is charged with protecting." Shaking her head, she changed the subject, reiterating what she'd already told us about the effect of sun on patients taking Thorazine. Since she didn't tell us how to know which of our patients might be taking it, how were we supposed to protect our patients? The hospital certainly contained crazy people, but in my opinion a good number of them weren't patients.

I left as soon as I could, but Bruce caught up with me. "I told you when we first met, don't do more than you have to. No one likes to be shown up."

I glared at him. "I didn't start the team to show anyone up. You should see how energized the women are. Doesn't that matter?"

He shrugged. "Let's go to Yanni's for coffee."

"No!"

"Why not? You like seeing Yanni."

"You're always talking about what friends do and don't do. Well, if you really were my friend you wouldn't shrug off what matters to me."

"Rennie, in case you've forgotten, we're paid to give patients exercise. You act as if it were some kind of mission. It isn't, it's just a job."

Bruce's words stung. That might have been true for me before I started working at the hospital but it certainly wasn't true now. As much as I wanted to see Yanni, I was too angry to go with Bruce. Before he could ask for a ride, I strode away. What should have felt like a celebration had turned into a trial. At least the women would be happy. I just hoped we would have enough time to practice before the first away-game.

22

Riding home in heavy traffic, I saw, far ahead, what looked like a thick brown line across my lane. There was too much traffic to shift into the left lane. By the time I got to the line, which turned out to be a downed telephone pole, there was nothing to do but jam on the brakes and hope I could stop in time. I didn't. The scooter hit the pole, stalled, and fell over—on top of me. The vehicle behind me screeched to a stop. Then, all the traffic stopped. People rushed over to where I lay. As I cautiously tried to move my arms and legs, making sure nothing was broken, I heard a voice yell, "Hey, that's 'Scootergirl.'" I looked up, stunned to see Mike, Russ, and Will running toward me.

They didn't hesitate. Will and Mike pulled the crumpled scooter off me, moving it to the side. Russ helped me stand up and practically carried me over to a strip of grass next to the road. Then the three of them, with help from some bystanders, lifted the telephone pole off the road and put it down on the roadside. "How are you?" asked Mike.

"Don't think I broke any bones, but everything hurts."

"Traffic's pretty backed up," said Russ, looking at the long line of cars, horns blaring.

"Mike, help me put the scooter in the back," said Will. He looked at me. "Think you can walk to the truck?" I nodded, but I couldn't have managed it without Russ, who was amazingly gentle as he lifted me into the passenger seat. Will and Mike, with the help of some drivers, loaded the scooter into the truck. Will got into the driver's seat and asked for directions to my house. Mike and Russ climbed into the back with the scooter. "Who the hell expects to see a telephone pole lying across the road?" grumbled Will.

"Not me. I'm lucky you guys were behind me."

"Funny thing is, we were just joking about how we rescued your scooter, and then, there you were, lying in the road with the scooter on top of you. Rescue number two."

"I sure hope there's no number three."

Will grinned. "Call us, we'll come. We're getting pretty good at this."

By the time we got to my house, moving was incredibly painful. Mike and Will made a seat with their arms and carried me into the house. Russ asked to use the phone. "I got a cousin who repairs cars. Maybe he can fix your scooter." All I could think about was the aspirin upstairs in the bathroom medicine chest. The stairs loomed large—an insurmountable obstacle.

"Think we should take you to the emergency room?" asked Mike. "You got some cuts on your face but they don't look too bad."

"I'll be all right." I hoped this was true.

"Hey, Russ, what did your cousin say?" asked Will. "If he can't fix it, I got a buddy who works on motorcycles."

While Will and Russ were talking about getting the scooter fixed, Mike kept looking at me. "Should I make you a cup of tea? Don't know how to make coffee."

"That sounds good. Make some for all of us." I told him where the tea bags were, ridiculously pleased I could offer them cookies I'd baked the night before. I had to go to the bathroom but was too embarrassed to ask for help. At least there was one near the kitchen so I didn't have to walk upstairs. How was I going to get to work tomorrow? I knew the women were counting on me, but the pain in my body was getting worse every time I moved. The guys turned down the tea but munched on the cookies, singing my praises as a baker. Will and Russ decided to take the scooter to Will's buddy and promised to bring it back as soon as possible. Mike asked once again if I'd be all right. I had no way of knowing, but I said I'd be fine. Will asked, "Think you'll be going to work tomorrow? We could pick you up and take you to work."

One way or another I will make it to work. "I'd really appreciate that." He nodded. I thanked the three of them for all their help and watched them leave.

Mike stood in the doorway, as if reluctant to go. "C'mon, Mike," yelled Will. "I want to get the scooter to Joe before he leaves the shop." Mike took one last look, waved, and then left with Will and Russ.

I locked the door, made my way up the stairs one step at a time, and tottered to the bedroom, where I slowly and gingerly took off my clothes. When I looked in the mirror, I gasped. There was dried blood on the scrapes on my cheek and neck but my body was turning black and blue. I took four aspirin—two more than usual because I hurt everywhere and moving only made the throbbing worse. There was no position that relieved the pain. When I closed my eyes I could feel the scooter flying out from underneath me, crashing down on top of me. There was no way I could force myself to go down the stairs to make something to eat. I felt alone. Frightened. The aspirin did nothing to relieve the pain. My stomach was grumbling and I was hungry, but walking downstairs was impossible. Morning was an impossibly long way off.

When the alarm rang I was wide awake. Pain kept me up all night. Moving was even worse than it had been the night before. Where my body wasn't black and blue there were red welts. My face wasn't so bad—a little makeup would cover the worst of the bruises. If I could get my body to function well enough to go to work I might not scare my patients. Probably taking a hot shower wasn't the most sensible thing to do but it got me going. Very slowly, I managed to get dressed and eat something before I took more aspirin. When the doorbell rang, I was downstairs and ready. Sort of. It felt miraculous that I'd made it this far.

Mike didn't hesitate. "God, you look awful!"

"And a good morning to you, Mike."

"I'm sorry, I didn't mean to say that, it just popped out. Are you really up to going to work?" His concern felt comforting and disconcerting. "At least you don't have to worry about your scooter. Will took it to his buddy's place last night. Joe says it's fixable. He thinks he'll have it ready in a couple of days—good as new." *Maybe I won't have to tell Jake.* "When he saw the damage, he asked how you were. We told him you were one tough cookie." *Not as tough as I wish.*

Although I didn't ask him to, he locked the door and helped me down the steps and into the truck. Will's reaction was equally frank. "Jesus, you look like hell. You sure you want us to take you to work?"

Russ was a bit more polite. "You look terrible. I'd call in sick if I were you."

"I'll manage. Thanks for the ride."

As we rode to the hospital, Will told me in graphic detail what Joe had to fix and how he planned to do it. I voiced my main concern. "Will the scooter look as good as it did before?"

"Don't want your boyfriend to know?"

"I guess it depends on how it looks."

"Don't worry, when Joe's finished it'll look like new. Might even look better than new."

"How much is it going to cost?"

"He won't know till he's done, but don't worry, I told him to give you a good price."

"I sure am grateful to the three of you."

"Kind of fun rescuing a damsel in distress."

In spite of the pain it caused in my body, I burst out laughing. "Damsel?"

Will grinned. "Thought it sounded good."

When we arrived at the hospital Will drove me as far as he could. Mike helped me out of the truck. "You think you can walk to building 5?"

What choice do I have? "Hey, I can hobble as good as anyone." I meant it to be funny but they didn't laugh.

"We'll meet you here at five if that's okay. You mind waiting half an hour?"

"You sure it's no trouble to take me home?"

Russ answered for all of them, "Your house is on our way home; it's no problem." He turned to the other two. "We need to get going. Bossman hates it when we're late." Mike and Russ squeezed into the front with Will, who waved and drove off to the construction site.

I walked with great difficulty to building 5, using every bit of the extra time I had. On my way I thought about what I would tell the women, but when I got onto the ward they rushed toward me, Liz yelling the news. "Our first game is Saturday. We're going with the men to Fairview State Hospital. We did it!" The women erupted into cheers. Mrs. Denby was actually grinning.

So soon? That's only four days to practice! I was about to congratulate them when Liz looked at me. "Jesus! You look like you tackled a truck and lost."

"Actually, my scooter tackled a telephone pole and lost. It and I went flying. The scooter landed on me. I'm told it will be fixed good as new. Hope I can say the same about me."

Barbara kept staring at me. "You sure you're up to working? We can practice without you."

Maggie shook her head. "No we can't. We need her help to work on strategies."

"You can do that, can't you Miss Weinstein?" asked Rita.

She looked so unhappy my heart went out to her. Her epileptic attack meant she wasn't allowed to go and I knew how much she'd been looking forward to playing on the team. "You'll still practice with us, won't you?" I asked. "Maybe if you don't have another seizure they'll let you go later on." I knew there was no chance of my changing the administration's decision, but she did look a little less upset.

The way Mrs. Denby studied me I began to wonder if I was worse off than I felt. "Miss Weinstein, I know how much you want to help the women, but I think you should go home. You can barely walk. Have you seen a doctor?" She turned to the women and I sensed she was about to tell them they'd have to postpone practice, so I interrupted her as she called the women together.

"I'll be fine, Mrs. Denby. Nothing's broken and I'd much rather be here working than moping at home." *I said it to reassure her, but I realized it was true.* The women will be doing all the work." I smiled, "I'll just tell them what to do."

Liz shot back, "She's real good at that."

Not sure how Mrs. Denby would take it, Barbara quickly added, "Thanks to Miss Weinstein telling us what to do, we have a team that's going to play another hospital for the first time in the history of Concordia."

Maggie asked, "Saturday's your day off. Are you still going to come with us?"

Mrs. Denby looked at me, studying my reaction. "If you decide to work on your day off, you won't be paid. I hope you know that." Everyone looked worried.

"Of course I'll be here. Nothing could stop me."

"Except a truck?" teased Liz.

"Not even a truck if I can help it," I retorted, already feeling better than when I'd arrived. "So, the first thing we need to do is decide who will play on Saturday. Those who aren't chosen can help by playing as hard as they can against the team in practice. Each time we play we'll choose a team, so if you're not chosen today, you might be the next time."

Maggie spoke for a lot of the women. "What if we lose and there is no next time?"

Exactly my question. "What if the sun doesn't come up?" I countered, pretty sure there'd be no next time if they lost. "Let's focus on playing the best we can. You have energy and spirit and ability. That counts for a whole lot."

I decided to ask for permission. "Mrs. Denby, may I take out any woman who wants to come? Even if they just want to watch?" I figured the players could use all the support possible.

When she asked whoever wanted to come with me to raise their hands, almost every hand went up, sometimes two hands from one woman. I was amazed that even the droolers and babblers and random movers raised their hands. Mrs. Denby looked as surprised as I felt, then turned to me and shook her head. "I don't have enough staff to let all the women go with you."

That set off a wave of voices. "I want to go! Let me go!" If Mrs. Martelli were in charge, she probably would have yelled loud enough to silence the group, but that wasn't Mrs. Denby's way. Instead, she motioned for them to sit where they were, put her index finger to her mouth, and quietly said, "Ssh!" The sight of the women quietly obeying after all the noise stunned me. How did she do it? What made them react as they did?

I was so moved by the women's reactions that I almost forgot the throbbing pain in my body. "Mrs. Denby, I think the women really want to support the team. I almost said, "and I think they'll behave," but looking at Barbara, the dignity with which she sat, I said, "Please, let me take whoever wants to go. It's good they care so much."

It took some time and persuasion but eventually Mrs. Denby said, "All right. Everyone who wants to go, line up." I was shocked. Nearly all the women got up and walked toward the door. I'd cleared the ward before to take people on a walk, in spite of their initial complaints, but I'd never tried to organize an activity with the whole ward. I said a silent prayer as the attendants interspersed themselves among the women and then led them down the stairs. Not one woman complained about anything. Walking was painful, going down steps even more so, but I managed to keep moving, buoyed by the women's support for the team—their team.

Once outside, Liz and Rita took over organizing practice. I explained what we were doing to the women who wanted to watch and asked if they had any questions. They looked at me blankly, waiting to be told what to do. The attendants didn't need instructions. They settled the women on the grass and the game began. I was worried about Rita. It was hot in the sun and I could see she was upset, but there was nothing I could do short of making her sit in the shade of a nearby tree, which would probably make her feel worse.

Carrie was up at bat, her body tense, her face red—too red—when we heard a loud voice, "Atta girl, you can do it. Whack it over the fence." We all turned to look. There was Shirley, beaming with joy as she strode toward us, an attendant just behind her. "Let's show those guys that women can play just as good they can." She patted Carrie on the shoulder, then stood back, smiling with satisfaction as Carrie hit the ball so hard and high that the two women on first and second bases ran to home base with Carrie following behind them. She and Shirley hugged as the rest of the team crowded around, asking how she was. Seems they all knew her. Did they also know her story?

The attendant was smiling as she walked up to me. "Ever since Shirley heard about the women's team she's been asking if I would take her out when they were playing. She's such a big help on the ward and in the laundry, where she works when she's well enough, so I promised I would. When Mrs. Denby said you were out playing, and I told her today was the day, she practically danced her way over here." Her eyes clouded over. "Such a tragedy. When she's well she's such a kind person."

"It's so nice that you were willing to bring her here." We both looked at the intensity with which Shirley was explaining some possible plays, and though I knew it was impossible, I wished we could bring her with us. Even if she didn't play, she seemed to know just what the women needed to learn and how to help them learn it. Better than I did, for sure.

But after Shirley and the attendant left, the women's spirit wilted; they played half heartedly, their enthusiasm gone. When I asked what was wrong no one spoke, nor would they look at me. The aspirin had worn off and the pain did not encourage diplomacy. I gathered the players around me. I spoke. Scolded. Yelled. "Look, if something's wrong you have to tell me. I don't read minds. What's going on?" I waited, looking at the women I knew best, watching them avert their eyes. "Damn it, if you won't talk I'll just take you all back to the ward and you can sulk in peace. I don't feel good, but I came because I thought you needed me. Well, it's clear I was wrong. So, line up, ladies, we're leaving."

I was furious at them, and jealous that Shirley could get them going when I couldn't. No one mentioned that it was too early to go back. No one reacted to my anger. No one looked at me. They had reverted back to their docile, passive behavior, and I had no clue why. Didn't I come to work in spite of the accident? Notwithstanding my pain?

I was full of righteous anger until I looked at their averted faces, their obvious unhappiness, their sagging bodies, their palpable despair, until I couldn't stand it. "Stop!" I yelled. They froze. I thought I saw Liz moving in the tense way she had when I first met her. Barbara, the one I could usually count on to explain a puzzling situation, was crying. Maggie, anxiously reacting to a woman moving too close to her, yelled at the woman to leave her alone. Some were babbling, others moving repetitively—all signs of distress. If I returned them to the ward in such bad shape, Mrs. Denby would be upset with me, and rightly so. She might even decide the pressure was too much for them and cancel Saturday's game. Despite my frustration at their incomprehensible behavior, I muttered, "I'm sorry," a miserable excuse of an apology, but I really wasn't sorry. Still mad, but desperate to return them in a better mood, all I could think to do was to tell a story. It had helped before.

"We have a little time before we have to go back so sit down," I ordered. Startled, the women obediently allowed the attendants to help them find places on the grass.

I thought about telling them a North American Indian story about Coyote, who felt a whole lot like me. In stories Coyote is smart and stupid, brave and cowardly, kind and cruel, silly and stubborn, all of which I am at times, as well as a shapechanger, which I'm not— though it certainly would have come in handy working here. But something in me rebelled. I didn't want to tell a story about someone else. Given their sudden change in behavior, I wasn't sure they even wanted to listen to a story.

Would you like to hear a story?" The women nodded warily.

"Why do you want to tell it to us?" asked Carrie.

I was too upset to lie. "Because I said something stupid. "

"What about us?" she retorted.

"I hope you'll like it and forgive me for what I said."

Liz piped up, bitterly sarcastic, "You don't have to apologize to us. We're only patients."

"Nobody is 'only' anything." What she said made me even angrier and I spit out my words. "So, is it okay if I tell you the story?" I asked Liz but I looked at the women. They didn't say no. I took this as approval and resorted to a beginning that always put me into a storytelling mood.

"A long time ago, in a place far away," words slowly came to me, "there lived a young girl who often felt lost and lonely. She wondered if something was wrong with her. She was different from the others in her large family. Where they were noisy, she was quiet. They laughed and tussled good naturedly, but she preferred being by herself. When they teased and called her 'Solemn Susan,' she smiled and pretended she didn't feel hurt and didn't care. Yet she was, and she did.

"When her chores were finished, she walked into the forest. In spring she collected shoots of plants to add to the soup she made for dinner. In summer she picked berries for jams and pies. In fall she made piles of brush and dead trees to use for kindling and firewood. Even in winter she bundled up and walked in the snow and cold. It was only in the forest that she felt free and fully alive.

"In every season she spent hours listening to the sounds of birds, wishing she understood the meaning of their songs. She often hid behind logs and in bushes watching animals play, trying to make sense of what she heard. She longed to know the meaning of the forest creatures' chirps and growls and barks and howls and hisses.

"One day, while mending a shirt, she asked her mother, 'Don't you wish you understood the language of birds and animals?'

"'No,' said her mother, 'it's hard enough trying to understand what people say.'"

"The girl took a chance and asked her sister, 'Do you ever wonder what squirrels are saying when we pick up their acorns?'"

"Her sister laughed. 'I know what they're saying: Don't touch our food.' The girl felt hurt that no one understood her yearning.

"One spring day, when the girl was walking in the forest, she heard birds chirping louder than she'd ever heard before. With the wind becoming stronger and the temperature dropping, she sensed a storm was coming and started to leave the forest, but when the chirping grew louder she changed her mind and walked toward the increasingly frantic sounds. She was so focused on the shrill squealing she almost stepped on a tiny baby bird that had fallen out of the nest. It lay without moving, but when the girl saw it was still alive she carefully wrapped it in her shawl, climbed up the tree, and searched for the nest. The sounds of the birds grew louder and so agitated she stopped climbing and looked around. Just above her head was the nest. She scrambled up to a branch near the nest and unwrapped the baby bird, carefully placing it into the nest. For a moment there was silence. As she climbed down the girl worried she had harmed the bird while trying to rescue it. But as her feet touched the ground, she heard a different bird song. The alarm in the bird songs was gone. She decided the baby bird was alive.

"Wrapping her shawl tightly around her, the girl ran home in the rain, her heart filled with joy."

There was silence after I finished the story. Many of the women looked bewildered, but it didn't take Liz long to find her voice, "So the moral of the story is that we're animals and you're trying to understand us?"

"First of all, I hate morals. Secondly, I have a hard time just trying to understand myself, much less trying to understand all of you," I quipped, thankful to hear a bit of responsive laughter from the women. "Thirdly, if anything, I hope you liked the story."

"Did it make you feel better?" asked Barbara, ignoring my question.

"Yes."

"How?"

"I can't explain. To me it's like a kind of magic."

"Should we call you Miss Magician Weinstein?" retorted Liz.

"The thing is, if no one's willing to listen, there's no story and no magic. You're all good listeners. You're part of the magic. That makes us all magicians."

"Better not let staff hear that. They'll think you've gone crazy, and before you know it you'll be on the ward." The woman speaking so bitterly had only been on the ward for two days and, according to Mrs. Denby, was there against her will. Her words stung. In the hospital the line between sane and crazy was murky.

Liz looked at the woman. "Sometimes it takes more than magic to get out of this place. Even when you're ready to be released you never know if it'll happen." She turned to me. "Have you heard any news about Carol?"

I shook my head, not willing to spoil the moment by telling them Coop had told me Carol continued to turn her face to the wall, refusing to eat or speak. Worse yet, there was talk of force feeding. What happened to her could happen to anyone, even me.

They walked back to the ward where Mrs. Denby was waiting for us. When one woman told her I'd told them a story, she nodded approvingly. I worried that someone else would tell her what I'd said before telling the story. Much to my relief, no one did. As I was getting ready to leave, a few of the women thanked me for the story and said they hoped my bruises would heal soon. It had been a long, exhausting day and I was grateful the guys were driving me home. When Barbara asked, "You are coming back, aren't you?" I nodded, surprised by the question. "We'll do better tomorrow," she said, quietly, so Mrs. Denby couldn't hear. "Sometimes we just have off days, but we'll be ready to play on Saturday. You'll see. Tomorrow will be better."

I took a chance and asked, "What happened after Shirley left? It was like she took all the energy with her. Did I do something wrong?"

"In this place things just happen. Telling a story was a good idea. You'll see, tomorrow will be better."

I needed to believe her.

23

As Mike helped me up into the truck, I recoiled in pain when his shoulder accidentally pressed against my black-and-blue arm. Will gave me a reassuring pat on my back, then put the truck into gear and drove away from the hospital, apologizing each time he hit a bump. During the ride home I asked Will when my scooter would be ready. "Why? You tired of riding with us?"

"No, but you might be tired of taking me home."

He shrugged. "You live on the way."

So far the guys seemed okay, but maybe letting them take the scooter wasn't such a good idea. I didn't know anything about them and had no way of finding out where it was, so I lied. "Well, my boyfriend's coming back soon and he'll want his scooter. Be good to have it before he arrives."

"Don't worry, I'll call Joe tonight."

"Think you could give him my number? Or, maybe I could call him."

"You worried?"

Yes. "No, just wondering when I'll get it back and how much it will cost."

"I told you, he knows you're a friend. He'll give you a good price."

"Thanks, Will. I appreciate your help."

"So, you and your boyfriend serious?"

I have no idea. "Yes. We're planning to be married when I graduate next year. You have a girlfriend?"

"Nah. Too much trouble," he said with an invented accent that made us all laugh. At my house, Mike opened the door to help me out of the truck. I was so stiff and the pain was so much worse after sitting for only twenty minutes that I was glad to have his help. Trying to keep my tone casual, I asked Will to give me a call after he spoke to Joe. He nodded. I hoped that meant he would.

Another long, pain-filled night. In the morning, I hurt so much I could hardly force myself to get up. Engulfed in self-pity, I swallowed four aspirin and soaked in the tub until my skin puckered. I felt a little better as I dressed and went downstairs. The honking horn announced the guys' arrival.

Despite my embarrassment, I had to ask for help getting into the truck. Both Russ and Mike lifted me up. "You sure it's a good idea for you to go to work?" asked Russ.

"No, but we only have three more days of practice before the game on Saturday. There's a lot of pressure on the women. Mr. Carson, the director, thinks the only acceptable outcome of playing is winning."

"Guess he's never played any sports," retorted Will.

"Don't know what he's done, but he sure doesn't seem to care about the patients. If we don't win it's likely he won't let them play away from the hospital again."

"That's crazy."

"You're right, it is, and there's nothing I can do about it."

"Bake them cookies. That can only help."

"Thanks, Will. Good idea."

I could feel the tension before I opened the ward door. When I saw the look on Mrs. Denby's face my worrying escalated. Maybe starting a women's team was too much for the women's emotional wellbeing.

She motioned me to follow her into her office. "Miss Weinstein, we have a problem, so it's good you've come early. The women are very tense. Rita had another seizure—she hasn't had two in such a short time since she's been here. Some of the players haven't been able to sleep. You either have to find a way to calm them down or I will request that we cancel the game on Saturday and all further away games. Do you understand?" *I do, but...*I nodded. "Now go and quiet them down."

The women were ready, waiting for me. The anxious expressions on their faces made me even more nervous than I already had been. My bruised and aching body didn't help. I took a deep breath, trying to think of something I could tell them that wasn't phony. Finally I just said in a mock-authoritative voice, "Let's go, ladies. We've got three days to practice." At least Carrie laughed. I knew I had to acknowledge what they were feeling, so when we were outside I gathered them in a circle; the grass was too wet to sit on. "I know you're worried about the away game. The worst that can happen is that we lose."

"Yeah, and if we do, that's the end of it," muttered one of the players.

"Maybe that's not the worst that can happen," said Barbara. "What if we get upset and lose control?" A stream of what ifs followed, all dire.

"Look," I said. "When I first came to work here there was no team. No excitement. No enthusiasm. Nobody cared about anything."

"We cared. We just didn't show it," countered Maggie. "But, you're right, it's given us something to look forward to."

"How many of us can go? And how're you going to choose?" asked Liz, more of a challenge than a question.

In addition to my bruises, my head was aching. What had seemed like such a good, even sensible, idea now felt like a huge predicament with too many unknowns. "Mr. Carson said I could take twelve women. You and Rita, as team captains, are going to choose who goes. I think that's only fair, don't you?" I almost laughed at the look of shock on Liz's face.

Rita stared at me, equally taken aback. "You should choose. That way no one will be mad at us."

"Right," I grinned, "they'll be mad at me." Liz actually smiled. "But, it's your team. You two know the players better than I do, so let's have a good practice game and afterward, if it's all right with the rest of you," I said looking at the women, "the three of us will talk about it. But, the two of you will make the decisions." Their bewildered looks reminded me that attendants made all the decisions and patients quickly learned that the safest way to survive was to keep their heads down, expressions vacant, and feelings hidden. Now I was asking them to do something dangerous. Was I pushing them too far? What good were principles of fairness if what I asked them to do made them sick?

While I was arguing with myself I heard someone yell, "Are you guys going to talk or play? We came to watch a game." We turned around and there was Coop with a group of women from building 6. Rosa and Georgia rushed over to say hello. Some of the building 5 women knew them and greeted them with hugs, something I hadn't seen before. I noticed Barbara walking over to Coop and I prayed she had some good news to tell Barbara about Carol. When I saw Coop shake her head, I guessed the news was still bad.

Rita and Liz organized their teams and the game began. Spurred on by the enthusiastic spectators from building 6, the women played better than ever, with spirit and energy that boded well for Saturday's game.

While we were watching the women play, Coop said, "You look like you battled Goliath and lost." I told her about the scooter accident, the guys picking me up, and Will arranging for the Vespa to be fixed. "You must be living right, girl, given what's been happening."

"I know, I was lucky they were there," I said, wondering what she'd told Barbara.

"I'm not talking about your scooter." My bewildered look made her laugh. "I've been working here almost ten years and never, not once, did anyone ever say that if the men had a team so should the women, not even me. And here you are a kid, just a summer employee, and you've started a whole lot of people thinking, even talking, about changes."

"Yeah, right. Like what? Haircuts? So a patient who's scheduled to go home, and looks presentable has the right to refuse to have her hair cut and no one will challenge her or cut her hair against her will?"

Coop shook her head. "Girl, you think change happens so fast? I said they're thinking and talking, not doing."

Even though I'd seen Barbara's reaction to what Coop said, I had to ask. "What about Carol? Any change?"

"Not really."

"What does that mean?"

"I'm not a doctor."

I was about to press her for more information, but loud yelling and a huge sense of excitement interrupted our talk. We watched Linda hit a home run with two outs and two people on base. The score was 3-2; Liz's team had won. The women from building 6 cheered, jumping up and down. I saw Coop watch them, closely monitoring their behavior, and I felt apprehensive as we ran to congratulate the players.

The women were too keyed up. Mrs. Denby was right. If I couldn't find a way to help reduce their anxiety she might well cancel Saturday's game. While I was wondering what I could do, Coop took charge, talking with them, telling them how proud she was of their accomplishment, and how sure she was that they would play well on Saturday. She reminded them that this was something they could do, that they needed to breathe deeply when they felt tense, and that they should remember how important it was to help each other. The effect was immediate and stunning. They visibly relaxed and listened attentively as she talked about her desire to play softball when she was growing up, how there weren't any girls' teams, and that she wasn't allowed to play on a boys' team. Much to my surprise, she told the women that their playing on Saturday meant a lot to her and she'd help them in any way she could.

Rita asked her, "Miss Weinstein told us we should choose the women who get to play on Saturday. Do you think Mrs. Denby will let us? She doesn't know who the best players are. I know she won't let me go, even though I'm a really good hitter and catcher." The women nodded in agreement. Coop stared at me. I felt stupid. She told the attendants from both buildings to take all the women back to the ward, leaving Liz, Rita, Coop, and me to talk about who would be on the team. Just before she left, Rosa found a way to corner me and asked in a loud voice if I was taking them out in the afternoon. I nodded, amazed by her spunk. "You should be taking us to play on Saturday," she whispered. "We'd win for sure." She was probably right. She also knew there wasn't a chance in hell this could happen.

While Liz and Rita were talking about who should be on the team, Coop took me aside and asked, "When are you going to learn? There's more to this than women playing softball." I cringed. She was right. All I'd thought about was fairness and giving the women a chance to decide something for themselves, but these women were in a mental hospital, mentally ill, no matter how normal they might seem. Coop was nothing if not experienced and prudent. She spoke to Liz and Rita. "Why don't you two make a list of the women you think should go and then decide on a few alternatives to suggest to Mrs. Denby if she has concerns. I'm sure Miss Weinstein has paper and a pencil."

My heart ached for them. A few had admitted they were afraid, but they all wanted to go, if only to get away from the hospital for a few hours and to have an adventure none of them imagined was possible. Slowly and thoughtfully they talked among themselves and suggested names. Although I felt terrible for Rita, who obviously wanted so badly to play, I admired the way she supported the players despite her disappointment. After a lot of back and forth discussion,

I told them, "We have twelve names. We need three alternates." I could only hope Mrs. Denby would approve.

Deciding who would play on Saturday took so much time we had to hurry back to the ward so they wouldn't be late for lunch. I gave the list to Liz, who'd been voted captain, and agreed to come back after telling stories to the children, to be with her when she showed it to Mrs. Denby. She surprised me by telling me she was nervous—she'd never talked to me before about how she felt. I was honest and said I was nervous too, which made us both laugh, recognizing the preposterousness of grown women worrying about who was going to play in a softball game.

The children were waiting for me, sitting quietly in a circle on the floor—such a change from their previous behavior I didn't know what to make of it. I sat down and asked if they wanted to hear a story. Jeffrey shook his head. "No. We want to go out, but not in the courtyard. It's too small. We want to go where we can run."

"If I could I'd take you, but all I'm allowed to do is tell you stories. Would you like to hear one?" They nodded, seemingly resigned. Unlike the women, they didn't interrupt or comment as I began telling them a Cherokee story about the coming of light.

Just then the door opened and a tall, heavy-set man with cameras around his neck, holding a tripod, strode in, almost pushing aside the attendant who seemed to be trying to stop him. The children immediately reacted, screaming, "Go away! Go away!" David hid behind me, shaking. I couldn't bear it. Even though I didn't know who he was or why he was there, I asked the man to please leave.

He didn't need to be asked. Turning toward the door, he muttered to the attendant, "These aren't children, they're animals."

"No they're not," I said under my breath, but hoping the kids would hear me. I took David's hand and we sat down, leaning against a wall. The others quieted down and joined us. I didn't feel like finishing the story and they didn't ask to hear the rest of it. The silence felt healing.

24

I left the children's unit feeling troubled. I believed them when they said they wouldn't run away, but what if I took them out and they did? I'd been asked to tell stories, nothing more. How could I go against Dr. Glassman? As I sat on the grass, leaning against my tree, ready to eat my lunch, I was relieved that the bruises weren't as painful as they'd been. At least I'd be able to travel on the bus without too much discomfort. So much was riding on how well the women did on Saturday. Not only the way they played, but also how they behaved—on the bus, on the field, with the women from the other hospital. It would be a long day and I didn't know if an attendant would be coming with us. What if there were behavioral problems or some kind of incident? Coop was right about me. I didn't think about ramifications when I suggested starting a team. All I'd thought about was that women should have the same rights as men. The men were mentally ill—why wasn't it too much for them? There was so much I didn't know about working with mentally ill women, but I was also discovering how little I knew about my motivation. More and more I was feeling I had to prove that I was a competent person, that I could do this job and do it well. Where was the pressure coming from?

I didn't hear Bruce approach, so when he spoke I was annoyed that my train of thought had been interrupted. "What happened to you? You're a mess! It couldn't have been a fight with a patient, I'd have heard about it."

None of your business. "You don't look so good yourself. Have you moved yet?"

"No. How's the team coming along?"

"Fine."

"Think you'll win on Saturday?"

"How should I know?"

"The men always win." He laughed wryly. "Carson never asks how it's possible they never lose."

"Not once? Not ever?"

"Nope. But if you saw the attendants who go with them, you'd understand."

"Well, I'm sure the women will play their best. That's all anyone can ask of them."

"In this place it's not about playing, it's about winning. I thought you'd have figured that out by now."

"So, I'm supposed to say nothing, do nothing, think nothing? Is that why you're here? Any more 'good' advice you'd like to give me?"

"I came to warn you. There's talk about you violating the rules of your contract."

My pent up anger exploded. "Contract? I don't believe I signed a paper that said I was forbidden to care about patients or give women the same opportunities as men, so exactly what contract am I 'violating?'"

"I told you when you first came here, do what's required, nothing more. People don't like to be shown up."

"Who am I showing up? I started a softball team, not a revolution."

Bruce sighed. "I'm trying to help you. I'm your friend, remember?"

"What's to remember?" I practically creaked as I stood up.

"Rennie, you were hired to work with patients in building 5—to take out women, give them exercise, and return them to the ward. You weren't hired to start a women's softball team or work with building 6 patients or with patients on ward 2. Everyone knows they're unresponsive except you. And now you're telling stories to kids in the children's unit. You need to stop drawing attention to yourself." I glared at him. "Look, it's been a while since we've seen each other. Let's go have coffee at Yanni's after work. He's been asking where you've been."

He has? For a moment I was tempted. "I can't. I'm busy." I looked at my watch. "I have to leave. Mrs. Denby and I need to go over the list of players for Saturday's game. The patients are really excited about being the first women to have a team."

"Let's just hope nothing untoward happens."

"Untoward? What's that supposed to mean?"

"These women are mentally ill and—"

I interrupted, in no mood to listen to a lecture. "I am fully aware of this, thank you very much." He was so critical of what I'd been doing that I didn't dare tell him how worried I was about the women's rising tension levels. Since there was no way to know ahead of time, I had to trust that Mrs. Denby knew the women and, whether I liked her choices or not, would only send those she thought could handle the stress of traveling and playing.

As I walked back to building 5, Bruce tagged along. "Rennie, I miss you. Let's have dinner at Yanni's Saturday night. Or we could go hear the Modern Jazz Quartet. They're really great."

"Saturday's the game, remember? I don't know when we'll be back." I was in no mood to tell him it was also my birthday. I would no longer be a teenager; I had looked forward to turning twenty. But now, without my family and with the game on Saturday, the birthday didn't matter.

"I can easily find out. I'll meet you at the bus."

"I might need to spend time with the women."

"It's your day off. You can leave whenever you want. You know you're working without pay, don't you?" *I volunteered to go with them.*

He misinterpreted my look of incredulity. "Bruce, don't you care about anyone? Or anything? When you needed help, you got help. Don't the women deserve help, or is caring reserved for the son of the Chief Psychiatrist?"

He turned away, embarrassed, mumbling words I couldn't hear. I walked away. "Rennie, wait." I wasn't moving very quickly. He easily caught up with me. "I'm sorry. I don't know why it happens, but it's like I turn into my stepfather when I'm with you. I can't believe the hateful things I say. I think it's great you care so much about your patients. I hope you win on Saturday so Carson will let the women keep playing other teams, but even if you don't, I'm sure they're grateful that you've given them a chance to do something no other women patients have had."

I stared at him. *Who are you?* "I'm not doing it for their gratitude. I'm doing it because it's only fair that the women have the same opportunities as the men."

"Please, have dinner with me Saturday night. I'll wait for you at Yanni's if you prefer. We can go hear music next week." *What if my scooter isn't ready?* "Oh, I forgot, I have something for you."

"Not a ring, I hope."

He managed a sardonic laugh and shook his head.

I didn't like feeling pushed by him and I didn't like what he said, even if he did apologize. "I'll have dinner with you Monday night, if I still have a job."

"You will, I'll see to that."

I muttered an ungraceful thanks and walked away, too worried about the women's stress to worry about being fired.

I always looked forward to being with the women in ward 2. My time with them was peaceful and interesting. I could concentrate on the women's reactions, or lack thereof, without stress. I even stopped calling them Zombies. But I'd promised Liz and Rita we'd talk about team choices, but Mrs. Denby had said to come to her office after lunch, so that took precedence over any of my choices. I stopped by the office on ward 2 to tell the attendant I wouldn't be coming today. When she saw me, she smiled and beckoned me to follow her. I stood at the entrance to the ward, too stunned to move. "Look! They're waiting for you." The women, most of them, were standing patiently in a circle in the middle of the room.

I was right. They were changing. I was so excited I wanted to rush out, pick up the balls, and play with them. They wouldn't understand if I explained why I couldn't. Mrs. Denby was waiting. My heart was with the ward 2 women. My head told me I needed to go. I felt so sick at the thought of disappointing them I rushed to find Mrs. Denby, hoping to explain the situation and come back in half an hour, but I had no chance. Mrs. Denby, Liz, and Rita were in her office. The players who hoped to go surrounded me, begging me to put their names on the list. Before I could speak, Mrs. Denby told me to come in, sit down, and listen. I sat. She explained that her criteria for choosing the women—those who were most likely to deal well with the stress and excitement—had nothing to do with who were the best players. Neither Liz nor Rita voiced any disagreement. I was afraid to say anything, aware that if I chose a woman who had an "episode," I'd rightfully be blamed and the woman might suffer serious consequences. I also realized that if I didn't say anything, they would blame me if we lost because we didn't have the best players.

Liz and Rita stared at me. Fear kept me silent. After an awkward silence, Mrs. Denby said, "Miss Weinstein, you will explain the criteria to the players and read out the names of those going. I understand some will be disappointed, but I am ultimately accountable for the health and welfare of my patients." She gave me a stern, all-too-familiar, look. "I will send one attendant with you, but you will be responsible for the patients' behavior, safety, and well-being. Winning is not worth the sacrifice of anyone's mental health."

Liz looked away and shook her head. I decided I needed to tie my already tied shoelace. Rita spoke up. "Mrs. Denby, I know I'm not able to go, even though I think I'd be fine, but Carrie isn't on the list and she's the best player we have. She hits and pitches and runs better than almost anyone. Please, can't you put her on the list?"

"And who should I take off? Maggie?"

Was Mrs. Denby being mean? She knew how close Liz and Maggie were. I was amazed at Rita's courage. "No, Maggie is the best catcher we have. In my opinion, if you have to take someone off, I think it should be Jane or Sheila—they're really good in the outfield but they don't hit as well as Carrie."

Mrs. Denby looked long and hard at Rita, but Rita didn't flinch. I felt so moved by Rita's bravery I asked, "Is it possible for Carrie to go?"

"Liz, Rita, please wait outside while I discuss the matter with Miss Weinstein." They had no choice. I felt both of them staring at me as they left. I could see them through the glass window, standing outside the door. "Three months ago Carrie was on suicide watch. There is a possibility she could run away or do something to hurt herself. I can't take the chance."

I saw Coop shaking her head, reminding me to keep my mouth shut. I couldn't. "Of course, you know the patients better than I do, but last week you remarked how happy Carrie looked every time she came back from practice. And, Rita's right, she is one of the best players on the team."

"Are you personally willing to take responsibility for her, Miss Weinstein?" *I could almost see Coop's face warning me, urging me to be sensible, to say no.* "Yes," I said, knowing how much her presence meant to the team, hoping her playing would keep her from going on a toot, or worse.

There was a faint smile on Mrs. Denby's face as she shook her head. "Miss Weinstein, what makes you so sure Carrie won't have an episode?"

I couldn't look at Mrs. Denby. "I don't know for sure." I knew the sensible thing to do was to agree that Carrie shouldn't go, but I couldn't. "If I've learned one thing working here it's that I can't be certain of anyone or anything, but I think it would be good for Carrie to go. She's worked hard. She encourages the others. Even to me she seems more, well, I don't know the word. She looks happier and has more energy than she did when I first came. I know she'll be very disappointed if she isn't chosen."

"Disappointment isn't the end of the world, Miss Weinstein."

No, but it can feel like it, especially in a place like this. I sat quietly while Mrs. Denby looked at the list again. So many thoughts were whirling around in my head, it was a wonder she couldn't hear them. "So, who do you think I should take off the list—Jane or Sheila?" I didn't want to make that decision and asked if we could take them both. She reminded me we could only take twelve—I needed to choose. Jane's name came first to mind, so I said, "Jane," feeling like an executioner. She nodded, erased Jane's name, and looked intently at me. "You are responsible for taking twelve patients off hospital grounds. You will be responsible for bringing back twelve patients in the same shape they were when you took them off the ward. It is not a responsibility to be taken lightly." *I don't need to be reminded of that. It already weighs so heavily on me it's a wonder I can still breathe.* She handed me a list with the schedule, said she would talk to the players, and that I was to be at the main gate at ten. The bus ride would take about an hour, and lunch would be provided by the host hospital. The game would start around 12:30. Did I have any questions? I shook my head. All I wanted was for us to have won the game, the patients safely ensconced in their ward, and the weight of worry lifted from me and gone.

There were cries of pleasure and disappointment as I read off the names. Both Liz and Maggie grinned when I read Carrie's name. I told the players that Liz and Rita would decide who would play what position and who would be subs. They looked surprised. I guessed they thought I would do this, but I was trying to give them some sense of empowerment. I left the ward feeling unaccountably depressed.

Even though it was too late, I walked to ward 2 and discovered, much to my astonishment, the women were still standing in a circle. "I tried to get them to sit down but they wouldn't leave," explained the head attendant. I told her why I was so late. "They wouldn't have understood even if you had explained the change in schedule."

I thought I detected a slight smile as I rolled the ball to one of the women, but I didn't react, especially since she didn't return it. The next woman put her foot out as the ball came to her, then watched it roll away. As before, most showed no reaction, but I was so tuned into the women, and so intent on the small but, to my mind, not insignificant changes, I lost track of time. Worst of all, I forgot about taking out Coop's patients.

On my way to the front gate, I stopped at building 6 and rang the bell, hoping I could explain, but no one answered. This wasn't unusual, but I felt terrible about letting down the women who I knew looked forward to playing softball. I wished I had my scooter so I could just go home and feel as grumpy as I wanted without having to interact with anyone. When I saw Will waiting, I asked where Mike and Russ were and felt a clutch in my stomach when he said they'd gone home in a friend's car. "I thought we could go out for dinner after we pick up your scooter. You know, celebrate its being fixed. I saw it and it looks brand new. Joe did a great job."

I didn't feel like celebrating. I didn't feel like there was anything to celebrate, but Will had gone out of his way to help me with the scooter and given me rides, so I thought I had to agree. Still, I was annoyed with myself for not saying no. As we drove I could tell he had something on his mind, but I was too preoccupied to pay much attention to him, grateful for the silence even if it didn't feel comfortable. "How are you and your boyfriend doing? Must be hard to have a long distance relationship."

The last thing I want to talk about is Jake. "We're used to it. You have a girlfriend?"

"Me? No. No time. I do construction in the summer. My uncle's a crew boss and he gets me and Mike and Russ the jobs. I'm in med school—going into my second year. Seems like all I have time to do is study and sleep. Working construction feels like a vacation." I asked what kind of doctor he wanted to be. As he pulled into the garage he said we could talk over dinner.

I was so happy to see the scooter I practically hugged it after paying for the repairs. Will offered to put it in the back of his truck, but when I told him I could drive home, he said he'd pick me up at six. I had already said I would go, and it was nice of him to offer, but I was too upset to eat. I forced myself to ask for a rain check. When he asked why, I took a chance and told him about having to choose the players to play on Saturday, the sense I had that a few of the women in ward 2 were beginning to react despite being told it wasn't possible, forgetting about Coop's patients, and my worries about the game. It came out in a torrent, with unexpected anguish. He listened without interrupting. When it had all poured out of me, I felt embarrassed that I'd said so much, especially to a guy I hardly knew, but saying no, even to a nice invitation, felt surprisingly good. It even gave me the courage to flirt a little. "After all you've done, and listened to, I think I should take you out to dinner."

He grinned. "I accept. Time and place of your choosing," then added, "I hope we can celebrate your team not only winning, but having many more chances to play."

"Thanks, Will. Thanks a lot." I remembered how preoccupied he looked when we met and asked him about it. He shrugged, said he didn't like the way his boss yelled at people, but there was nothing he could do and there was no sense talking about it. We stood looking at each other for a second, then with a wave, we both took off. As I was driving home I wondered why it was so hard for me to say no. Why did I always feel guilty if I didn't do what someone wanted me to do?

25

I couldn't eat. I couldn't sleep. To distract myself I looked through sports textbooks to find advice that might help with tomorrow's practice. Instead, I woke up on the couch, around two in the morning, still dressed, a book lying on my chest. It hadn't offered any good ideas, but at least I knew what to do the next time I had trouble sleeping.

Despite all the strategies I devised for the women, nothing I offered energized the women like Shirley's suggestions. She knew them from the inside, whereas I had to rely on what I'd learned in coaching class and playing softball as a kid. Even though I knew it was an impossible dream, I wished I could take her with us when we played. With her enthusiasm and ability to talk to the women, I was sure we could win. Thinking about my lack of experience was depressing. Trying to calm my nerves by breathing deeply made me even more anxious, so I got up and baked chocolate chip cookies, packed them in a container, and put them in the freezer, ready to take with me on Saturday. At least the women would know I cared about them, if they didn't know it already.

The next three days passed in a whirl. My body hurt less each day, but my anxieties about the women's tension increased, as did my worries about the children. I had to work to calm myself before I entered their room because their tension antennas worked overtime. I talked once again with Dr. Glassman but he was adamant—the children could not be trusted to obey the attendants if they left the courtyard. Nothing I said made any difference. Maybe I was learning to be more careful; I wasn't willing to go against his orders, even though the children accused me of not trusting or caring about them.

Mrs. Denby talked with the women about the importance of staying calm and composed no matter what and told them that no game was worth sacrificing their health, but my tension added to theirs and I knew they felt it. I even began each practice with deep breathing, something recommended in the sports textbooks, though I couldn't see that it made any difference in their anxiety. Certainly didn't relax me. Still, it was something to try and it did help focus the women. Before practice on Friday, Rita asked what made me think to start a women's softball team when no one else had. At first I shrugged the question off, but when I saw that she really wanted to know, I said it wasn't a story with a happy ending. "Tell us anyway, " she retorted. "One thing we know about is unhappy endings."

"Don't get personal," warned Mr. Carson. I ignored his voice. "I was at a camp, only for three weeks, but they had a softball team and I noticed there were no girls on it. When I thought no one was looking, I posted a note on the bulletin board: This camp is a chauvinistic camp because there are no girls on the softball team.

Unbeknownst to me, a counselor saw me, read the note, and announced at dinner that evening, 'Rennie thinks it's chauvinistic to have only boys on the softball team so I'm inviting her to join us.'"

The women gasped. Barbara looked at me with such admiration, I had to turn away. Just remembering what happened filled me with shame. I wished I'd I fought discrimination and won.

"Did you join the team?" asked Liz.

"I didn't have much choice. Just before practice, the athletic director found me and brought me to the playing field. The boys stared at me. One of them finally asked what position I played. Position? The only games I'd ever played were pickup games and we played whatever position needed to be filled. The captain asked if I could pitch. I said yes. I'd pitched a lot of games because that was the one position almost no one wanted to play. So, we chose up sides and my team took to the field with me as the pitcher."

"Uh-oh," muttered Barbara. "I can just imagine what happened next."

"Well, if you imagine that I was so tense I could barely hold the ball, much less throw it, you'd be right. The catcher threw me some warm-up balls and although I managed to catch them, I could hear the snide comments and jeers and knew none of the boys wanted me to play with them. At that moment I was more than sorry I'd written the stupid note. When the game began, I pitched; the batter swung and hit a home run. Even though I struck out the next two boys and the first baseman caught the third out, the hostility was more than I could bear.

"What did you do?" asked Carrie.

Still feeling the old shame, I muttered, "I quit. It was either that or throw up in front of everyone. I ran from the field, ran down to a patch of woods and hid for hours, wishing I'd never been born."

"And that made you want to start a women's team?" asked Rita, astonished.

I nodded. "I was never a great ball player but I was pretty good, and maybe, if the boys had been more accepting, I might have been able to play with them. I wasn't as good as the best but I was certainly better than most of them. I just couldn't stand their resentment and nasty remarks."

"Sounds awful," commiserated Barbara. Then, she grinned. "But, if it gave you the idea to help us be a team, I'm glad it happened."

Surprisingly, her words took some of the sting out of the memory. "Happy to be of service," I grinned back. "Now, let's play ball."

The morning of the game, I was so wrought up, my birthday didn't matter. I was glad not to be a teenager, but being twenty didn't feel any different. The only present I wanted was for the women to win the game, and I wanted that too much. Unable to make myself eat, I put a bag of sliced apples, almonds, and dried fruit in my purse and drove to the hospital, delighted to be driving my scooter despite momentary bouts of fear when I saw potential hazards. I arrived early and walked to building 5, hoping my unexpected presence would not be unwelcome. As I trudged up the stairs I heard an unusual amount of noise coming from the players' ward. As soon as one of the patients saw me, she yelled, "She's here! She's here!" Patients weren't supposed to yell, and I cringed, knowing Mrs. Denby would not be pleased by my arrival; she had specifically told me where and when to meet the players at the administration building.

When I walked into the ward I understood why Mr. Carson, Mrs. Denby, Coop, even Bruce, had warned me about the dangers of creating a team. I didn't know what the men were like before leaving the hospital on game day, but the women players' behavior verged on hysteria. Mrs. Denby and the attendants—there seemed to be more than usual—were like firemen rushing around to put out brush fires. One woman complained her sneakers were too tight, another couldn't find her socks. Rita was crying. Liz, normally outspoken, was huddled in a corner. Carrie was marching up and down the ward, waving her arms as if acknowledging a crowd of admirers. Mrs. Denby looked at me as if to say, "I warned you."

I was ready to admit I'd made a mistake, or worse, that she was right and I was wrong, when Barbara came up to me and said, "Miss Weinstein, could you tell us a story?" I looked at her as if she were crazy, then of course I realized she was crazy, according to someone, and that maybe I was crazy as well for causing so much trouble. I laughed, probably out of nervousness, and couldn't stop. The women closest to me started laughing and pretty soon almost everyone, including Mrs. Denby and the attendants, was laughing. Just as soon as some would stop, others would start again. It took a few minutes, with women rushing to the bathroom, before all the laughter stopped.

Afterward, everything changed. Some came up to me to wish us luck. Women helped each other dress. The hospital had no pants for the women to wear, so I buttoned dresses, zipped up skirts, tied shoelaces, braided and brushed hair—even tied a bow in a woman's hair. In the midst of the preparation, Mrs. Denby asked for everyone's attention. The women stopped what they were doing and stared at Rita, standing next to Mrs. Denby, practically leaning on her. With tears running down her face that she didn't bother to wipe away, Rita managed to say, "You know how much I wish I was going with you. I want you to know I'll be with you in spirit. All of us here will be cheering for you. If you're feeling scared or nervous, just remember that we're thinking of you, wishing you the chance to play well and win."

And then there was no more time. Two attendants walked with us to the administration building parking lot where the bus was parked. Mr. Carson was standing near it checking in the men. As we approached he frowned. Had he changed his mind? I tried to hide my apprehension, waiting to hear what he had to say. He spoke curtly. "There are seats for the women at the back of the bus. No woman may sit next to a man and there will be no fornication or talking between the women and the men on the bus." *Fornication?* I hoped he didn't see me rolling my eyes. "I expect the women to behave properly." *And what about the men? They can behave improperly?*

What I said would have pleased Coop. "Mr. Carson, the women appreciate the opportunity you're giving them and we hope to do Concordia proud."

He harumphed, "Good luck," as the women, their attendant, and I boarded the bus. When we were all seated, he got on, wished us well, warned the women once again about behaving properly, which infuriated me, then left. The bus driver closed the door. Some of the men were sitting by themselves, which meant there wasn't enough room for the women to sit two in a seat. I asked one of the male attendants if the men could double up so the women wouldn't have to sit three in a seat. He told me the men had a right to sit where they wanted. I was so mad I didn't think, just went up to a couple of men and told them in my most authoritative voice to please double up. Enough men moved so that the women didn't have to triple up, but it left me sitting next to a male attendant who sprawled over the seat, leaving little room for me. Two women noticed and invited me to sit with them. I took it as a good omen. Despite the discomfort, the closeness felt reassuring.

The men, used to the ride, dozed or talked among themselves, but the women commented excitedly on everything they saw, from what was happening on city streets to the increasingly tree-and-meadow-filled countryside. After the first annoyed looks and complaints from the men, the women kept their voices low, still managing to convey the intensity of their excitement at seeing life outside the hospital. When the bus drove into the grounds of Fairview an hour later, the men gathered their things and prepared to leave. The women remained seated, paralyzed by fear. I stood up and smiled, hoping I looked composed, aware that I was probably as anxious as they were, or more so. The male attendant who had spread himself over most of the seat yelled, "You ladies gonna stay on this bus all day? Move!" Accustomed to responding quickly to an authoritative voice, they quickly filed out of the bus, heads down, eyes focused on their feet. Even the female attendant looked cowed. Not the way I wanted this outing to start.

I glanced at his nametag. "Mr. Dobson, you are not in charge of my patients." I was about to ask him to use a kinder tone of voice, that the women were scared, but I could tell from the women's rigidity they wanted no trouble. If he wanted them to move, they would move. Ignoring my comment, he joined the other two male attendants and led the group to the administration building where the patients were to check in. Rose bushes and a colorful variety of flowers, attractively planted, scented the air. The patients tending the flower gardens made me think of Bruce trying to persuade Mr. Carson to allow patients to grow flowers and vegetables with no success. I decided to tell him about the Fairview program. Maybe it would help him convince Mr. Carson that gardens made the hospital grounds more appealing to visitors. He didn't seem to care much about what it might do for patients' morale or wellbeing.

Miss Ryback, an attractive young woman with a welcoming smile, clipboard in hand, checked off names, welcomed the women, then asked us to follow her. We walked to a small building near the playing fields where a buffet lunch of juice, sandwiches, salads, and fruit was set up on a table covered with a white tablecloth. "You have about an hour to eat and rest up before the warm-up starts. The game will start about half an hour after that. Do you have any questions?"

Liz asked, "Are the men and women playing at the same time?" Ms. Ryback nodded. "How many teams have the Fairview women played?"

"I don't exactly know. There are three or four hospitals within a couple of hours from here, so these women have played other teams a few times." The women exchanged glances. I could feel their tension rise.

"Do the women from Fairview always win?" asked Carrie.

Miss. Ryback laughed. "Usually, but not always."

So they can keep playing no matter if they win or lose? Well, today they're going to lose. There were no more questions. Miss Ryback left, promising to be back in time to lead the women to the field.

"Time to eat," I said. No one moved. "Aren't you hungry? Breakfast was a long time ago." They shook their heads. I didn't blame them. I wasn't hungry either. "Well, how about chocolate chip cookies I made for you. I thought we'd eat them after the game but maybe now's a better time." I put the cookies on a plate and passed them around. In seconds the plate was empty. While they were munching, I talked with them about the importance of helping each other, not getting upset if they missed a play or struck out. Liz went over playing positions. I reminded them that no matter what Mr. Carson said, winning was great but not everything, that this was a time for them to enjoy being away from Concordia, to meet new people, and to have a good time. Time dragged. When Miss Ryback came back she noticed the food had hardly been touched and said there would be time for them to eat something after their game, that the women's games usually ended before the men's because the women only played seven innings; the men played nine. Although the attendant who'd come with us didn't say much, she tried to relax the women by gently touching a shoulder, or smiling at a woman who looked scared. I was grateful she was with us. I hoped that if anything bad happened, she would know what to do. I hoped even more fervently that nothing bad would happen, we would win, and Mr. Carson would be so pleased he'd buy the women's team uniforms like the men wore.

As we walked to the playing area, I couldn't help comparing the well-kept, newly mown grassy field the Fairview women played on with the lumpy, weed-filled field the Concordia women used. I had previously tried to talk with Liz about strategy, but she said she and Rita had talked a lot as captains and had made decisions about what they would do in as many circumstances as they could imagine. Even now Liz made it clear she did not want me to coach or make suggestions, so I sat on the bench the Concordia women would use and watched, hating how stressed I was. Coaching would have given me something to do and might have helped reduce my concern, but I was pleased that Liz was taking charge and the women were responding well to her suggestions and comments.

At first, while warming up, the women made a lot of wild throws and missed catches, but the focus with which Liz pitched and Maggie caught calmed the team. When the Fairview women approached, Liz gathered the women and gave them a pep talk. The two captains tossed for which team would bat first. Liz won the toss and quickly said her team would bat second.

The game began. I watched with the women not chosen to play initially—more edgy than the players—who were obviously enjoying themselves. My anxiety grew with each play, even though Liz struck out three of the first four players. The Concordia team ran off the field, big smiles on their faces. At the end of the first inning the score was 1-0. Carrie had hit a hard ball to left field, allowing the runner on base to score. Concordia was ahead. I breathed a small sigh of relief, but there were still six innings to go. The teams were well matched and I was pleased to see how happy the women looked, exchanging good-natured bantering with the other team.

Then, at the top of the fourth inning, Fairview scored three runs, leading 3-1. Liz switched the women who had not yet played with players who said they were tired. I was impressed by her determination to use whatever strategy she could to win, but nothing worked. At the top of the seventh inning, when it was Fairview's turn to bat, the score was still 3-1.

I called a time out. After the women gathered around me, I suggested that Liz might be tired. "I'm a good pitcher. Maybe if I played, we could win." Liz reacted as if I'd punched her in the stomach. The team turned to her. She looked away. Linda, who was playing first base, hesitated, then said, "That might be a good idea, Liz." Carrie turned to Maggie and asked what she thought. Maggie asked Liz if she was tired. There was a long silence; our time out was almost over. Liz said nothing, just threw me the ball, and strode over to where the Concordia women were sitting. I threw a few warm-up pitches to Maggie and then threw the ball to the women around the field several times until I felt we were all connected.

Two Fairview players got on base, but our Concordia shortstop caught a pop-up fly, I struck out one batter, and Maggie tagged one out before she reached home plate. It was the bottom of the seventh inning—our last chance to score. The first Concordia batter struck out. The next two hit line drives; we had a woman on first and one on second. The fourth batter struck out. It was my turn to bat, with two outs. I was so tense that every part of me was shaking. I swung at the first ball and missed. Taking a deep breath, I swung at the next ball and hit it far into left field. The two women on base ran home. Despite my bruises, I ran as fast as I could and smashed into home plate, not sure if I'd scored or been tagged out. Then I saw the Concordia women running to Liz and their teammates sitting on the bench. We'd won, 4-3.

While the Fairview team congratulated our team, their captain shook hands with Liz and said she hoped Fairview could come to Concordia, that they'd had a great time. Miss Ryback brought punch and cookies for the women, who mingled, chatting amiably, as they ate and drank. Everyone avoided me. I felt sick. We'd won, but at what cost? Yes, I'd asked, but now that I had time to think, I felt sure they heard my suggestion as a demand. They had learned only too well that saying no to someone in power, even a summer employee, was dangerous. Coop was right when she told me to recognize I had total power over my patients. Why hadn't I listened to her? Why had

I acted without thinking or caring about the women? How had I so easily turned into a Mr. Carson?

The team walked to the building where the buffet lunch was still laid out. No one ate. No one looked at me. I had transgressed in a way that allowed no apology but I apologized anyway. Linda tried to help by saying that since they'd won, they'd probably be allowed to play other teams. A heavy silence followed, only broken when Miss Ryback came by to congratulate the team. Liz, as captain, thanked her for Fairview's hospitality. The other women echoed her. After Miss Ryback left, Liz, her face and body tight with anger, walked over to me. She looked as if she'd aged ten years. Her hands were shaking like they had when I first met her, but her voice was clear and harsh. "We wanted to win, but we wanted to do it ourselves." The women nodded, clearly feeling the same way.

I apologized again. "I acted without thinking. Next time, I promise, I won't interfere, no matter what happens." *What happened to all my fine principles?*

Carrie took pity on me. "At least you were trying to help us." I thanked her, but shame engulfed me. When it mattered most, in spite of my fine words, I cared only about the result and not the women. Some birthday present I'd given myself.

The bus ride back to the hospital was agony. My bruises hurt more than they had while I was playing, and the jostling of the bus didn't help. None of the women spoke to me, nor did they make room when I had to sit next to Mr. Dobson, so pleased with having hit the winning home run for the men that he spread out even more than he had on the way to the game.

Back at the hospital, Bruce and Mr. Carson were waiting for the bus. He greeted the news that both teams had won with the promise of a celebration. He even congratulated Liz for doing such a great job as captain. *How did he know she was the captain?* I couldn't bear to hear Mr. Carson's praise and told him I would walk the women back to building 5. Bruce reacted to the news of our winning with a big smile and offered to walk with us. I said no. He said he'd wait for me at the administration building. I told him not to wait. As we left, I saw him talking with Mr. Carson. They were both grinning.

26

The walk back to the ward could have been a funeral procession. The weekend attendant attributed their behavior to exhaustion and suggested they lie down and rest before dinner, behavior usually prohibited during the day. I apologized once again, then left. All the way back to the administration building, walking as slowly as I could, I tried to figure out why I'd acted as I did, against every principle I believed in, against everything I thought I knew about myself, against everything I'd said to the women.

Bruce had ignored my telling him not to wait. Even worse, his enthusiasm about the team's accomplishment blinded him to how I was feeling. "Rennie, great work. Carson's really pleased—and amazed. He's already figuring out where your team can play next. Boy, was I wrong about you starting a team. You certainly knew what you were doing. I just spoke to Yanni. He said to bring you to the restaurant for a celebration dinner."

"There's nothing to celebrate. I'm going home."

Bruce stared at me. "What are you talking about? Concordia's first women's team won. Everyone's talking about you. What's wrong?" I shrugged and told him what happened. It was his turn to be astonished. "You won! That's all that matters. You should be jumping for joy."

"Well, I'm not. At the moment I'd rather be jumping off a bridge."

He gasped. "You don't mean that."

"What I mean is that I don't much like myself right now."

"All the more reason to come with me to Yanni's. I've seen the way you change when you're with him. He always makes you feel good." I couldn't deny that. "Besides, Yanni asked me to bring you." Reluctantly, I drove us to the restaurant. Yanni's welcoming smile filtered through some of my despair and I responded with a less than whole-hearted smile. He silently questioned me as he seated us at the counter and brought coffee, but I felt too miserable to explain. After drinking the hot, fragrant coffee, savoring its smell and taste, I told

Bruce I was leaving. He stood up and blocked my way. "You can't go. I sold two of the paintings that were hanging in the dining room and it's Yanni's birthday. I think we should have dinner together. We all have something to celebrate." *Yanni and I have the same birthday?*

"Congratulations," I said, and meant it, "but you thought wrong."

"Please, Rennie, there's so much to tell you."

All I could think about was the softball game. Why hadn't I talked with Liz? Why had I just acted? Both Mrs. Denby and I noticed that after being chosen team captain she'd become less sarcastic and more friendly. I felt like I'd trampled on her soul.

I started to leave, but Bruce stopped me. "I bought you a present." *For what? I didn't tell you it was my birthday?* He handed me a small box. *Please, let it not be another ring.* "I was walking with my dad on a funny little street in Greenwich Village and I thought of you." I stared at him. "Go on, open it." He was looking at me so intently, so anxious to please, I felt sorry for him. The package, wrapped tastefully in gold print paper, with a gold bow, was too pretty to spoil. I undid the paper carefully. As I took off the top I gasped. Inside, nestled in velvet, was a pair of gold earrings with a tiny cascade of stones that changed colors in the light. They looked expensive. Too expensive. I needed to give them back to him. I loved them.

"Try them on. There's a mirror over there," said Bruce, utterly delighted with himself. I couldn't accept such a luxurious gift, but they were so much more beautiful than any jewelry I'd ever owned, and, it was my birthday, even if he didn't know and I didn't feel like telling him. What would it mean if I accepted them? I was afraid to ask.

I could feel Yanni's presence before I saw him. In the mirror I watched him looking at me, both of us admiring the earrings shimmering in the light. I was taking them off when Bruce said, "Please, wear them. They look really nice on you." Before I could tell him I didn't deserve such a gift, given what I'd done, he spoke as if he could read my mind. "The earrings are a present. My way of acknowledging that you were right about starting a team and I was wrong. And, if you're worried about people finding out that you played, I'm absolutely, positively sure none of the women will say anything about what happened. Why would they spoil all the accolades they're going to get? As far as Carson and Denby know, the women won. That's all Carson cares about and Denby won't ask.

Just think how self-serving it would seem if you boasted that you, the great Miss Weinstein, hit the winning home run."

"I would never do that."

"And the women will never tell. In fact, I bet the story of how the first Concordia women's team won their first away game will take on a life of its own. No one will ever know that they had help from a summer recreational therapist."

"So what? I know I didn't do right by the women."

"Even if that's true, you meant well, I'm sure," said Yanni.

"What I meant, and how the women feel, are completely different," I countered.

"Please, tell me. I'd like to know," he said, in such a caring manner my eyes teared up.

I told him briefly what happened. "I saw the looks of disappointment and frustration on their faces when the game was over. It was the first chance they had to be in charge of themselves, to have some control over their actions, and I ruined it for them. I let Mr. Carson's probable reaction if they lost be more important than the women's feelings. I did something I never thought I would do. I let the score be more important than the women's sense of accomplishment." From the expression on his face it seemed he agreed with Bruce, so I said, "I thought you of all people would understand."

"What makes you think I don't?" asked Yanni.

"You were talking about my reaction as if I'm being stupid, making a big deal out of nothing." I turned to Bruce, glaring at him. "You don't care about the patients, which surprises me since you were one of them once."

Bruce reacted as if I'd whacked him. Yanni put his arm around Bruce's shoulder. Even though what I'd said was true, I muttered, "I'm sorry, that was a low blow." He nodded, accepting my apology, but I was so filled with self-disgust that I challenged Yanni. "Didn't you ever do anything you were sorry for and couldn't make it right no matter how many times you apologized?"

"Yes, of course. More than once."

"So what did you do about it?"

"Tried not to make the same mistake twice."

"That's all?"

"What else can we do? You helped people who didn't want your help—that's not the end of the world. And what about hitting a home run with two women on base?"

I shrugged, caught between feeling horrible about playing, proud that I'd hit the winning home run, wanting the earrings, knowing I shouldn't keep them, wishing I could take back what I'd done. Yanni touched my cheek so gently that I wanted to bury my face in his chest and feel his arms around me. "Rennie, it's good you care so much about your patients. Stay for dinner. It's my birthday. Please help me celebrate. I have some time before it starts to get busy."

On a shelf near the counter was a ceramic bowl of water in which two burning candles floated. The bowl sat on a large matching ceramic plate filled with yellow roses. Next to it was a birthday cake decorated with chocolate frosting and yellow candied roses. Unable to take my eyes off the flickering candles, I wished the birthday cake was for me, but that wasn't possible. No one knew it was my birthday.

I turned to look at Yanni staring at the bowl. He caressed one of the roses and a petal fell into his hand. He pressed it to his cheek, his eyes full of tears. "Happy Birthday, Yanni," I said, wishing I knew why he was crying, wanting to know the meaning of the candles and the roses. Not a normal way to celebrate a birthday. He nodded and thanked me as we stood together watching the quivering light.

I didn't want to move—the moment felt so private and special—it was a shock when Bruce joined us and wished Yanni happy birthday in a loud and intrusive voice. He had no hesitation about asking the question I wanted to ask. "Would you tell us about the candles and the roses?"

Yanni cleared his throat, wiped his eyes, and said, "Let's eat. The food is ready."

I noticed how adroitly he avoided answering the question, which only made me more curious. When we walked into the dining room I was surprised by the change in the space. Bruce's paintings had been taken down and in their place was an amazing variety of woven textiles: tapestries, blouses, shawls, woven scenes of shops and family life, even jewelry. The bright, cheerful colors transformed the space, making it seem larger and brighter. Yanni saw me staring at the pieces and explained, "A few weeks ago, one of the guys who washes dishes—he's from Guatemala—told me his mother and sisters were weavers and asked if I would show their work. The exhibit's only been up a few days and almost half of the pieces have been sold." I could see why. All of the work, but especially a stunning shawl woven in shades of red, purple, and blue, called out for appreciation. When I walked over to have a closer look, Yanni took the shawl off the wall and draped it around my shoulders. "It matches the earrings. Go look at yourself in the mirror." I had to agree. The shawl felt and looked lovely. "If you want to buy it," he offered, "I have another piece I can hang in its place." He saw me looking at the price—almost a week's salary. "Don't worry about the cost, I'll sell it to you for what I paid for it." I hesitated. It was my birthday. I could call it a birthday present, but I didn't deserve the shawl or the earrings. I sighed, shaking my head, longing to say, "I'll buy it."

"Rennie, why are you so hard on yourself?"

Because I cared too much about a score and not enough about my patients. "Because I let the women down."

Bruce was quick to respond. "No, you didn't. You have keys. That gives you power. A staff member says do something, they do it, no matter what. It's the only way to be safe, if you can call it that in a mental hospital. Remember Carol?" I shuddered. The memory of her being taken away in a straightjacket was etched in my brain. "Believe me, she's no exception. I know from experience."

Yanni changed the subject. "Let's drink. I've opened a wonderful bottle of wine." Without waiting for us to respond, he led us into the private dining room where I'd slept off the migraine headache weeks earlier, then left to bring us food. Bruce and I put three folding chairs around a small round table and while I arranged the napkins, he brought back a small vase of daisies. "It's his birthday. He should have flowers on the table." *It's my birthday too.* Yanni returned with three glasses, a chilled bottle of Israeli white wine, a basket of freshly baked rolls and bread, dishes of hummus, eggplant dip, and olive oil and a strange, dark, aromatic liquid that he said was balsamic vinegar, for dipping. I'd never tasted vinegar by itself. When my parents made salad dressing they used apple cider vinegar, which, if they used too much, made me cough. But when I dunked small chunks of bread into a little dish each of us had for mixing the oil and vinegar, it was even better than eating bread with butter. My evident hunger surprised me, and pleased Yanni, who told me to make sure I saved room for dinner and dessert.

When Yanni left to get our dinner, Bruce told me how relieved he was that people bought his paintings. "I'm glad to see them go. They reminded me of what it was like— being hospitalized."

I needed to take my mind off myself. "What was it like, being in the hospital?"

"It was horrible. Seeing my father and Yanni made me feel a little better, but after they left I lost whatever self-control I still had. I was furious that my stepfather had had me locked up and outraged that Yanni and my father left me there. When an attendant came in with supper I told him I didn't want any. He told me that I had to eat, and if I didn't, they had ways to make me." Bruce sipped some wine, trying to compose himself. "No one had ever spoken to me like that. I was so livid I took the tray of food and threw it at him. He yelled for help. Three huge guys came running in, wrestled me into a straightjacket, called me a bunch of dreadful names, took the tray of food, and left me. I lay on the cold concrete floor—shivering, humiliated, frightened, enraged. The harder I tried to get out of the damn thing, the tighter it got, the worse I felt. I was in hell and nobody cared."

"Oh, Bruce." It was impossible for me to imagine something so horrendous."

"I'll spare you the rest of the gory details, but I finally figured out that nothing I said or did mattered. Even in a private hospital, what the attendant says is what the staff believes. And what the staff believes is true is true, even if it isn't." He looked at me, his eyes filling with tears. "I'm sure you did what you thought was right, Rennie. I know how much you care about your patients. But you're staff. Even though it would have been all right with you if Liz said no, she's learned to do what you say no matter what." His words did not make me feel better.

Whoever said ignorance is bliss never worked in a mental hospital.

Yanni brought in a strange-looking set of pots stacked one on top of the other. "It's what we use to make couscous, a dish my mother served when our family needed comfort food." I inhaled the delicious smells and watched with fascination as he piled yellow bits on each of our plates, topping it with chunks of meat and roasted vegetables, then ladling a sauce over it. I was used to eating "foreign" food— the only restaurants my family ever ate in served food from other countries. But Bruce stared at it, asking what it was. Yanni explained that couscous was a kind of grain and he had used spices common to the Middle East to roast the lamb and vegetables. He urged him to try it, which Bruce did, reluctantly, but it was not a big success with him. Yanni had piled so much food on my plate that when I was too full to finish or even mop up the great tasting sauce with the bread, I asked if I could take the rest home. Yanni said, "Of course," with such obvious pleasure that his warmth eased the hurting places inside me a little. I hated myself a little less.

Bruce gave up trying to eat what he obviously didn't like, apologized to Yanni, who shrugged it off, then said to me, "I hope you'll celebrate my selling two paintings and you starting the first Concordia women's softball team." Yanni didn't wait for my answer. He told us he'd be back in a minute and returned with champagne cooling in an ornate silver ice bucket.

"The ice bucket is so beautiful. Doesn't seem like it belongs in a restaurant," I said, astonished by the intricate silverwork.

"It doesn't," he said. "I only use it for special occasions, for special people."

"Where did you get it?" I asked, pleased to be thought special.

"It was my grandmother's—one of the few things she took with her when we had to escape the riots against the Jews in Baghdad."

"When was that?" I knew about the Holocaust in Europe but I'd never heard about riots in Iraq.

The expression on his face was grim as he answered. "The first two days in June 1941. We call it the *Farhud*. In English I guess you could say it was a pogrom—similar to what happened on Kristallnacht in Germany in 1938, as well as many places in Eastern Europe. Hardly anyone knows about what happened in Baghdad. Nazi sympathizers burned every property they could find that was owned by Jews. A lot of people we knew were killed." He closed his eyes, his face clouded with pain. "We were lucky. My father found a way for us to leave in the middle of the night. We didn't even have time to pack." He shook his head; the intensity of the memory silencing him for a moment. "Afterward, when we were safe in Jerusalem, my father asked her why, of all the things she might have taken, my grandmother had chosen the ice bucket. She said it was to help her remember the good times of her life, before the troubles. Her father had had it made for her and had given it to her the morning of her marriage to my grandfather."

Bruce and I stared at the ice bucket, as if the fierceness of our gaze could make it talk. I was full of questions. I wanted to know how Yanni got it, and what it meant to him, and why he brought it with him, and why he kept it at the restaurant instead of at his home, but I was afraid questions might upset him even more.

"Well," he said, as if shaking away the memory, "that was a long time ago. This is a celebration." He poured each of us a glass of champagne. Bruce and I wished Yanni a happy birthday. Bruce made a toast to Yanni, for being his friend, for helping him connect with his father, and to me for being his friend. My mood quickly changed. What had happened with the women that afternoon paled in comparison to people fleeing for their lives, having to leave everything behind, grateful to be alive.

Yanni toasted Bruce for choosing to be an artist despite all his difficulties. I drank to that. Then he turned to me and said, "And here's to Rennie, who cares about what matters most—kindness and compassion."

I blushed, and mumbled, "Thank you," too embarrassed to look at either of them. Bruce and Yanni's glasses were empty, so while Yanni was refilling them, I found my voice and congratulated Bruce. I couldn't bear to just toast Yanni for being kind and caring. He'd been so much more, yet I didn't have the courage to tell him what he meant to me. I thanked him for being such a good cook.

Yanni brought coffee, fruit, and a variety of cheeses. While we ate, Bruce told us about the paintings he'd sold and some of the new ones he'd been working on since moving to his father's apartment, the first place he ever felt safe. When Bruce talked about his art he was a different person. His harsh, critical, and sarcastic remarks were replaced by thoughtful, sensitive, insightful comments. I envied him. He knew what he wanted to do with his life and had found a way to do it, even a person to help him. When I thought about who I wanted to be and what I wanted to do with my life, all I could see was what I didn't like or want. I had secret dreams of writing books, but the one time I'd told my parents, they made such fun I pretended I was kidding. As for who I wanted to be, today's experience with the women had made a mockery of my supposedly firmly held principles, sending me into a tailspin of doubt and self-loathing. It was the kind of experience that usually ended with me sinking into a bottomless dark place inside myself where there was neither kindness nor compassion, the very qualities Yanni had toasted.

In the past, when I sensed I was spiraling downward, I had found a way to be alone, to crash with my privacy intact. At home I locked my bedroom door. At school I either hid under my covers or walked to a small cave I'd found in a nearby forest that I had camouflaged so no one else would find it. Here, in Yanni's restaurant, with Bruce and Yanni staring at me, there was no place to hide. Yanni kept looking at me with concern. "What's going on, Rennie?"

I shrugged. "It's nothing compared to what happened to you, or even the hard times Bruce went through." I stood up, trying to keep from showing how bad I felt. "Yanni, thanks for the delicious dinner. Bruce, it's really great that you sold two paintings. Maybe we can meet for lunch at the tree on Monday."

"Rennie, sit down and talk with us," ordered Yanni. Bruce nodded in agreement. "I don't know why you're so upset but I know how it feels to keep everything inside."

"How?" I asked, remembering the times when he refused to talk.

"After our escape to Israel, and the loss of so many family members, I stopped talking. We all felt terrible—why talk about it? One morning before dawn, about a month after we found a place to live, my father woke me up and said to get dressed, that he had something to show me. He took me to a place in the desert and said, 'Look! Tell me what you see!' I looked but I didn't see anything unusual. Sunrise. Boulders. Sand. A few nomads on camels in the distance. I wanted to please him. It was the least I could do after everything we'd been through, but nothing I saw seemed worth mentioning. Frustrated, I finally spoke. 'Abba, why did you bring me here? What is it you want me to see?' He took my face in his hands. I asked myself, When had his hair gone from brown to gray? Why hadn't I noticed the deep lines in his face? He reminded me that when I was a little boy we'd gone to Jerusalem to visit family and he'd taken me to this place and that I'd been so excited I couldn't stop talking about all the things I saw. 'So, my son, tell me what you see. I need to hear your voice. The dead don't talk. You're alive. Talk!'

"You're alive, Rennie. You need to talk. There's no point in comparing what happened to my family and what's happening inside you. Suffering is suffering and silence is not the answer." He took my face in his hands, just as he described his father doing to him, and it helped me feel safe enough to talk. I briefly touched his hands with mine, wishing he would hold me until I felt better about myself but who knew how long that would take.

"I'm in a school I hate, learning to teach what I hate, so that when I graduate I'll have a job doing what I hate. I have a boyfriend…" I stopped, ashamed at how trivial it sounded, powerless to describe the inner depression with which I lived for reasons I couldn't figure out. I was tired of being told I was too serious, too concerned about right and wrong. I certainly couldn't talk about how envious I was of Bruce, who knew what he wanted to do, who knew how he wanted to live, and who had had the guts to stand up to his stepfather, even after being accused of killing his mother with all his questions about birth certificates and passports. I stopped talking, too self-conscious to continue. I looked at their faces and decided their intense looks masked their judgment of me, that my concerns were insignificant. "I know what you're going to say, my boyfriend tells me it all the time, 'If you don't like the school you're going to, change schools. Study what interests you.'" I braced myself for their agreement.

Yanni shook his head. "That is not what I was going to say. Not at all. You've been attending that school for three years. Something must be keeping you there." *Yes. I'm not smart enough to go to a good college, and even if by some large miracle I did get in, I could only go if I got a scholarship, which I had no chance of getting, so I persuaded myself that having a job when I graduated is worth the misery of studying subjects that don't interest me. A terrible bargain for sure, but I couldn't do anything about it.* I was too ashamed to talk about any of this.

While I was thinking of a response, Bruce spoke up. "Rennie, you may hate the college you're going to, but you got to work at the hospital because of what you're studying, and you're doing a terrific job. That should count for something."

"It does. It pays for my tuition." I didn't mention that I was still ashamed that I'd signed the loyalty oath.

Both Bruce and Yanni were talking about symptoms, not causes. It wasn't only the college that I hated, I hated myself for being a coward, for deciding I wasn't smart enough to go to a liberal arts school when I'd been getting decent enough grades in high school and had won awards for dances I choreographed and performed in the annual dance club concerts. Worst of all, I didn't see how I could change any of this. I'd go back to school in the fall, graduate, and teach dance if I was lucky, physical education most likely.

I'd been encouraged by one of my professors to apply for a dance scholarship at Connecticut College's Summer Dance Program after graduation, but I had dismissed her suggestion as kindness rather than support for my dance ability. Although I liked to move, I wasn't a great dancer. I wasn't even sure I liked the world of dance with its fierce competition. Everything I liked to do—writing, making pottery, dancing, creating music, all depended on talent. I was afraid I had more enthusiasm and interest than skill. As for Jake, if he wanted me to be his girlfriend, I would be his girlfriend, even though I hated that I needed to have a boyfriend so badly I put up with behavior that sometimes made me feel even worse about myself.

Yanni was looking at me so intently I couldn't bear to meet his gaze. "Rennie, please." I waited for him to say more. "I'll be right back." He put the dirty dishes on a large tray and left the room. When he returned, he was carrying the plate with the candles and roses. The candlelight shone brightly in the dimness of the room, illuminating Yanni's face. He looked older and more tired than I'd ever seen him. We were silent while he stared at the candlelight for what seemed a long time before he spoke. "I had a wife and a daughter. During the 1948 war I was supposed to be in 'harm's way' fighting on the so-called front line. They were in a kibbutz, surrounded by soldiers, supposedly safe. Except they weren't. A bomb fell on the kibbutz kitchen where my wife and daughter were helping to prepare lunch. My wife and daughter were killed. Today is also my daughter's birthday. She would have been fourteen." He stopped talking and looked at the candles before turning to me. "There's something about you, Rennie, that reminds me of Adit, something about the intensity with which you live life."

I couldn't keep it in any longer. "Today is my birthday too. I'm twenty."

"Really?" I nodded. "Well then, I need to light another candle." A tender smile replaced his look of sadness. "Perhaps sharing a birthday gives a special connection between the living and the dead. I'll be right back."

"Why didn't you tell us before?" asked Bruce.

"I don't know." *I never celebrated a birthday without my family.*

"Well, now I'm really glad I gave you the earrings." He laughed. "Maybe I'm psychic and didn't know it. Happy Birthday, Rennie. I'm glad you told us."

"Me too." And I was. Surprisingly so.

Yanni came back with another candle, lit it, and placed it in the dish. Two of his kitchen helpers came in, one carrying the birthday cake with three lit candles, the other carried a tray with coffee, small delicate cups, plates, and silverware. Yanni asked me to make a wish and to blow out the candles. They didn't ask what I wished for but it welled up in me—I wished I could feel better about myself. We sang "Happy Birthday" and both Yanni and Bruce kissed my cheek. Then, giggling, a release from the tension I guess, Bruce and I kissed Yanni's cheeks, which made him laugh as well.

Yanni and I cut the cake and gave pieces to everyone. The kitchen help squeezed in as we oohed and aahed over the delicious chocolate cake, perfectly accompanied by Turkish coffee—hot, strong, and sweet, a new taste treat. When it was time for Yanni to go back to work, he asked the kitchen help to box up food and cake for me. Knowing Bruce hadn't liked the food very much, Yanni told them to box up slices of cake for Bruce and his dad.

As I was getting ready to leave, laden with food and the earrings, which I'd been persuaded to keep, Yanni brought the shawl. "Here, this is my birthday present to you." He saw me shake my head, the "no," forming on my lips and said, "You must take it. When I think of you wearing it, I will smile."

"I don't have a present for you," I said, my eyes tearing.

"What is the cliché? Your presence is my present? No more talk." He brought paper and I carefully wrapped the shawl, managing to fit everything into the carryall on the back of the scooter. My twentieth birthday turned out to be the most memorable birthday I'd ever had.

27

Driving home, the cool night air felt so good I rode through the park instead of going straight home. The smell of fresh grass, mingling with the scent of roses, reminded me of the roses around the candles. I parked at the recreational area, brightly lit and filled with people listening to a band concert. Although I normally don't like Sousa marches, the energy of the music got to me. I thought about the talk with Yanni and Bruce, about my giving up before I'd even tried. Maybe I could have gotten into a better college had I applied, but it was too late to do anything about that, too late to redo what had happened this afternoon with the women. Still, I could do something about me, now. I made a promise to myself. I would apply for the dance scholarship, regardless of the odds. Maybe I could also apply for a graduate school dance fellowship and not teach physical education—an idea that hadn't occurred to me before.

Feeling peaceful, I pulled into the driveway, turned off the motor, and was about to get off the Vespa when I thought I saw someone on the front porch. I put the gear in neutral and was backing down the driveway when I heard a familiar voice. "Where've you been? You told me you didn't work on Saturday."

"Jake?"

"You expecting someone else?"

"I thought you were in Europe."

"I tried calling you all day. Where've you been?"

"Thanks for wishing me a happy birthday." I tried to slow down the thoughts and feelings whirling inside me, but chaos reigned. During the time he'd been away, especially after his last letter, I had had fantasies of what our reunion would be like when he returned from Europe. Mostly I imagined us hugging, him telling me how much he loved me, how he wanted to marry me when I graduated. I even envisioned me forgiving him for the way he'd been with other women, certain that now he'd be faithful and attentive and supportive. This reality was so far from my fantasies that I was unable to move, barely able to hold up the scooter, staring at him as if he were a stranger.

"Sorry, I forgot. Happy Birthday. Aren't you going to invite me in?" His voice became softer, more seductive. "Your family's still in Mexico, right?" I nodded. He moved toward me, a familiar smile on his face—the one that preceded a hug, some kissing, making love. "Babe, you look terrific. It's been a long few months. Good thing we've got the rest of the weekend to catch up." His voice became seductive. "Actually, I do have a birthday present for you—one that has to be delivered in person."

I know what that means. "No." It was as if the word came from someone else's mouth, taking me by surprise as much as Jake.

He treated it as a joke. "Are you crazy?"

I found my voice. "No, I am not crazy." *And never was!*

"What do you mean, 'no'? No you can't wait for us to be together? No you're sorry I've been waiting all day? No what?"

The day had been too long and too full of emotion. When Jake put his arms around me, I buried my head against his chest, feeling his desire and my own lack of response, which contrasted sharply with what I used to feel the moment he touched me. I pulled away, bewildered by my not wanting to make love with him. "I didn't expect to see you so soon."

He looked and sounded annoyed. "Rennie, I'm here. That's what matters."

"Let's go inside," I said curtly. "It's so dark I can hardly see you." I didn't want to invite him in and I also didn't want him to leave. Besides, I had to give him the insurance papers and title for the scooter. "Want some tea and birthday cake? It's in the scooter bag, I'll get it."

He moved toward me but I evaded him and went to unpack the scooter. When I came back, I put the shawl on the dining room cabinet and offered the slices of cake to Jake. I busied myself putting water on to boil.

"This cake is great? You make it?"

"No, Yanni made it." Jake looked confused. No wonder. I wasn't behaving like the Rennie he'd known for the past three years. I felt like a stranger to myself. "He's a friend of mine. Someone I met this summer." Instead of waiting for Jake to respond, I opened the loose tea leaves and inhaled the scent of apple and cinnamon, willing myself to think about what I wanted, not what Jake wanted. My resolve quickly disappeared when Jake turned off the stove and held me, kissing me insistently, his knowing hands seducing and arousing. My body responded. It felt like betrayal. I told him to stop, even tried to pull away, but I didn't do it with enough conviction to challenge him. Then I just waited for it to be over. For the first time I understood the difference between making love and having sex.

When it was over, feeling dirty and disgusted with myself, I took a long hot shower while Jake slept in my bed. It didn't leave me feeling clean or comforted. I went down to the living room, cradled myself in the shawl and lay on the couch. The only way I could make myself feel less ashamed was to tell myself, out loud, "Not again. Not with Jake. It's over unless things change a whole lot between us."

The next morning, while I was making coffee, he came down, grinning. "Hey Babe, how about a quick one before breakfast?"

Still reeling from our time together last night, I spat out the words before I could change my mind. "No, Jake." I took a deep breath, and gave him the keys and the papers. "Everything feels different between us. Could we talk about—"

He interrupted, not bothering to hide his anger "I don't get it. I leave for Europe with you as hot for me as any woman I've ever known, who can't get into my pants fast enough." I winced, knowing there was truth in what he said. "Now you act like all that never happened."

"We've known each other for three years, can't we talk about what's happening now?"

"What's there to talk about?"

"What about the summer. I'd like to know about your trip. I'm guessing you met other women, and I— "

Jake exploded. "You're guessing? Why the fuck would you say something like that?"

I could feel myself retreating, thinking how to placate him, but then I remembered what Yanni and Bruce had said to me over dinner. "I know you've been with other women while I was away at school. Are you going to tell me you didn't have sex with other women while you were in Europe? I think it would be good if we could talk—"

"There's nothing to talk about. Sure, I met some women and we had some good times, but I'm here, aren't I?"

"And I'm not supposed to care?"

"This conversation is pointless."

"Do you love me, Jake?" The question took him aback. His hesitation told me everything I didn't want to know. I wasn't his girlfriend, at least not in the way I wanted to be. Maybe I never was. His response took forever and he didn't answer my question.

"I guess it depends on what you mean by 'love.' Didn't seem as if you wanted to be with me last night. Do you love me?"

I did. Do I? I hesitated. "I guess the truth is I don't know what I feel for you right now. A lot happened this summer. To you and to me. That's why I thought we should talk about it." The conversation was making me anxious. A spasm of dread washed over me. Habitual fear took over. "What about coffee and something to eat? My stomach is rumbling."

His response surprised me. "Sure. What about eggs and orange juice? Got any bagels? I'll toast them."

Feeling a spurt of relief, I handed Jake the carton of juice to pour into two glasses and took out three bagels from the freezer for him to toast, then scrambled six eggs. When he was hungry he ate a lot. I thought, hoped, that making breakfast together would ease the tension between us, or at least the uncertainty I felt. While we were eating, I asked what had brought him home two weeks earlier than he'd planned, and discovered he'd been accepted as an intern with a prestigious law firm and was beginning work on Monday.

"That's great. When did you apply?" *How come you didn't tell me?*

"Just before I left. One of my professors told me about the possibility. I was one of thirty-seven guys who applied. Only two got picked. It's a big deal, with pretty good pay. Might mean a great job for me when I graduate next year." He finished eating a bagel that he'd smeared with cream cheese and topped with sliced tomatoes.

I felt a need to counter his success. *Maybe saying it will make it true.* "I'm applying for a dance fellowship next summer. Also thinking about going to graduate school rather than teaching." He nodded, more interested in breakfast than what I might do after graduation. My spirits plummeted when he had no questions, no response. I couldn't help contrasting the way Yanni, Bruce, even Will, listened to what I said, asking questions that gave me something to think about, making me feel they cared about me. If I didn't feel as attracted to Jake as I used to, what was left?

Jake finished eating, took his plate and cup to the sink, and washed them while I put the food away. He left my dishes on the table. Not anything unusual, but it seemed like a metaphor for our relationship and it didn't feel good. He stretched, smiled, and put his arms around me. "Thanks for the breakfast. Just what I needed." I leaned into his chest, feeling his warm, strong body, smelling his familiar scent. Maybe we could still reconnect. He caressed my neck and said, "Hey, Babe, let's go upstairs and say 'good morning' properly."

"It's a gorgeous morning, let's go to the park. I'd like to hear about Europe." I felt Jake move away and when I turned to look at him his face was hard and closed.

"You've changed, Rennie. You met someone this summer? You have another boyfriend?"

"No, there's no one else. How have I changed?"

Jake shrugged. "Hard to put in words but you sure as hell don't seem as loving as you were before I left."

"So much has happened, to both of us. We're not the same people we were before you left. How could we be? You've been with other women and I have a job that's a thousand times more difficult than I ever thought possible. I think it would help if we talked. I'd really like to know about your trip and the internship."

Jake stared at me. Like he was seeing me for the first time. Maybe I was seeing him, not for the first time, but from a different place. What I wanted was for him to give me a loving hug and say, "You're right. Let's go to the park and talk. I want to hear about what you've been doing."

What Jake said was, "You need to talk, find someone to talk to. I'm leaving, but you might at least thank me for letting you use my Vespa."

I quelled any thought I had of telling him about the accident. Will had assured me that his friend repaired it so well no one would be able to tell. "I do thank you, Jake. It made life easier and it was fun to drive. I even learned to change the spark plug in the rain on the Queensboro Bridge—something I didn't think I could do."

I wasn't ready for him to leave. We'd been together for three years. I tried again. "Please, let's go to the park. We don't have to talk; the rose garden is really beautiful."

He shook his head. "You don't have to walk me to the door, I know the way out." He turned and marched out of the kitchen. We didn't even say goodbye, although I wished I had. The roar of the scooter made Jake's leaving final. The reality of never seeing him again hit me hard.

I washed the dishes and cleaned up the kitchen, feeling as if I'd been anesthetized against pain I knew was coming but didn't know when it would hit. I just knew it would be terrible. I thought about life without Jake, about not being a virgin. In spite of everything, I thought about the wonderful times Jake and I had had hiking and camping in the wilderness, sharing a love of theatre and classical music, cooking crazy concoctions. Maybe I could have been nicer, responded differently? But what was wrong with wanting to talk about what had happened? I was feeling so miserable and muddled that I didn't hear the front door opening.

"Rennie?"

I turned around, wondering if I was hallucinating. "Jake?"

"The very same."

"I thought you left."

"I did. But I kept thinking about our hiking trip to the White Mountains."

"What's that got to do with anything?"

"Remember when the cop stopped me because you were slicing tomatoes on the back of the scooter—with the knife pointed toward me?"

I nodded, too confused to speak.

"When the cop asked you what you were doing, you said, 'Making lunch.'"

"So?"

"So…" he looked as nonplussed as I felt. "I'm not sure what the point is."

We stood looking at each other. The tension was making me nervous. "Why did you come back?"

"I guess I'm not ready to say goodbye."

"You guess? What does that mean?"

"Maybe you're right. Maybe we do need to talk."

"Maybe?" *You guess. You think maybe. What am I supposed to say?* "What do you want, Jake?" *What do I want?*

"I don't know. I just had to come back."

I shrugged, feeling muddled. "Well, let's walk to the park. It's too nice a day to stay in the house." He nodded and we left, walking silently, the tension between us palpable and awkward.

Lots of colorful flowers were in bloom, perfuming the air. Blossoms danced in the breeze. People were throwing Frisbees, sitting on blankets having picnics, kids were playing ball—a perfect summer morning, yet it felt perfectly awful to me. I didn't know how to break the silence or if I even wanted to. Walking felt safe, so I led us to the paved path that circled the outer edges of the park. Jake walked beside me seeming to take no notice of anything or anyone. When he suddenly stopped, turned to me and asked, "Rennie, do you love me?" I wished I could disappear.

All I could mutter was, "I don't know what I feel about you."

"You used to tell me all the time how much you loved me. What changed?"

"Everything and nothing."

"What's that supposed to mean?"

Can I tell him that I wished he'd wanted me to go with him to Europe? That his having sex with other women upsets me? That I feel different now than I did before I started working in the hospital? That the talks with Yanni, and even Bruce, helped me think differently about who I am and what I want to do after I graduate?

I tried.

Jake listened, but soon interrupted, telling me what I should do. I tried not to lose my temper. He did come back. He did come to the park. But I couldn't stop thinking about his having slept with other women while he was in Europe. When I mentioned it he exploded. "I told you. They don't matter. None of them did. If I cared about them I wouldn't be here now, with you, trying to make sense out of nothing."

"Well, they matter to me. It doesn't feel good to know you're sleeping with other women. You're supposed to be my boyfriend."

"Is that what this is all about? You've always known there were other women. Why bring it up now?"

"Maybe I didn't have the courage to say anything before."

"So, if I may ask, what's giving you the courage now, if that's what it is."

Yanni? "It's hard to explain. I think it has to do with working at the hospital, which is so much harder than I could have imagined."

I started to tell him a little about the talks Yanni and I had but he immediately interrupted. "Is he the reason you don't want to make love with me?"

"Jake! Stop it. You're not listening. He's a friend, a person who listens. He cares about me."

"You think I don't care about you?"

"I don't know how you feel about me. Maybe I never did."

"That's your problem. I told you lots of times that I love you."

"That's true. And I told you I love you, but that was before you went off to Europe and I started working at a job that is really difficult and challenging." He started to walk away. I caught up with him and said, "This whole conversation—you never once asked about how I'm doing."

"That's not true."

"Yes, it is."

"How long do you plan to walk and argue? I have a lot to do to get ready for my job."

It was on the tip of my tongue to tell him if that was the case, he should leave. The conversation was going nowhere and I was feeling bad about myself—not that I needed help from Jake—but I kept thinking how easy it was to talk with Yanni. Why was it so hard to talk with Jake? "Okay, so at least tell me about your job." Jake's stony face made me desperate to find a way to ease the tension between us. "If you don't want to talk, could we walk for a while? We don't have to talk. Maybe that would help us find our way back to each other."

"I don't need to find my way back. I came back. The question is, where are you?"

I tried to make a joke. "I'm here, walking in the park with you."

"I used to know you, Rennie. I remember how happy you were to see me. To be with me. Now, you're like a different person. I don't know who you are or what you want from me. You walk. Figure out what you want. When you do, call me."

He gave me a light kiss on the cheek and walked away. I watched him go until I couldn't see him anymore. What troubled me the most was that I didn't know what I wanted. I didn't know why I didn't want to make love with him. Worst of all, I didn't know how I was going to know. At least he said to call him.

28

I walked for a long time, filled with sadness and pain, not paying attention to where I walked. I was about to sit near a bush when I felt an arm tighten around my neck, a hand cover my mouth, a deep voice say, "I have a knife." He reeked of liquor. Instinctively, I elbowed him in the stomach. Hard. It surprised him enough that he briefly loosened his hold on my neck. I yanked myself away and ran, running until I reached my house, unlocked the door, locked it, and collapsed on the couch, panting. I cowered under the shawl, shivering, alone, and scared. What had been a miserable day had suddenly become much, much worse.

It was dark when I woke up. I turned on the lights, searched for the bus schedule, and set the alarm for almost an hour earlier than when I drove the scooter. Although my parents' car was in the garage, and I started it regularly to keep the battery charged, I hadn't asked for permission to drive it. With the way things were going, driving seemed like asking for trouble. Better to take the bus despite the extra time it took. At least if there was an accident, I wouldn't be responsible.

Even after a long bath filled with lavender salts and two cups of my mother's calming tea, I couldn't sleep. Nightmare images of Jake intermingled with the faceless man in the park. Drenched with sweat, I changed my nightgown twice, then realized, despite changing the sheets, I could still smell Jake. I got out of bed, went downstairs, lay down on the couch, snuggled under the shawl, and eventually felt safe enough to fall asleep.

The bus schedule I'd found was for winter, not summer, so when I arrived at the bus stop the next morning, the bus was just pulling away, exhaust clouding the air. I worried I'd be late. I worried that my despondency would show. I worried about the women on the team. By the time a bus did come, I groaned. It was a local bus that stopped every three streets and so crowded I almost didn't get on. At each stop, people got off, others squeezed on. The smells of perspiration and perfume made me dizzy. I finally got a seat three stops before mine and almost missed my stop because I couldn't see through the mass of standing riders. I practically ran the four blocks to the main gate. "Where's your putt-putt?" asked the guard. In no mood to talk, and too late for comfort, I shrugged, said good morning, and hurried to building 5, dreading the effort it would take to pretend that I felt fine, nervous that the patients would see right through me.

A grim-looking Mrs. Denby was waiting for me in front of the building. Had the women complained about my playing? Was I later than I thought? Had I done something wrong? After such an awful weekend, the thought of being fired was too much to bear. I froze. She spoke tersely. "Mr. Carson wants to meet with us." *Oh no!* Mrs. Denby led the way. I followed, barely able to make myself walk. By the time we arrived at the administration building I was a sweaty mess. We walked into Mr. Carson's office. A stone-faced Miss Hempner told us he was waiting in the reception room. I had to force myself to keep going as I walked behind Mrs. Denby. When she opened the door, a cacophony of voices yelled, "Surprise!"

In a daze, I looked around, unable to comprehend what was happening. The women from building 5 were grinning and clapping as Mr. Carson walked toward me, holding a newspaper, his face lit by a smile I'd never seen. "Congratulations, Ms. Weinstein. You've given Concordia the best publicity we've had in years." Even Mrs. Langstrom was smiling.

I looked at Mrs. Denby, who winked and said, "Fooled you, didn't we."

I barely managed to nod.

Liz, Rita, Maggie, Barbara, and everyone who'd played or wanted to play, were there, so full of excitement they barely managed to contain themselves. Not only was I not being fired, the team and I were being honored at a party organized by Mr. Carson. I couldn't make it make sense, even though I saw the big sign that read: Congratulations to the FIRST Concordia Women's Team. *What happened to the team's disappointment when I helped them win?*

I turned and saw Bruce, a huge grin on his face. "Told you no one would say a word. Look at this." He showed me the article about the women's team. I suppressed a snort when I read how Mr. Carson had encouraged me to form the first women's team, had supported their practice games, and was delighted they not only won, but now had a chance to play other hospital teams. There were no photos, but Liz, first name only, was given credit for inspiring her team to keep focused even when they appeared to be losing. I couldn't suppress my laughter when I read that a patient's late inning home run had allowed the women on base to score and win the game. I wondered who told this to Mr. Carson.

"So much for truth," I muttered, but what I read next astounded me. The writer quoted Mr. Carson: "It is my hope that every hospital with a men's team will also create and support a women's team."

"See what you started?" chortled Bruce. Still stunned, unable to take in everything I was seeing and hearing and reading, I asked Bruce if he could get me a copy of the article.

Mr. Carson asked everyone to please help themselves to the food—all sorts of baked goods, cheeses, jams, butter, fruit, as well as coffee, tea, and orange juice. The women, accustomed to lining up, lined up and waited patiently for their turns. As soon as a tray was almost empty, two women dressed in blue uniforms with white aprons replaced it with a new tray, the food beautifully arranged. I was impressed. Someone had spent a lot of money on this party and I couldn't help wondering why, until I saw a reporter taking notes. Mrs. Denby and Bruce were right. Good publicity mattered.

When everyone was seated, Mr. Carson, Mrs. Langstrom, and Mrs. Denby stood at the front of the room. Without being asked, the women stopped talking and eating. I stood in the back, dazed by the unexpected celebration.

Mrs. Langstrom welcomed the group, acknowledged the historic nature of the occasion and then nodded to Mrs. Denby, who spoke first. "When Miss Weinstein told me she wanted to form a women's team I told her she had to get permission from Mr. Carson before going further. She admitted she had, without permission, already spoken to the women about a team and that they were so enthusiastic they had begun practicing, to see which players would be on the team. As you all know, acting without permission is not standard operating procedure." I would have been worried about what she was saying but she was smiling. "Miss Weinstein, please come up to the front of the room." I walked up and stood next to Mrs. Denby." I think Miss Weinstein deserves a round of applause for caring enough to turn what could have been merely a dream into this wonderful reality." The women cheered.

When the room quieted, Mr. Carson spoke, congratulating the team, even mentioning that it was a historic occasion. "Liz turned, caught my eye, and winked. I grinned. I guessed she was the one who'd told Mr. Carson about the winning home run. Her response was absolutely perfect, better than anything I could have thought of—had I been asked.

Mr. Carson shook my hand, congratulating me one more time before he and Mrs. Langstrom left, giving no sign that he remembered our first encounter, when he'd yelled at me for allowing the women to sit under a tree and tell stories rather than play games on a sweltering afternoon. Had it not been for Liz and Maggie I would have quit. I needed to thank them. They had helped me develop the confidence and courage to act on the caring I felt for my patients. Had I quit I would have missed working in a place with shifting rules and contradictory attitudes that I was learning to negotiate—no mean feat. Maybe this was what I needed to tell Jake. But would it change how I felt about him?

Mrs. Denby called the women to attention and waited until they quieted down. "It's time to walk back to the ward. Miss Weinstein will lead so please line up, two by two.

Liz and Maggie and Rita and Barbara rushed to be the first two pairs behind me. There was no way to talk privately with them, but their good humor said a lot. Even Rita, who hadn't been allowed to go, yet who'd worked so hard during team practices, glowed as if she'd played Fairview. Barbara, who wasn't much interested in sports, gave me a look as if she were bursting with news, but when we got to building 5, Mrs. Denby told me the women were too worked up to go out, that she wanted them to rest. She suggested I take out women from building 6. I thought this was strange, but everything about the day had been extraordinary, so I left, hoping Coop was on duty. I wanted to see her, to tell her about what happened.

Still high from the team's celebration, I ran to building 6, determined to ring the bell without worrying. Coop answered quickly, almost as if she were waiting for me, but I knew that wasn't possible. Her beaming face made me happy, yet there was something about her demeanor that struck me as odd. Worrisome. Had I done something wrong that I didn't know about? But then, why would she be smiling? Before I could ask, she said, "Congratulations, Weinstein. Not only did you start a women's team, they won!"

"How did you know?"

"No secrets around here. Ready for my folks?" I nodded and went to get the equipment.

When the women came out, I stared.

Obviously I was seeing a mirage.

I rubbed my eyes.

I stared harder, but she was still there.

In person.

Smiling.

"Carol!" I screamed, running over to her, probably breaking all rules, hugging her, tears streaming from my eyes. "Oh, Carol, I'm so happy to see you." I couldn't stop hugging her. I couldn't stop crying. I couldn't stop saying, "Oh, Carol. Oh, Carol."

"Okay you two, time to stop hugging and start playing." Rosa's mock serious command made everyone laugh.

I looked from Coop to Rosa, full of wonder, but it was Georgia who spoke. "You did it, you know."

"Did what?" I asked, still not able to believe my eyes.

Carol looked embarrassed. "You tell her, Georgia."

Georgia hesitated. "Well, I guess you know how upset Carol was after the haircutting." I nodded. "After a while, Coop and Rosa and I and a couple of other women got permission to talk to her. We kept telling her about how you were starting a women's team. At first she didn't care and wouldn't react. It was like she was waiting to die."

Rosa interrupted. "Sure was a hard case. Took us plus a whole bunch of attendants talking to her to even get her to turn her face from the wall."

Carol blushed. Georgia shook her head in mock exasperation. "When they brought her to our ward, we kept telling her how bad Barbara felt and how she kept asking about her."

"Yeah," agreed Rosa, "and it didn't do one bit of good." Her mischievous eyes belied her words. "But then, we told her how Liz was the captain and Maggie was catching and Barbara was coaching and after us saying it about a thousand million times she finally turned her face to us. Still not saying nuthin'." Rosa shook her head in teasing disapproval. "Sure was a hard case," she repeated.

I couldn't wait. "So then what happened?"

Georgia chimed in. "Coop told her she had to stop thinking about herself and start thinking about the team."

Nothing they said made sense. How could my starting a women's team account for the change in Carol?

Coop gave Carol a look as if to check that it was okay to speak. When Carol nodded, Coop said, "I told her that if she wanted the team to win she had to tell me, 'I want the team to win.'"

I gasped. "You didn't!"

Coop grinned, "I most certainly did."

Carol sighed. "She kept saying it over and over and over. All I wanted was for her to go away. But everyone kept at me and at me and at me. Then, when I finally tried to talk, nothing but a squawk came out. Coop spoke to me so gently and patiently. She never gave up on me and kept repeating, 'You can do this,' looking at me until I squawked, 'I want the team to win!' She made me say it a bunch of times until I sounded like I meant it." She wiped away tears that streamed down her face. "It was the first time I cared about anything since—"

I gave her another hug. "Carol, I am so happy to see you. I can't wait to tell the others. Barbara will be so happy."

Coop grinned. "She already knows. I told them about it after you all left to play on Saturday. Best medicine in the world."

"How come they didn't tell me at the party?"

"Sworn to silence, they were," said Rosa, boogying with delight. "They sure kept the secret good. Best day I've had in forever."

She wasn't the only one. Just looking at Carol made me feel clean and clear, as if seeing her washed away the wretchedness I'd been feeling. Coop assured me that Carol was on her way to recovery. But then, when the two of us were off by ourselves, I thought about the haircutting, and some of my happiness drained away. "What if something else happens that she doesn't want?"

As usual, Coop didn't mince her words. "Obviously, I can't answer for sure, but I have to have hope. I have to believe that she'll remember what happened and what it did to her and not let it happen again. If I didn't have hope I couldn't work here, especially in this building. I've seen lots of women move to building 5 and then be well enough to leave—and not return, I might add."

"But how do they get well? My title is recreational therapist but I don't do therapy, I play games with patients well enough to play. What's that worth? There's one psychiatrist for 900 patients—no treatment or therapy once patients get to building 5 and hardly any for patients in 6.

"Rennie, stop! You think Carol didn't remember how you tried to help her? Why do you suppose our talking to her about the team helped her turn her face from the wall? I admit, some attendants are downright mean and power hungry, but most of us work here because we care about helping people—just like you do." I tried to tell her I'd taken the job for the money but she shook her head, dismissing my words like annoying mosquitoes. "It doesn't matter why you took the job. What matters is how you do it. You haven't worked here long enough to know, but I can tell you, you've given more women than you can imagine a bit of hope that things can change in good ways." I blushed, uncomfortable with Coop's praise. "Now, let's play ball." The women cheered. I brushed away bothersome tears.

When it was time to take Coop's patients back I managed to tell Carol, once again, how happy I was to see her. Then I probably broke all sorts of rules by asking her if there was anything I could do for her or any way I could help her. She asked if it would be too much trouble to bring a barrette for her hair. I told her I would. It occurred to me that someone might ask how she got it, so I broke more rules by telling her to lie, to say she found it on the field. The smile on her face as she nodded filled every dark and broken place inside me with light.

29

I had a lot to think about. When Jake walked away, I felt as if I were losing a part of me that I would never find again, even if I somehow figured out how to reconnect with him. Today, the women in 5 and 6 helped me to feel good about myself—needed and useful. Working with them was giving me a sense of accomplishment I could never have predicted. Even though I hadn't yet convinced Dr. Glassman that I could safely take the children out beyond the enclosed area, I was certainly going to keep trying.

The world outside hadn't changed. People were still making rampant and hysterical accusations, labeling people as Communists with no proof. The world inside the hospital hadn't changed either. What had changed was me. I felt stronger, more sure of myself and more clear about what mattered to me. I still regretted having to sign the loyalty oath, and swore I would never do it again, but I couldn't regret working at the hospital.

I picked up a few big rubber balls and went to meet the women in ward 2. As soon as they saw me, almost all of the women formed a circle in the center of the room. Although there was no interaction, a few women smiled, I hoped in response to my smiling at them. I threw the ball to three women with no response. When I threw it to a woman who was still smiling, much to my utter astonishment, she picked it up and threw it to another woman, who then threw it to me. The two women laughed. A few more women laughed. I wanted to run to the attendant on duty and ask her to watch, but I was afraid to spoil the mood. Only one other woman returned the ball to me, kicking it with her foot, perhaps accidentally, I couldn't tell.

When it was time for me to leave, I put the balls back into the bag and realized one was missing. I looked around. No ball. Had I miscounted? I counted again, trying to figure out where it could be. A woman who'd thrown the ball back was holding something behind her. As I walked toward her she ran behind another woman and crouched down, terrified, clutching the ball tightly against her chest, holding it with both hands. Tears filled my eyes. I knelt down next to her. "It's okay, don't worry." Breaking another rule, I told her, "You can keep the ball and play with it. It's okay, it's okay." I had no idea if she understood what I was saying, but I gently helped her stand up and told her, "I'll be back tomorrow." I repeated it to the group and added, "We'll play ball tomorrow." The women watch me leave with no expression on their faces.

30

A warm, soothing rain fell on me as I walked to, and then past, the bus stop. It had been an unexpectedly momentous day after such a shattering weekend that I needed to put the pieces into some perspective. I had less than a month to work at the hospital before it was time to go back to college for my senior year. The next away game was already scheduled and the women were practicing hard, looking forward to it. They were more confident and relaxed about playing. No one ever mentioned or alluded to the way I had interjected myself into the game. Liz even asked if I had any strategies to suggest.

The day's joy had temporarily muted thoughts of Jake, but now, as I sloshed through puddles, I thought about him, wondering how I would know what to do, if it was still possible to do anything. No matter how I tried, I couldn't feel what I used to feel when I was with him. One thing I knew for sure, I didn't want a relationship with him if he was going to see other women, which might mean the end of our being together.

"Hey Scooter Girl, where's your scooter?"

Startled, I looked up and there was Will in his battered truck, with Mike and Russ squeezed into the front seat, irate drivers honking their horns just behind it. Mike yelled, "Meet you round the corner." I nodded, delighted to see them and ran to catch up with the truck, ignoring spraying pools of water that drenched me.

"Where's your scooter?" asked Mike.

"You're soaking wet," fussed Russ.

"Get in or you'll drown," ordered Will.

Before I could answer, although I wouldn't have believed even two could sit comfortably in the front of Will's truck, somehow the three guys squeezed together and Mike put me on his lap, unfazed by my sopping wet clothing.

"You have another accident?" asked Will, sounding worried.

"No, Jake came home early and took back his scooter."

"Why didn't you call me?" asked Will. "We could have picked you up like we did before."

"It just happened Sunday."

"He take anything else?" asked Russ.

Sitting squushed in the truck, soaked, with rain pounding so hard the windshield wipers couldn't keep up, I quipped, "Only a piece of my heart," feeling strangely at ease, one among four.

"Jerk!" muttered Will.

"Asshole!" sneered Mike.

"You're better off without him," said Russ.

I laughed. The scene felt surreal. I hardly knew these guys but they'd come to my rescue three times, with no hesitation. I felt I owed them something. "Will, if you don't mind, how about all four of us going to Luigi's on Friday—my treat." Russ and Mike immediately accepted. Will graciously agreed. By the time we arrived at my house, the rain was gushing down too fast to see clearly, so I invited them in for coffee. Just the short run from the truck to the front door left us dripping water all over the floor. While they toweled themselves off, I put out cookies, started the coffee, then went up to my room to change into dry clothes.

When I came downstairs, they were looking at my birthday cards. Mike shook his head. "Hey, Scooter Girl, looks like you've been having a birthday. You even got cards from Mexico. How come you didn't tell us? This calls for a celebration. We'll order a cake when we take you out to dinner. Right guys?" They nodded. I blushed.

Russ said, "First things first," showing me the empty cookie plate. "Any more cookies?"

"Yup," I said, feeling unaccountably cared for. I refilled the plate and poured coffee into four mugs. Russ took the cookies, Will brought the milk and sugar, Mike held the napkins and we went out to the porch. For a while we sat quietly and companionably, watching the rain, listening to the sounds it made hitting the tin roof.

Russ broke the silence. "You okay?"

"Right now I am," I grinned.

"According to my Buddhist teacher," said Will, "now is all we got."

"Well, right now, now feels pretty good."

Mike raised his coffee mug. "A toast, to Scooter Girl."

Will and Russ echoed him, "To Scooter Girl."

"And to the three of you, the best rescuers of damsels in distress, ever," I toasted in response before offering them more coffee.

I might not have a scooter any more, but I liked the name—Scooter Girl. I liked that I was able to conquer my fears and drive the Vespa anywhere I chose to go.

In fact, I liked everything about the moment—the rain dancing on the porch roof, our camaraderie, the coziness of their presence. It all helped me feel like I was coming home to myself.

Acknowledgements

I thank Andrew Adleman, Linda Dickson, Harriett Rynberk, and Diana Wolff for their willingness to read early and late drafts, offering advice, support, and encouragement.

I am grateful for the presence of Suzan Hall in my life. She is a marvelous and discerning editor as well as a good friend.

I appreciate William Abrashkin, Phil Eagleton, and David Pody for their suggestions, friendship, and unique points of view and insight.

Claudia Redder and Judie Fein are always ready to read and respond to my writing. I count on their honest responses. What would I do without them in my life?

I thank Pam Knight, the publisher of Plain View Press, who continues to support and publish my novels.

Although *Opening Gates* is a work of fiction, when I was 19 I was employed as a recreational therapist in a large mental hospital for three months before beginning my senior year of college. I began the job as a frightened, naïve, young woman who knew almost nothing about mental illness, thrust into wards with no orientation or training. By the end of the summer I had learned how to work in an institution where the unexpected was a fact of life, where incredible kindness and unbelievable cruelty co-existed. I am mindful of how much I learned from my patients and some of the attendants. I wish I could go back in time and thank them all.

Readers Discussion Guide

1. *Opening Gates* is set in the summer of 1956. Birth control was not readily available for women. If a man didn't want to use a condom, the woman risked becoming pregnant. What do you think about Rennie's relationship with Jake at the beginning of the novel? What does she gain by being with him? What, if anything, does she lose?

2. The McCarthy era hysteria is a character in the book. What does that mean? How does it affect Rennie? She worries that she is crazy. What does being crazy mean to you?

3. In 1966, ten years after Rennie signed the loyalty oath, the Supreme Court ruled that the New York State loyalty oath was unconstitutional. What do you think about Rennie's decision to sign the oath although it was against her principles? What would you have done in that situation?

4. Instead of an orientation before beginning work, Rennie is thrust onto the wards with no preparation except for receiving a chain of keys around her waist. What helps her survive her first days? What do you think about her promise to Maggie and Liz? How might you handle a situation where you are hired to do a job for which you have no direct training?

5. In the mental hospital the patients are powerless. Attendants have the power. How does Rennie react to this? If you have been in a position where you were totally powerless or powerful, how did this affect your sense of self? Your choices? The actions of those around you?

6. Why do you think Rennie has no friends? What makes her feel so different from other people her age?

7. What do you feel about the episode with Carol? How might you have reacted? If you have ever been in a situation where you were not able to help, what was it like for you?

8. From her first day on the ward, Rennie interacts with Liz, Maggie, Carol, and Barbara. How do they affect Rennie—as a person and as their recreational therapist?

9. What do you think about the women's behavior before and after they are allowed to form a team and play women patients in other mental hospitals? What do you think about Rennie's behavior when the Concordia women were losing?

10. What do you make of the relationship between Rennie and Bruce? Between Rennie and Yanni?

11. What has Rennie learned from working at the mental hospital? How did working at the hospital affect her sense of self? What most impacted her?

12. How do you account for the changes in Rennie's feelings for Jake before and after his trip to Europe?

13. Explore some of the ways in which various attendants influence Rennie's choices. What effect, if any, did her encounter with the molester in the park have on Rennie?

14. The title, *Opening Gates*, refers to the gates attendants have to open and close in order to take patients in and out of buildings, but what might it mean in terms of the characters' development in the book? In your life?

15. What role does storytelling play in the novel?

16. What roles do Bruce and Yanni, as well as Russ, Will, and Mike play in the novel? How do they affect Rennie's sense of self and her relationship with Jake?

17. What do you know about the treatment of mental illness today compared with the treatment of mental illness in 1956? What do you think about large mental hospitals as a center for treatment of mental illness? How might the treatment of mentally ill children differ from the care of mentally ill adults?

18. *The Feminine Mystique* by Betty Friedan, was published in1963. It became an influential book that described what Friedan called "the problem that has no name," the widespread unhappiness of women in the 1950s and early 1960s. How do you account for Rennie's strong sense in 1956 that women patients should have the same rights as male patients?

19. After reading *Opening Gates*, what aspect(s) of the story impact you most strongly?

20. What gates would you like to open in your life? What might keep you from opening them? Does the novel offer you any new ways to think about this?

Selected Resources

Information about the "Red Scare," McCarthy, and McCarthyism

In 1950, fewer than 50,000 Americans out of a total US population of 150 million were members of the Communist Party. Yet in the late 1940s and early 1950s, American fears of internal communist subversion reached a nearly hysterical pitch. Government loyalty boards investigated millions of federal employees, asking what books and magazines they read, what unions and civic organizations they belonged to, and whether they went to church. Hundreds of screenwriters, actors, and directors were blacklisted because of their alleged political beliefs, while teachers, steelworkers, sailors, lawyers, and social workers lost their jobs for similar reasons. More than thirty-nine states required teachers and other public employees to take loyalty oaths. Meanwhile, some libraries pulled books that were considered too leftist from their shelves. The banned volumes included such classics as *Robin Hood*, Henry David Thoreau's *Civil Disobedience*, and John Steinbeck's *The Grapes of Wrath.*

> **"Anti-Communism in the 1950s"** by Wendy Wall, The Gilder Lehrman Institute of American History

Archibald MacLeish, an American poet, writer, and the Librarian of Congress, who received three Pulitzer Prizes for his work, wrote about this period: "American foreign policy was a mirror image of Russian foreign policy: whatever the Russians did, we did in reverse. American domestic policies were conducted under a kind of upside-down Russian veto: no man could be elected to public office unless he was on record as detesting the Russians, and no proposal could be enacted, from a peace plan at one end to a military budget at the other, unless it could be demonstrated that the Russians wouldn't like it."

By the spring of 1954, Senator Ralph Flanders, a Republican from Vermont, had denounced Senator McCarthy on the Senate floor and Edward R. Murrow on CBS critically profiled him. When McCarthy's committee began to investigate the United States Army, the Army hired Boston trial lawyer Joseph N. Welch. He subjected McCarthy and his aide Roy Cohn to a cross-examination that anyone making charges in a criminal trial would face. For years, McCarthy had waved mysterious lists of subversives. Now Welch asked him: What is the source of your evidence? How was the evidence treated? Whom exactly are you accusing? And of what?

The following fall the Senate condemned Senator McCarthy's tactics by a vote of 67 to 22. He died three years later, in 1957.

The blacklist resulting from the anti-Communist hysteria lasted though the mid-sixties.

Point of Order—a film

In 1964, documentary filmmaker Emile De Antonio and art-film impresario Daniel Talbot, edited the kinescopes of the 1954 Army-McCarthy hearings, cutting down six weeks of testimony into the 97-minute film, *Point of Order*. Anyone wanting to know about McCarthyism would benefit from seeing this movie.

Selected Fiction

The Lacuna, a novel by Barbara Kingsolver

Barbara Kingsolver takes the reader on a journey from the Mexico City of artists Diego Rivera and Frida Kahlo to Pearl Harbor, FDR, and J. Edgar Hoover. *The Lacuna* is a novel about a man hurled in various directions by political winds, in a plot that turns many times on the breach—the lacuna—between truth and public presumption, and art and politics.

The Crucible, a play by Arthur Miller

The Crucible, first produced in 1953 by the American playwright Arthur Miller, is a dramatized and partially fictionalized story of the Salem witch trials that took place in the Massachusetts Bay Colony during 1692 and 1693. Miller's play was written at a time when the government of the United States blacklisted people accused of being Communists, often with no proof of subversive activity. Miller himself was questioned by HUAC (House Un-American Activities Committe) in 1956 and convicted of "Contempt of Congress" for refusing to identify others present at meetings he had attended.

Selected Nonfiction

A People's History of the United States: 1492–Present, Howard Zinn. Harper & Row, Harper Collins, 1980 (1st edition); 2009 (most recent edition).

Thirty Years of Treason, Eric Bentley. Viking, 1971.

Report on Blacklisting, John Cogley. The Fund for the Republic, 1956. Reprinted by Arno Press, 1972.

A Journal of the Plague Years, Stefan Kanfer. Atheneum, 1973.

Weblinks

Popular Mccarthyism Books—Goodreads
https://www.goodreads.com/shelf/show/mccarthyism

About the Author

Photo by Paul Ross

Nancy King, Ph.D., is also the author of the novels *A Woman Walking*, *The Stones Speak*, *Morning Light*, and *Changing Spaces*. Her books, plays, and novels have won numerous awards. *The Stones Speak* has been optioned for a movie.

A prolific playwright and essayist, Nancy King has written seven nonfiction books that explore aspects of creative expression. She teaches creative writing, storymaking, drama, and literacy workshops in the US and abroad.

Living in Santa Fe, New Mexico, she finds inspiration in storytelling, weaving, writing, and hiking in the mountains. She is a contributing writer for the online journal *Your Life Is A Trip* at www.yourlifeisatrip.com/home/author/nancyking.

Please visit Nancy King's website at www.nancykingstories.com for more information on her books and workshops. She can be reached at nanking1224@earthlink.net.